Thaddeus Longworth has lost his parents, but he does
have
drive
trails
dies,
reco
Thad
into

Julia
has
tocra
fossi
field

In th
field
in c
able
real

DATE DUE

T·H·E
BONE WARS
KATHRYN LASKY

PUFFIN BOOKS

FOR MOTHER

PUFFIN BOOKS
Published by the Penguin Group
Viking Penguin, a division of Penguin Books USA Inc.,
40 West 23rd Street, New York, New York 10010, U.S.A.
Penguin Books Ltd, 27 Wrights Lane, London W8 5TZ, England
Penguin Books Australia Ltd, Ringwood, Victoria, Australia
Penguin Books Canada Ltd, 2801 John Street, Markham, Ontario, Canada L3R 1B4
Penguin Books (N.Z.) Ltd, 182–190 Wairau Road, Auckland 10, New Zealand

Penguin Books Ltd, Registered Offices: Harmondsworth, Middlesex, England

First published in the United States of America by William Morrow and Company, Inc., 1988
Published by arrangement with William Morrow and Company, Inc.
Published in Puffins Books 1989
3 5 7 9 10 8 6 4 2
Copyright © Kathryn Lasky, 1988
All rights reserved

LIBRARY OF CONGRESS CATALOGING-IN-PUBLICATION DATA
Lasky, Kathryn.   The bone wars / Kathryn Lasky.   p.   cm.
Bibliography: p.
Summary: In the mid-1870s, young teenage scout Thad Longsworth,
blood brother to the Sioux visionary Black Elk, finds his destiny
linked with that of three rival teams of paleontologists searching
for dinosaur bones, as the Great Plains Indians prepare to go to war
against the white man.
ISBN 0-14-034168-4
1. Indians of North America—Great Plains—Wars—Juvenile fiction.
[1. Paleontology—Fiction.   2. Indians of North America—Great
Plains—Wars—Fiction.   3. West (U.S.)—Fiction.   4. Black Elk,
1863–1950—Fiction.]   I. Title.
PZ7.L3274Bo 1989   [Fic]—dc20   89-33720

Printed in the United States of America
by R.R. Donnelley & Sons Company, Harrisonburg, VA
Set in Palatino

"Know the Power of Peace."
Black Elk

*Black Elk was a warrior and medicine man
of the Oglala Sioux. At the age of thirteen,
he witnessed the Battle of the Little Bighorn
and as a grown man he was present at the
massacre at Wounded Knee.*

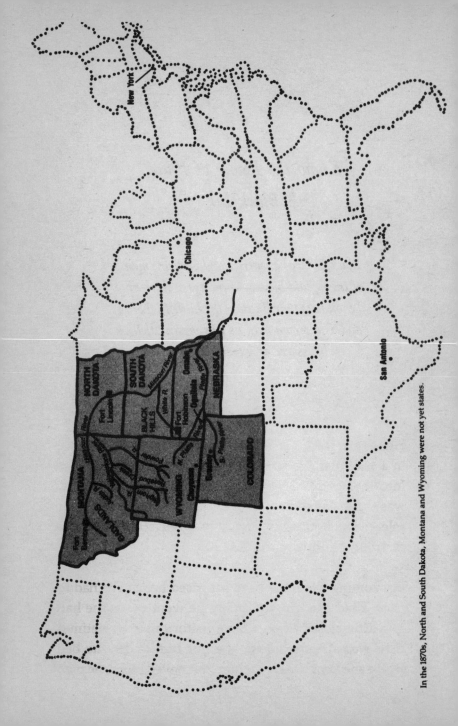

In the 1870s, North and South Dakota, Montana and Wyoming were not yet states.

No Creek, Texas
1865

PROLOGUE

He would always remember the waking-up part. That in a way was the worst. The low rank smell weaseled into his nostrils and he knew that the buffalo hunter was there even before he felt the shaking. He had been asleep under the bed and a piece of straw from the mattress fell down on his cheek.

His ma must not have known that the buffalo hunter was coming. He must have surprised her so she had to stash Thad real quick. Usually he went down the hall to a little closet when a man visitor came. Sometimes if he was already asleep, she put him under the bed where she kept a quilt for him, but never when the man called Hutch came. He used her real rough. She didn't like Thad around then.

The whole room suddenly seemed to be jumping about and the dark space under the bed swirled with bits of straw. Then there was the awful pounding sound, but he never heard his ma scream. He saw one thin white hand lop over the edge of the bed, the fingernails torn and bloody. Then there was a low grunt. He saw the huge boots. Thad pressed harder against the quilt on the floor, willing himself to disappear into the patchwork and become the tiniest figure in one of the thousands of cloth pieces.

This must be a bad dream. He'd wake up very soon, but how come it kept getting more and more real? Commonplace things like furniture and walls seemed to melt away from Thad's vantage point while the figure of the buffalo hunter loomed up with frightening intensity. There were four bloody streaks where his ma's nails had raked across the hunter's back. Then the red tracery disappeared as the man swung on his huge shaggy buffalo coat. The smell washed across the room like a wave. Now he was just a huge dark shape in the doorway. Then the shape vanished. The door slammed. Objects seemed to return to their ordinary positions. The door still wore its coat of peeling yellow paint. The cracks in the walls were exactly the same. Everything was in its usual place, Thad assured himself. Now he would crawl out from under the bed and the dream would be over. His ma would be quiet, like always, and she would get up and put the money in the hiding place. Just now, she must be resting a spell. He'd rest a spell himself. Just a little bit.

So he went to sleep and when he woke up, the nightmare began again.

"Where's Thad?" the voice said. It was Mr. Ditmore, or "Ditty" as he was called.

"He's not down the hall?" That was Pascal, the bartender. "Hell, he's such a tiny tyke, Hutch could've just ground him into the floor like a cigar butt."

Thad's eyes flew open. Someone was lifting his mother's hand, which still hung over the edge of the bed.

"Poor Miss Delia!" Pascal sighed.

"Poor little boy!" Ditty said.

Was he awake or asleep? Why were they calling him "poor"? Then Thad heard a big familiar voice on the stairs.

"Is it true?"

" 'fraid so, Jim."

"Where's the boy?"

"Beats me."

Thad recognized the spurs on Mr. Jim's boots.

"Did ya try under the bed?"

"Nope."

Mr. Jim's voice grew low. "Close her eyes and stick her tongue back in. Wipe that blood off her," he whispered. "No need for him to see her like that."

Then Thad heard a groan and saw one of Mr. Jim's knees sink down to the floor. Then he saw the two big fists with their knuckles braced against the floor. Then he saw Mr. Jim's face with the brushy salt-and-pepper mustache.

"C'mon, little fella." Mr. Jim sighed. "Sad times."

And now here was Mr. Jim pulling him out gently, not from a bad dream at all but just deeper into a sad life. It was when Mr. Jim was lifting him up into his arms that Thad made up his mind right then and there not to see and to start forgetting. So he buried his face in Mr. Jim's shoulder.

He had been five years old when the buffalo hunter murdered his ma. But there had been no forgetting. He stopped talking, though, for almost two years. He liked the silence. It was soft and comforting. He wrapped himself in the silence the way he wrapped himself in the old patchwork quilt at night. For it was within the silence that he came closest to becoming a tiny figure, unnoticeable in this violent patchwork that grown-up folk called life.

CHAPTER

1

Thaddeus Longsworth sat bolt upright in his sleeping bag. The four bloody streaks had raked his dreams once more. He blinked. This time there was no huge dark shape, only a Colorado sky poured full of stars.

Phew! He sighed and brushed his hair off his brow. Back in No Creek, he could have sworn that he dreamed about it every single night since it had happened. Nine years of bad nightmaring and then not once since he had been on the cattle drive north with Mr. Jim. This time, just the four bloody streaks came back, not his ma's torn nails or her protruding tongue. He only knew about the tongue from what he had overheard, but it made it worse somehow and it had come back to haunt him as much as anything he had seen.

It helped a lot to try to forget while looking up into a star-thick sky. Maybe that was why he woke himself up so early in the dream. Thad never did dream it completely from start to finish. It was usually jumbled with parts floating up out of the swamp of the nightmare in no particular order. Maybe the stars were looking out for him tonight.

Mr. Jim had told him something about the movement of the stars. "The transcription across the heavens" he called it. According to Mr. Jim, the stars marched about in an orderly fashion up there, so orderly that if you really knew arithmetic, you could figure out where on earth you were by just looking at a star. Mr. Jim told Thad that sailors navigated across oceans that way. Thad wasn't sure whether he really believed Mr. Jim or not on that one. Mr. Jim was plenty smart, though. If anyone could figure out where he was by a star, it might just be Mr. Jim. He had gotten a crew and two thousand head of cattle from Texas to Colorado in record time with no loss of human life and very few losses of cattle. This was no small achievement.

Thad would always think of it as something of a miracle that Mr. Jim had wanted him on the drive at all. He had gone into the Hole in the Hat saloon, where Thad was sweeping up, and scooted around the question for a while. First he asked Thad how old he was.

"Thirteen, I reckon."

"You reckon—don't you know for sure?"

"Not exactly."

"Well, when's your birthday?"

Thad hesitated. It had been one of those things he had tried hard to forget, because once his mother had made a real fuss about it. He remembered candles burning on a little cake in a room over some saloon, and a little bag of wintergreen candy and some shiny coins. Thad didn't like to remember the good times. They were almost more painful in their way than the bad ones.

"Summertime, I think," he finally answered.

"You be fourteen then?"

"Yes, sir."

"Well, I reckon that's old enough to go on a cattle drive." Thad had nearly dropped his broom. "Unless, that is, you're set on sweeping saloon floors and mopping up after cowboys who can't hold their liquor for the rest of your life."

Thad had swallowed. "No, sir!" He had stood real still and not said another word. This was a good dream and he did not want it to go away.

"You ever been on a horse?"

The dream fractured. Thad could hear it in his head shattering like glass.

"Don't go looking all slobbery, son." Mr. Jim seemed almost to be shouting. "And don't go mute on me. Lordy, you were a case back then. We'll teach you to ride. It'll be easier than teaching you to talk again."

Mr. Jim taught him how to ride that afternoon. He

was a "natural," Mr. Jim said. He was "part horse, born in the saddle." And he had given Thad a horse of his own, a sturdy pinto named Jasper.

This was the first time Thaddeus Longsworth had been praised for doing something well. From the time his ma died, Mr. Jim had always been plenty nice to him, but he didn't come into the saloon that much. He had a ranch of sorts, but had, as he put it, spent more time dealing with Comanches and Mexicans than cattle. Now the Comanches were gone and things had become "exceedingly dull" for Mr. Jim. Everybody else was getting rich driving cattle to the railroad heads in the north. A Texas longhorn steer could bring as much as thirty or forty dollars. It was Mr. Jim's notion to split the herd in Colorado, shipping part of the cattle north right then and using the rest to start a ranch in Colorado near Greeley and the South Platte to feed into those rail heads in Nebraska.

Thad had never really reflected on the "dullness" of life. He had just supposed it was a condition and nobody could do much about it. He had certainly never expected to go far from No Creek, Texas—not since his mother had died. He was never clear on why men gave his mother money after visiting her in her room, but she had always told Thad that they would save that money and someday they'd just take off. He once asked her whether that meant they were going home. He didn't know where home was, just that the Hole in the Hat saloon was not it. But when she didn't answer, he never asked again. Then after his mother was killed, he tried to stop thinking about it altogether—until that day when Mr. Jim asked him to join the drive.

Then his life really changed. One week after learning how to ride a horse, he had signed on with the J. W. Dundee outfit as assistant to the cook. The cook was a surly Mexican named Paco Paco who cooked the worst food imaginable. But Thad had loved every minute of it, even Paco's scowling and his leather-tough food. And even when a fierce wind blew up and the figures of the cowboys faded to become shadows in swirling rivers of sand, and it would have been an easy trick to get snagged, then trampled by a confused longhorn, the sand shadows were never as fearsome as the dark shape in the doorway of his mother's room nine years before. If he could not forget that dark shape, at least he was moving farther away from No Creek. And if he did not know what he was moving toward, he at least knew it could never be worse than that from which he had come.

Thad proved himself well. Not only could he endure sandstorms and the cook's scowls, but he possessed an uncanny ability to "read" the landscape. His visual acuity was phenomenal. He could spot figures in the endless grass oceans of the prairie that no one else could see. Once at high noon, he caught the flash of the sun against the silvery band on what turned out to be a horse thief's hat. They were a bad lot—three notorious bandits who were dedicated to thinning out remudas, the accompanying herds of horses on cattle drives. But Mr. Jim; Sport, the scout; and two other top hands thinned out the horse thieves before they had a chance to do their work. Mr. Jim presented Thad with the silver hatband. Thad felt good that Mr. Jim thought he deserved it, but he felt foolish with a dead man's hatband.

Ever since that day, Mr. Jim had let Thad ride scout with Sport. "Food ain't going to improve no matter what. You might as well ride scout with Sport and improve our chances for living."

Mr. Jim had said that when they got to Colorado, Thad could stay on and help set up the ranch. He would be a top hand in no time. But Thad wasn't sure he wanted to be a top hand, and as the last red streaks of his nightmare flickered out like dying coals, he looked up at the bowl of stars overhead and thought about what he might become. *Might become*—the words seemed as open as the night sky. Mr. Jim said he was a natural scout and Sport was teaching him how to track. Put it together and maybe he could sign on with one of those big outfits that took fancy eastern gentlemen with their beautiful Remington rifles into Wyoming territory for grizzly, elk, and buffalo. Now that would be a job, Thad thought excitedly. Tomorrow in town, he would keep an eye open for gentlemen's hunting outfits.

That was the last clear thought Thad was to have for the next several days. Not twelve hours later, just as he was standing outside the dry-goods store in Greeley, Colorado, Sport came racing out of the Tumbleweed saloon shouting for Thad. It was as if Thad somehow instinctively knew and had willed himself deaf and his brain numb. But then Sport's lean ruddy face was crammed right up to his and the words slammed right into him. "Mr. Jim's in there dying. Took a heart seizure right at the bar."

But by the time Thad had made his legs move him across the street and into the saloon, Mr. Jim was dead. Thaddeus Longsworth got busy trying to forget again.

CHAPTER
2

Julian DeMott was trying to remember exactly where under the rhododendron bush he had buried the fossilized tooth of the castoroides. He could have sworn he had buried it just under the lowest limb, the one that pointed toward the sundial in the middle of the walled garden. But he had now dug eight or nine holes, something that old McGuff the gardener would not like at all, and he had found nothing but spring bulbs. He hoped he had not disturbed them too much. The little flotillas of pink and lavender blossoms that hovered beneath the rhododendron in the spring were beautiful, but it was a terrible nuisance to mislay such a lovely specimen.

"Is this what you're looking for, laddie?"

A wisp of a man stepped out from behind the rose trellises that hid a potting shed. He held a rather large curved tooth in his hand.

"That's it!" Julian leaped to his feet. "My lovely castoroides incisor! Where ever did you find it, McGuff?"

"Under the rhodo while I was digging up last season's candysticks."

"Candysticks? Is that what you call those flowers?"

"I do." McGuff answered and then paused. "Castor oil—is that what you call the creature this belongs to?"

"Yes. It's an extinct giant beaver."

"Glad it's extinct, I'd say." McGuff held up the tooth in the sunlight. "Reckon it could do quite a job on a bloke—like them dinosaurs."

"I don't think there were any blokes living then," Julian said.

"Lucky, I'd say." McGuff walked over to Julian and tousled the boy's pale orange curls. "You'd probably not make much more than a quick snack. The good Lord knew what He was doing when He set us down long after those giant beasts were gone. And there's your father, a-digging them up in every shire 'tween here and Wales. So many bones there is!" McGuff sighed.

"Not nearly as many as in America," Julian replied.

"Eh? They got them there, too?" McGuff raised a snowy eyebrow.

"Do they have them!" exclaimed Julian. "The bones are practically leaping from the ground. Seems one can hardly walk a meter without stumbling upon a dinosaur fossil out in the wild territories."

"Whatcha mean, 'wild territories'?"

"Well, they don't have shires over there, you know, with the land all divided up neat and nice with roads and hedgerows and villages and churches. In the Wyoming and Montana territories, the land's unsettled, with nothing but wild Indians and stampeding buffalo."

"Wyoming . . . Montana . . ." McGuff repeated. "They never have proper names, those Americans. These sound like a moaning wind. Wyoming, Montana—howling, crying names if I ever heard one."

"Well, the cry has been heard, I'd say. It's a veritable shout that the big bones are over there in the American wild west."

Julian's father, Dr. Algernon DeMott, was England's most distinguished paleontologist. Dr. DeMott's specialty was the "terrible lizards," the dinosaurs of the Mesozoic era. The ancient creatures had first revealed themselves through the fossilized bones found less than one hundred years before. By now, 1874, fossil dinosaur bones had been popping out of the earth's crust from England to the European continent to North America, and Julian's father was the man who knew more about what they were than anyone else.

It was a controversial time. Scientists were beginning to believe that some living things evolved, or changed, over time and that some were linked to others through a common ancestor. DeMott refuted as preposterous the notion that fish from an earlier time might be ancestors of the reptiles of a later era, any more than apes could be linked to humans. *He* believed that God had formulated a divine plan, for which He had created separate groups of animals, each one an improvement over the group before. All were part of a highly complex design. And the ultimate aim of the Creator? It was to introduce the most complex and divine form next to His own—man.

Professor DeMott had lectured on this "Divine Intelligence" at the British Society for the Advancement of Science. But Julian on this occasion had suffered a terrible tummy problem and had had to depart rapidly. Julian's father had just been expostulating on the divine design that constructed the archetype and also "anticipated all its alterations." It did not anticipate, Julian remembered thinking as he bolted from the lecture hall, the effects of three servings of plum pudding on his rather undivine guts.

Julian had heard the lecture enough times that he didn't miss much that evening. He thought the plan was awfully clever on God's part and took it for granted that if anybody could figure out its meaning, it would be his father who was, he guessed, nearly as clever as God.

McGuff, of course, had no understanding of the Divine Plan. "Yes, laddie," he was saying. "Hardly a midnight snack you would have made for them creatures. But now when your mum was alive, she had a ladies' maid, pink, plump, and dimpled, with bright goldy curls." McGuff smacked shut his nearly toothless mouth as if savoring a most delectable memory. "She would have made a right proper Devonshire cream tea for one of them beasts. Come to think of it, she was from Devon."

"Maggie's from Devon," Julian replied, referring to the scullery maid.

"Oh, but she's as stringy as a blue heron. They'd spit her right back."

Julian and McGuff laughed at this. "Can't you just see her, McGuff, flying out of a megalosaurus's mouth—char bucket and all? If I were a dinosaur, I think I would find Mrs. Oliver quite tasty," Julian said, reflecting on the cushiony qualities of the cook.

"No," McGuff said. "Just because she cooks good don't mean she tastes good. Not with them hairs sprouting from her chin and that wart above her eye. Quite prickly, I'd say."

"Oh dear, I forgot about that." Julian had mostly been thinking of Mrs. Oliver's soft puffy arms and plump cheeks, which always seemed slightly damp and pink from her hovering over steaming pots.

Julian and McGuff continued to discuss from a dinosaur's point of view the relative merits of each of the members of the household staff from the butler to the lowliest parlor maid.

"Well, laddie," McGuff finally said, "I got to be getting on with me work. We'll be bedding out in another week and I don't have that east-crescent bed half turned yet."

"Bedding out" was the springtime ritual in which those flower beds reserved for annuals, or flowers that only bloomed one year—such as pansies or petunias or Johnny-jump-ups—were planted in intricate geometric patterns.

"And what will it look like this year, McGuff?"

"Oh, I thought I'd take the plan your dear mum did up the year she died. The one with the verbena and dusty miller and some nice bright purple pansies. Pink, purple, and silver—nice colors, eh?"

"Yes, I suppose," Julian said absently. It was odd how everyone spoke of 1861 as the year his mother had died rather than the year he had been born. But then again, the business of this house seemed to be that of extinction. Wasn't his father one of the world's greatest experts on extinct creatures? True, he had married the beautiful and genteel Lady Pamela, but unfortunately she had died giving birth to Julian, and now there was no lady of the house to provide for the lighter, social side of life. Still, Algernon DeMott pursued his science brilliantly, and because of it the whole house, in spite of the death of the lovely Lady Pamela, was highly regarded in London. And London, after all, was the hub of the Empire on which the sun never set. So if extinction was the business of this house, no wonder death dates took precedence over birth dates.

"Julian! McGuff!" A plump rosy lady with a wart above her right eye bustled down the pebble path. She was wiping her hands on her apron. "You two, palavering away! Julian, Mr. Fry's been upstairs a quarter hour already waiting for you."

"Oh dear!"

It had completely slipped Julian's mind that his tutor was waiting for him. He had not quite completed his Latin translation. Perhaps he could distract Mr. Fry, who was quite distractible actually, with the giant beaver incisor. He found that if he could distract Mr. Fry in the beginning of lessons, it often disrupted his tutor's plans. If this happened, Latin could very easily be postponed until the afternoon and Julian could finish his translation during lunch, which he usually ate by himself or with his father when Dr. DeMott was not taking lunch at his club. On those occasions, the meal was more or less an extension of lessons. Most regrettably, his father had decided that they should speak Latin during the last third of the meal when pudding was served. It was an exquisite way to wreck a very lovely dessert. His father would look on benevolently while Julian tortuously phrased: *"Hoc crustulum gloriosum; multae et mirae res ex manibus dominae Oliveris."* (This glorious tart: many and wondrous things from the hands of Mrs. Oliver.)

Julian really wanted to say, *Quae molestia!* (What a bother!)

Julian thought about all this as he raced upstairs. He burst into the music room. Mr. Fry was pacing up and down impatiently in front of a glass case containing

fossil specimens from a giant ground sloth, mega-
therium or Big Beast, as he had been named by the
great French paleontologist Georges Cuvier. In the case
were a femur or thighbone and a few random foot
bones, as well as 90 percent of its skull, the eye sockets
of which seemed to stare down at Mr. Fry, who paced
feverishly. His blond hair swirled about his head like
the spume from a force-eight Channel gale. Poor fellow, Julian thought. He's been pulling on his hair again,
all because of me. Teaching England's greatest scientist's only son was really a task designed to shred Mr.
Fry's already fragile nerves.

The tutor whirled around. "Julian, where have you
been! I really must insist—"

Julian quickly drew out the castoroides specimen
from his pants pocket. "It's a beauty, isn't it, Mr. Fry?"

Mr. Fry stopped his pacing. His eyes cleared as he
focused on the gleaming incisor caught in shafts of
sunlight that poured through the large French windows.

"Well, I say, Julian. A rodent of some sort, I take it."

"Right-o, Mr. Fry." Neither Julian nor his tutor
heard the footsteps that then stopped in the hallway
outside the music room. "I thought, sir, we might use
it for a drawing lesson. You know, in developing techniques of light and shadow."

"Well, perhaps, perhaps. I had thought actually it
might be a nice outing if one day we went to Synden-
ham and drew the marvelous sculpted beasts of Mr.
Waterhouse Hawkins."

Julian's stomach turned slightly, but it was too late. A tall man with an enormous head and bulging eyes strode into the room.

"And tell me, Mr. Fry, what is it that you imagine Julian drawing—iguanodon, perhaps?"

Julian felt a hot dark feeling well up in the pit of his stomach. How could Fry not have known about his father's running battle with Waterhouse Hawkins? For a park outside London, the sculptor had designed full-scale replicas of many of the recently discovered prehistoric beasts. At the time, his father had had a bitter disagreement with another distinguished paleontologist over the shape and form of the iguanodon's head. Hawkins had consulted with DeMott's rival and the result was a creature with the appearance of a rhinoceros, which in DeMott's words was "patently wrong, anatomically disastrous, and a betrayal of the reptilian legacy." But the beast had already been cast in iron and it was deemed too expensive to redo.

That his son's tutor was now standing in front of him proposing the preposterous beast as the object of a drawing lesson was an unparalleled affront. Trembling with apprehension, Julian waited for the inevitable. Although his father never raised his voice, there was something almost volcanic in his anger. When he felt challenged in any way, Algernon DeMott's voice would become softer as it acquired a slicing white-hot edge. Julian had witnessed only a few such scenes, but he was gripped with a terrible fear that seemed to wash through the room, threatening to drag him down into its powerful undertow.

The trick was to try to hang on mentally, to anchor oneself. He did this by focusing his attention on a very small piece of the physical environment. At this moment, it was a dust mote circulating within a shaft of sunlight in some seemingly preordained dance. As he concentrated on the dust mote, it was as if he could become a part of a pattern worked out by some higher order or force.

Julian was concentrating so hard that his father's voice sounded as if it came from quite far away.

"So you call yourself a scholar? I call you a sniveling . . ."

Julian's eyes glazed over as his father continued. "Suppose, Mr. Fry, some scientist thousands of years hence digs up your own fossilized bones. Now, how do you suppose they would reconstruct you? I would imagine that with that rather small brain case of yours, they might mistake it for half of the pelvis."

Mr. Fry looked toward Julian in despair.

"Dismissed!"

The word came crisp and clear.

Julian was not sure how much time had elapsed. It could have been minutes or it could have been an hour, but as soon as Mr. Fry left the room, his father clapped Julian on the back in a hearty manner.

"Well, that's done!" he said almost gaily.

Julian stopped looking at the shaft of sunlight and

the slowly circulating dust particles. He blinked once or twice. "But I didn't say good-bye, Father."

"Well, no need for that. I have to go over to the academy now, my boy, but I'll keep my ears open for a new tutor. We'll find a much better one than Fry. In the meantime, I'll try to make it back in time for luncheon, at least dessert, so we can keep our Latin up to snuff. Cheerio!" He gave his son another clap on the back and turned and swept out the door.

Julian sat alone in the cream-colored and gilt dining room. There was no need to finish his Latin translation now. He suddenly realized how awfully tired he was of eating alone. David Bartholomew, his next-door neighbor, had told him how he and his older sister and brother had had a food fight once, flinging gooseberries at each other. It had all started as a dare. Julian imagined how much fun it would be to sit at a table with other children, having food fights and telling riddles. He was sick of doing riddles with Wirth, the butler, or McGuff. They always laughed politely and said, "My! My! How clever!" He wanted somebody to laugh so hard that they fell down; to think the riddle was so outrageous, they would repeat it to a friend and then come back and tell Julian one even funnier. But there was no one to fling a gooseberry at or tell a riddle to. He thought of the giant beaver tooth in his pocket. Perhaps he would try cutting his chop with it.

At just the moment Mrs. Oliver entered through the swinging service doors carrying a lemon tart, Algernon DeMott burst into the dining room. He was in a froth of jubilant agitation. His bulging eyes danced. "Julian! *Peregrinatio a nobis paranda est. Necesse est iter facere ad Americam ut inveniemus fossila dinosaurorum. Veniemus, videbimus, vincemus Medicinem Buttesem in Montana!*"

Mrs. Oliver stood stock-still holding the lemon tart, her eyes transfixed by the agitated creature she knew as her master spewing unrecognizable words. "Would you care to translate, Julian, for the enlightenment of Mrs. Oliver?" Professor DeMott asked jovially.

Julian was stunned. The Latin translation was trickling into his brain at about the rate that the average sedimentary deposits took to make a fossil—several thousands of years.

"Uh . . . uh . . ."

"Well, don't sit there like a fool, boy. Didn't that idiot Fry teach you anything? Go on! Go on!"

"Well, yes. I believe, Mrs. Oliver, that my father said. . . ." Could it be true, Julian thought. Could he have correctly translated it? If so, the slow dance of the dust motes in the shafts of sunlight had suddenly gone screwy in a most delightful and wondrous way. "My father says, if I am translating correctly, that we are to prepare to travel. It is necessary to go to America to find the fossils of dinosaurs." Julian hesitated, trembling with excitement. "We will come to, we will see, we will conquer Medicine Buttes, Montana!"

CHAPTER

3

The herd could not be split. There were legal complications. Thad hardly understood any of it. There were a lot of -ate words—like *intestate* and *probate*. Thad reckoned the upshot of it was it would have been a whole lot easier if Mr. Jim had died in Texas. But then, Thad would never have learned to ride, never learned to scout—and never learned to miss Mr. Jim. That's what it always came back to—missing again, hurting again, and trying to forget again. He wasn't as good at it this time. Must be age, he thought. Like older people who grew bent over and creakier with the weight of years, he had grown creakier with the weight of memory and had a harder time forgetting.

Sport said he should wait around until the will was probated. He might get something out of it, Mr. Jim favoring him as he did. But Thad couldn't really see what there was to wait around for. Cattle? Cattle were of no real use to him unless Mr. Jim left him enough money to buy a ranch. But how could a fourteen-year-old boy, especially one who could barely read, run a ranch? He would never know whether someone was cheating him or not. He wouldn't know how to keep records and write letters to shipping agents and brokers. No, he would lose a ranch faster than it took a cow to drop a calf.

Thad was sitting on the steps of the only hotel in Greeley, Colorado. He held the silver hatband in his hands. Mr. Jim had said he deserved it. Mr. Jim had given him what he needed and what he deserved, and now he was gone. Sport had disappeared into the Tumbleweed saloon two days before and had yet to emerge. Beezus, another top hand, had actually emerged from the saloon so drunk that he was now in the jail. This was probably a blessing, Thad thought, because he would have more pay left than Sport. There were ways to pass time when one was older, surefire ways to forget, and it must beat sitting on the steps of the only hotel in town stroking a dead man's hatband.

Suddenly, there was the smell of very good leather

mixed with a sweet pungent fragrance. Thad looked up. It was as if he were an ant looking up at a stand of giant trees made of leather and finely loomed broadcloth. A group of men had just walked up the steps of the hotel and were standing on the front porch. Their accents were so peculiar, it took Thad several seconds to realize that these men were actually speaking English.

"Well, you're certainly not going to find grizzly south of the North Platte River." The man flicked his cigar, and ashes drifted down beside Thad's foot.

"It's a damn shame that these Indians are making life so inconvenient for us. Is there any talking with this fellow Crazy Horse?"

"Forget Crazy Horse. He'd cut your tongue out and scalp you before you could say a word." A third man was speaking. "No," he continued, "the only one that you can deal with at all is Red Cloud."

"Are you proposing then, Mr. Carroll, that we go all the way up into Sioux country to talk to Red Cloud? It seems rather off course from our intended prey."

"It would be somewhat of a detour." The first man spoke again. "But then again it might be worth it."

"You could probably pick up a good scout at the government agency there—one of the hangabouts."

"Hangabouts?"

"Yes, that's what the Indians call their brothers who stay around the forts and the agencies. The wild ones don't have much use for them."

Scouts! Grizzly! These were the fancy eastern gentlemen that Mr. Jim had told Thad about, the ones with
the beautiful Remington rifles. And there were the
beautiful rifles stacked up just by the door in sleek
cases the likes of which he had never seen. Thad was
filled with resolve. He could scout near as well as Sport.
He could track. He would find grizzly and elk for these
fine gentlemen and keep them out of the way of Cheyenne and Sioux as well as any man. Mr. Carroll, the
man who knew so much about Crazy Horse and Red
Cloud, was no scout. He was slow and fat; his eyes
were dim; and although he smoked the same cigars as
the rest of the men, his clothes were not quite as good.
Thad couldn't smell the trail on him, the pungent dusty
smell of horses and worn saddle leather. The men were
going into the hotel now. This was his chance. Thad
jammed the silver hatband in his back pocket and followed them through the door into the lobby of the
hotel.

"Pardon me, sir. Sir!" They were all busy with their
bags. The hotel manager had come out to greet them.

"Mr. Russell's and Mr. Galbraith's bags go up to
rooms 20 and 23. Mr. Richardson, we have reserved the
governor's suite on the third floor for you."

Thad did not know how to get the men's attention.
The hotel seemed filled with their presence. It was like
riding through a sandstorm on the trail when the entire
world was wrapped in wind and sand. While the storm
lasted, there was nothing else. In the hotel, of course,

there wasn't any sand. But these gentlemen brought
their own weather, and the very air around them rus-
tled with money and importance and power. What was
he supposed to do, Thad wondered, tug on somebody's
sleeve? He was short, but he wasn't that short! However, he was scared of his own voice. Sometimes it did
funny things, squeaked out like a mouse squeezing
under a grate. He couldn't help it. These men had
voices that were rich and low and the manager was
bending close to hear them. Thad had controlled cattle
with his voice, but he could see how these gentlemen
controlled people with theirs.

"Boy! Get that bag over there." It was the hotel manager.

"What?"

"You deaf, boy?"

"No, sir!"

"You with the Galbraith party, boy?"

"Uh . . . no, not exactly."

"Not exactly! Boy, get your hide out of here. We
don't need you lazing around."

"I'm a scout . . ." There, he'd said it. "I was figuring
these gentlemen might need someone, seeing as they're
fixing to go hunt grizzly."

Mr. Carroll turned around slowly. So the words had
penetrated the gentlemen's weather. His eyes were pale
and tilted up like pig eyes. Thad had always heard that
pigs were smart, but he found it difficult to believe that
when he looked hard at one. He felt the same way now.

"Scout?" He snorted. "Boy, you look more like grizzly bait to me."

A dreadful feeling crept up through Thad. He felt as if he had somehow become transparent, a clear kind of container into which this man with the pig eyes was pouring his contempt, and the contempt was turning to some kind of shame within Thad.

"My name's Thad Longsworth." His voice came like a rough wind out of a canyon. "I rode scout for Jim Dundee. Came up from Texas just above the Rio, south of San Antone, all the way to here. We drove two thousand head. We only lost twenty and not one man. We did it in record time. I can scout. I can track anywhere." By this time two of the other gentlemen were listening. And then he said the fatal words, "Give me a chance." He saw the four men exchange glances. The fat man came forward. "Uh, boy," he spoke quietly. "These are gentlemen and not gamblers. We don't deal in chances. Now you run on."

He knew it was over. One of the gentlemen came forward. "Here, son." He reached in his pocket and drew out a silver piece. "Go on, son, take it."

"No, sir." He turned and walked out.

He hadn't gone more than fifteen yards before Mr. Carroll came running up to him. "Boy, I don't know what kind of a fool you are, turning down good money." He paused. "Look. Mr. Galbraith said that a professor friend of his is up in Ogallala trying to convince Will Cody to scout for him."

"Buffalo Bill?"

"Yeah."

"But what about his show?"

"He still does the show, in the winter. Summers he scouts for General Philip Sheridan, and I guess sometimes for this professor fellow."

Thaddeus had heard about the show when the cattle drive got to San Antone and he had met a gambling-man friend of Mr. Jim's who had actually seen it in Chicago. It was billed as the Scouts of the Prairie, with Texas Jack, Buffalo Bill, and the beautiful Mademoiselle Giuseppina Morlacchi.

Thad looked hard at the fat man. "If I'm bait for grizzly, how come you think I could help scout for Cody and this professor fellow?"

"They're not going after grizzly."

"What they going after?"

The little pig eyes squinted. "Bones."

"Bones! Whose bones?"

"Dead animals, prehistoric beasts."

"Prehistoric beasts!" Thaddeus was not even sure what *prehistoric* meant. The man called Mr. Galbraith had walked up behind them. "Giant lizards," he said, smiling at Thad. "From long before there was man."

"They're dead, though, boy," the fat man offered.

"They are extinct, Mr. Carroll."

"Yes, they are extinct." The little pig eyes blinked rapidly.

"Extinct?" Thaddeus said. "What's extinct?" He

looked toward Mr. Galbraith, for he realized that this Mr. Carroll probably didn't know any more than he did.

"More dead than dead," Mr. Galbraith said coolly. "Gone forever as a species. My old friend George Babcock from Harvard University is about to commence his fourth expedition in search of the fossil remains of these 'dinosaurs,' as they are known. He has always had great luck in Wyoming and has decided now to prospect in the Black Hills. Buffalo Bill Cody was with him four years ago. I hear he's not anxious to go again. Perhaps the Harvard expedition needs a scout. You can tell Babcock I sent you." He handed Thad a small card. "Now don't give this back, son. I admire a young boy with your kind of get-up-and-go."

"Thank you, sir." Thad paused. He would not give the card back, but there was one thing that was bothering him. If this Mr. Galbraith thought he was good enough to scout for some fancy professor, why wasn't he good enough for going after big game? He reckoned it would be a three-day ride over to Ogallala, Nebraska, and here was a hunting party ready to go. "Uh, sir, I just have one question."

"Boy!" the fat man started to interrupt.

"Just a minute, Mr. Carroll. What's your question?"

"If you and your gentlemen friends were so worried about me getting et up by a grizzly, how come you're not worried about me being scalped by Indians? The Black Hills, that's their sacred land. They don't like people going in there."

"You're right. They don't like people looking for gold, but George Babcock tells me they think he's some kind of a holy man, because he goes about picking up bones. As a matter of fact, they call him 'The-Man-Who-Picks-Up-Bones.' "

CHAPTER

4

So far New York hadn't been that different from London, except that the people were very outgoing. All of their hosts had made a terrific fuss over Julian. They loved his accent. They loved his manners. He had just now gotten up from dinner at one of the grand mansions of Fifth Avenue, streaming with the other guests from the marble-and-gilt dining room. As he had been taught, he gave his arm to an elderly woman whose gnarled and heavily veined hand resembled a claw except for the jeweled rings she wore. A large square-cut emerald glittered fiercely in the flickering gaslight of the paneled library. The woman was the ninety-year-old mother of their host, Cyrus Snow.

"This is where we must part, dear boy," she said. "It's that dreadful moment when the ladies must retire to the gentler diversions—playing poker!—while the men of course have all the real fun planning the world."

Julian bowed. "I've enjoyed your company, Mrs. Snow. Good luck with the cards."

"Oh, wish them the luck." She nodded toward her daughter-in-law and the other fashionably dressed women. "I've taken pots from these ladies." She smiled and disappeared through a portiere, a velvet drapery that hung across the doorway. Had he imagined that she had winked at him? Julian wasn't sure.

"Well, Algernon, you are going to have some competition out there. Harvard and Yale have been sending expeditions for years." Julian's father and Cyrus Snow were standing a few feet from him, lighting up their cigars.

"Babcock and Cunningham, I presume," DeMott responded.

"Yes. But it's not only them," said Cyrus Snow. "The New World Museum is turning its eye in that direction, too."

"New World Museum? What in heaven's name is that?" Algernon DeMott's face darkened.

"As a matter of fact, Louis Woodfin, who was—let me see—yes, at the other end of the table from you at dinner, is one of the New World's biggest benefactors. Things are just getting under way there, actually."

Julian tried to stifle a yawn. He got up and walked toward a window overlooking Fifth Avenue. His father was about to begin his diatribe against museum collections. He had heard it all before: Fossils belonged in private scientific collections or universities. The general public did not have the intellect to understand or appreciate them. DeMott, an expert, after all, on Divine Intelligence, had a very keen sense of where the Divine ended and the public began. His father wouldn't rant. He would control his temper in the home of his New York host, for Cyrus Snow seemed to find no fault in Algernon DeMott's views on this subject.

"I quite agree with you, Algernon, about the inappropriateness of a museum for these finds."

A servant was passing through with a tray of bubble-shaped glasses filled with brandy. He didn't even bother to stop and ask Julian whether he wanted one.

"That'll have to go," a man said, lightly touching the winged collar of Julian's shirt.

"You mean my shirt, sir?" The man was a pleasant-looking fellow, a bit younger than Julian's father. His hairline receded some but his muttonchop sideburns and bushy eyebrows gave him a rather hairy appearance. He had soft brown eyes that made the cragginess of his face more gentle. "I doubt you'll be too comfortable in that getup where you're going."

"Oh, to Montana. No, sir, I doubt I would. Luckily

my father and I spent yesterday getting outfitted at Hoofner's & Mason's."

"Ah. I understand you are to go out with Sheridan's party?"

"Yes, through the graces of my cousin Lord Haversham."

"Have you met the estimable General Philip H. Sheridan?"

"No, sir, I haven't. I look forward, of course, to meeting him."

The man lifted an eyebrow and took a puff on his cigar. "Let me tell you an amusing story about the general."

"Oh, what's that?" Julian asked, startled but gratified that someone was paying attention to him.

"When he first heard that your distinguished father was coming to this country, he asked who he was, and when told that he was England's foremost paleontologist, he asked his secretary to fetch a dictionary to look up the word. 'Damnation!' he is rumored to have exclaimed. 'He's like those other two idiots—the ones from Harvard and Yale.'"

Julian's eyes widened. He hardly knew how to respond. "What two idiots are those, sir?"

"George Babcock and Nathaniel Cunningham, of course." There was a slight pause.

"And what treasures do you dream of bringing back from the great expedition?" the man continued. "You are, after all, in the tradition of the western dreamers, I imagine."

"Dreamers?" Julian asked. He thought he had misheard the man.

"Of course! Dreams of conquest, dreams of riches. It is our destiny, as decreed by God, to conquer the west and gain its treasures!"

Was this destiny, Julian wondered, similar to his father's theory of Divine Intelligence? This man did not sound entirely serious.

"So no dreams of glory? Of treasure?"

"Oh, none, sir. I just hope to be of some service to my father and his students."

"And their booty, where will it go?" Then, as if he felt he was being somewhat forward, the man said, "Oh, pardon me. My name is Louis Woodfin."

"Are you a paleontologist, Mr. Woodfin?"

"I was a student of paleontology. So by interest, yes, by trade, no. I am in the railroading business now."

Julian thought he had an odd way of answering questions. By trade, he was in the railroading business. Did that mean he was a train engineer, a stoker, or a conductor? More likely, he was an owner of railroads, a magnate, a word that Julian had never heard until he had come to New York, where there were no lords or dukes, but everyone he had met so far was either a professor of science or a magnate—a magnate of steel, or of coal, or of shipping.

"Are you, sir, if you don't mind me asking—a railroad magnate?"

Mr. Woodfin laughed heartily. "Well, if the defini-

tion of a magnate is someone who owns railroads, or
other industrial concerns, I guess I am one."

"But you said you had at one time been a student of
paleontology."

"Correct. I studied at Harvard with Louis Agassiz."

"Oh, yes. I've heard of him. I think actually he dis-
agrees with my father's theories."

"Which must mean, of course, that one must be quite
distinguished in his own right if he chooses to disagree
with your father."

This was absolutely the oddest man Julian had ever
met. He had, of course, been thinking the very same
thing himself but would never dare say it. Yet Mr.
Woodfin spoke without malice and absolutely radiated
a kind of warm, jovial sense of life and well-being.

"Why didn't you continue in the field of paleontology?"

"No money. Not a growth industry."

"But I believe, sir, that I just heard it mentioned
minutes ago by our host, Mr. Snow, that you were
involved in this New World Museum."

"I am indeed! And never expect to make a cent from
it. High time people saw the wonders of the previous
world—the magnificent creatures who used to roam the
earth, those behemoths of the past that were the size
of buildings, even New York buildings!" Woodfin
stopped speaking for a moment and began to relight his
cigar. As he cupped his hands around his match, he
resumed speaking in a lowered voice, barely above a
whisper. "In this room there are men with millions of

dollars invested in the west. Dreamers. But this west, said to be our destiny, has a past, a history that is so mysterious and profound that it could make our brashest dreamers tremble."

Riding back to their hotel that evening, Algernon DeMott inquired whether his son had enjoyed the evening.

"Oh, quite, Father. I had a very interesting discussion with a railroad magnate."

"Mr. Louis Woodfin." There was the curl of a sneer in his father's tone.

"Yes. Did you meet him?"

"Briefly. But I felt it better not to pursue any conversation. He is a great supporter of this New World Museum, and you know how I feel about museums."

"Well, yes, Father, but . . ."

"But what?"

"Nothing, Father."

Julian sank back against the upholstered seat as the hansom rattled down Fifth Avenue.

The next morning sharply at eight, Julian was standing amidst a throng of distinguished and well-turned-out people waiting to board a special train arranged by General Sheridan, the commander of the western frontier.

Among the group on the station platform were one steel magnate, a newspaper tycoon, a Russian grand duke, two Wall Street speculators, the commodore of the New York Yacht Club, and Lord Haversham, a cousin of Julian's mother. Lord Haversham had arranged with General Sheridan to include the DeMott party on this special train outfitted to carry big-game hunters to the west.

General Philip H. Sheridan, the man who had proclaimed that "The only good Indians I ever saw were dead," had met with extreme success during the course of his military career. Those Indians he had not succeeded in killing, he was moving wholesale onto reservations, with the notable exceptions of Sitting Bull, Spotted Tail, and Crazy Horse.

He made a business cultivating the rich and the influential. He had become proficient in catering to their needs and paving the way west for them, whether it was for business or pleasure. He arranged for everything, even the shipments of black magnums of their favorite champagne, which he had succeeded in delivering to the most desolate of hunting campsites. He helped these people and they in turn helped him. They gave him entry into the world of wealth and lavish living. It was a tidy and profitable arrangement on all accounts. So he had helped Lord Haversham not because he had any particular fondness for paleontologists but because he liked the English aristocracy, who were becoming increasingly more captivated by, and thus were investing in, the west.

There were four others in the DeMott party besides Julian and his father—students Albert "Bertie" Blanchford and Ian Hamilton-Phipps; a young cleric, Samuel Wilbur, who was a naturalist by hobby; and another professor, Charles Ormsby, who was younger than and certainly not of the rank or renown of Algernon De-Mott, but his father was a member of Parliament.

It was just after noontime on the second day of the journey, and Bertie Blanchford had come back from walking through General Sheridan's private car.

"I am staggering from the motion of the train," he reported, "and not from spirits, as is our esteemed leader Philip H. Sheridan at this very moment." Bertie looked toward Algernon DeMott and Samuel Wilbur, who were sitting next to each other poring over a map. Wilbur looked up with a wry smile.

"At this moment? He's been that way for several moments, I daresay."

"I think," Bertie continued, "one can safely say that for the general there are two states of existence—war and celebration." Bertie paused. "I heard an awfully funny joke about him, you know."

"What's that?" Julian asked.

"The cavalrymen apparently refer to their two most famous leaders, Custer and Sheridan, as Iron Butt and Lard Butt. We all know which one Sheridan is!"

"What else do you hear of this Custer?" Samuel Wilbur asked.

"Quite a chappy, he is. He's the one who really takes care of the Indians for the general. Made a name for himself in the Civil War, known as the Boy General—the man who goes into a charge with a whoop and a shout."

CHAPTER
5

Thaddeus was riding alone now. It felt strange. When he rode scout for Jim Dundee, he had always been alone. So he couldn't figure out why this felt so different, except that on the drive there were things to come back to—the camp and the other wranglers. And there was nearly always that familiar cloud of dust kicked up by the herd. He'd bet he could actually spot that dust from eight miles away. It did something weird to the horizon, smudging it up a bit in different ways, depending on the time of day and the weather. If it was a really clear dry morning just an hour or so after dawn, the horizon would be a deep pinky-gray smudge like his mother's lips.

He'd realized that one morning after he had first started scouting, and the very thought nearly bucked him out of the saddle. He had been surprised at himself for remembering. And he didn't like it one bit. He didn't like being bucked by thoughts or horses. He couldn't mind his business then, and his business was watching the horizon, watching the weather, watching the terrain. That was how he had spotted the sun glinting off the horse thief's hatband, and how he smelled the rain before it fell. That was scouting.

Sport had said that soon Thad would be able to track a prairie hen all the way to Chicago! And Mr. Jim had boasted that Thad must be half-hound and half-eagle with those sniffer and eyes that the good Lord gave him. There would be no more of that talk now. He wasn't really complaining, he told himself as he rode down the middle of a dried-out creek bed. Buffalo had been through here in the past week and so had Indians, a small group with some dogs, a few loaded travois, or pony drags. No, he wasn't complaining, but this was what made the ride different this time, more alone than just alone.

It was in the late afternoon on his second day out from Greeley that he caught up with the Indian party. The country was barren. There were not many places to hide, but suddenly, from behind a hillock, three Indians seemed to melt out of the twilight. Sioux. "I'll be!" Thad whispered to himself. His hand went for his gun and froze there. Stupid, he thought. Four of them, one of me with a one-shot Winchester. And who knew with whom they were traveling—maybe Sitting Bull, or worse, Crazy Horse. Thad had heard about Crazy Horse, the warrior chief who was as cunning as he was fierce. Stories of him had spread far beyond the Sioux nation.

One minute the Indians had been figures on the bluff, their earthy skin colors blending perfectly with the rocky outcrops, but the next minute they were beside Thad, their ponies' flanks pressing against his. A bright white line of foam landed on Thad's chaps, flung from the panting mouth of one of the ponies. They were closing around him, and then they were moving as seamlessly as if they were one. And his own horse Jasper, whose intelligence he had never questioned before this, had fallen into an easy pace with the Indian ponies. By gum, he thought, they've done it. They've charmed my horse with one of their fool spells and I've been captured alive by wild Indians. But nobody had laid a hand on him yet. Nobody had drawn a weapon or said a harsh word.

At first he watched for gaps, gaps big enough for him to slip through, but with each stride of the horses, he knew there was no escape. They were riding farther and farther away from the few things he had known and trusted, toward everything he feared. Every muscle in his body urged him to break away, while his brain told him it would end with an arrow between his shoulder blades.

Their pace slowed as they approached a clear-running creek, the first good creek Thad had seen since he'd left Greeley. The warrior who rode on Thad's left side was not much older than he was—perhaps eighteen or nineteen. Thad wasn't too scared to notice that the Indian's skin wasn't really red after all, not to one who had seen the clay of a Texas riverbed. It was a deep ruddy brown. He wore his hair in two braids. In one braid, a hawk's feather had been fastened. Around his neck was a bear-claw necklace. It was his eyes, though, that made Thad the most uneasy. They seemed masked, without a flicker of expression.

Thad coughed a little and cleared his throat. He bit his bottom lip lightly. He felt a word form somewhere in the back of his throat, but he couldn't push it out. He tried again. It was like trying to bellow up a spark into flame. "Howdy!" It was such a strange sound that he barely recognized it as a word. Could have been Sioux for all he knew, except he had felt it stagger up his throat and out his mouth, so he guessed it was his, particularly since these Indians didn't look like talky sorts. Indeed, they continued on in stark silence.

They were not pressed so tightly against him now. Escape lay on the creek side, which had now broadened into a churning stream. He counseled himself to keep calm—*sit tight! Your scalp is still on your head. Your butt is still in the saddle.* He kept up this talk with himself for some time.

Then, as suddenly as the Indians appeared, there was a small encampment a short distance ahead. Ten or

twelve tipis were scattered on either side of the creek.
Three or four children were playing a game with what
looked to be buffalo ribs, flipping them across the
ground. A couple of dogs seemed to patrol the edge of
the game, letting out yelps along with the children. The
activity in the camp stopped instantly as the men entered with Thaddeus. They motioned to him to dismount. A boy of about eleven walked forward. Beside
him was another young man. The boy looked gravely
at Thad and spoke. Thad couldn't understand him, but
the boy's eyes were not a mask. They were like dark
shining pools shot through with light.

"Black Elk." The young man spoke carefully, nod-
ding toward the boy. "He is a spirit traveler. In his
vision, he has known you. In his vision, he has followed you for two sleeps and now you are here." The
sound of the English startled Thad. He didn't know
about any such visions. He only knew that the last
rays of the sun were slipping over the horizon behind
him.

"Who are you?" Thad's voice croaked.

"Standing Eagle," the young man replied. He put his
hand on the boy's shoulder. "Black Elk has special
medicine."

Thaddeus had heard Mr. Jim speak of such things.
He was never sure what it meant. It was not the same
kind of medicine that white men had—castor oil or
liver pills. It had more to do with the spirits of the dead,
Thad believed, and holiness and sacred things. This kid
looked kind of puny to him to be the possessor of such

stuff, but then who was he to talk—old Grizzly Bait himself!

Black Elk was saying something to Standing Eagle.

"Where are you going?" Standing Eagle asked, and as he spoke, his dark eyes bore into Thad.

"I'm fixin' on going over to Ogallala and talk to Mr. William Cody 'bout some business."

"Pahuska?" Thad recognized the Sioux name for a long-haired man. A ripple of amusement seemed to pass through the Indians.

"Yes, sir," Thad answered. "To scout."

"Scout for what?" Standing Eagle asked fiercely, and now there seemed to be no amusement in the air at all. The other Indians became immediately sober, and now Thad felt a score of dark eyes piercing him.

"Bones." His voice was barely a scratch in the air. Standing Eagle leaned forward to hear him better. "Bones," Thad repeated, this time louder.

"Bones? Not gold?"

"No," Thad said. He seemed to have recovered his voice. He could think of better ways to make a living than squatting in a creek all day getting his feet wet while hoping to pan up some gold. Thad knew he might die poor, but at least he'd die with a good back and dry feet.

Standing Eagle turned to Black Elk and repeated what Thad had just said.

Black Elk now took two steps toward Thad. His face was inches away, and he spoke in his own language directly into Thad's face.

"Black Elk want to know, Who are you?" Thad had known the question before Standing Eagle translated it. The eyes of the young boy had an old light in them, older than time, it seemed, or at least the time that could be counted in years, and this light seemed to be searching for something deep within Thad.

Thad replied softly, directly to Black Elk. "I have no people."

Black Elk paused for a while and then turned to Standing Eagle and spoke.

"Black Elk say, come share campfire and tipi with him."

Black Elk then stepped forward and lightly took hold of Jasper's bridle. Thad took a deep breath and felt something relax inside him. He followed Black Elk to the place where the Indians hobbled their ponies. He took off Jasper's saddle and Black Elk brought over some grass and what looked like cottonwood bark to feed him. Thad hoped that Jasper wouldn't be too finicky about his eats. Indian ponies were a tough lot, known to be able to survive on practically anything.

A few minutes later, Thad was staring into a bowl of soup with some of the weirdest stuff floating in it he had ever seen. He was sure he had seen some of the ingredients growing along the trail. It made him nervous. He guessed there was nothing to do but eat the soup. It would be impolite not to; besides, he was hungry. And he realized he was grateful.

They were eating around a campfire just outside of Black Elk's tipi. His mother, White Cow Sees, seemed pretty nice, although she never did look straight at him. The soup was actually good. It was flavored with some grassy stuff that had a nice strong spicy flavor to it, kind of like onions but better.

When they had finished eating, Black Elk took a skin bag hanging from a hook and nodded for Thad to follow. Outside, Thad noticed that the colorful markings on the tipi were not simply designs but actual pictures and scenes. An especially intriguing one showed a fallen warrior with his leg trapped under the belly of his pony, which had been shot. Thad stopped to study it.

In several of the other drawings, there was a small boy whom Thad supposed to be Black Elk. In one, he appeared to be floating in the sky. In another, he stood under a rainbow, carrying his bow, and faced six tiny figures. Two birds flew outside the rainbow like guardian spirits. In a third drawing, the boy stood on the top of a peak that rose sharply to a flat tabletop. In the center of the flat summit stood the boy's small figure. Birds swirled about him. The figure held a decorated stick in his hands. Thad was not sure whether the stick was a weapon or a kind of holy instrument. Was the boy protecting the earth below or was the stick part of the trappings of a spirit traveler? He didn't want to ask. He felt that it wasn't right to ask questions about holy things, things of the spirit. They were best kept private.

Thad followed Black Elk down to the creek to fetch the water. They were alone now. The horses were nearby. It would be easy for Thad to slip away. He knew that Black Elk would not stop him. Yet he stayed. They sat by the creek for a spell, saying nothing, and watched the stars come out. The reflections of the stars danced like fireflies on the black surface of the water. Soon Standing Eagle joined them.

Black Elk began to speak to both Thad and Standing Eagle. It was as if he did not believe that language was any barrier at all, that Thad could somehow pick up some strain of what he was saying. There were certain words or phrases that seemed to recur. *Tashunka Witko* was one. Then Black Elk spoke the only English words Thad would hear from him that evening: "Crazy Horse." The boy's face lit up. Thad instinctively knew that Tashunka Witko was the name of the great Sioux war chief.

"Crazy Horse?" Thad whispered, and turned to Standing Eagle.

"Yes, Tashunka Witko. He is cousin to Black Elk."

"He is!" Thad was stunned. No wonder this kid had strong medicine.

"We go to meet him in the *Paha Sapa*, our sacred country, the place you call the Black Hills. But we are late. We must be there by the Moon of the Red Cherries. Black Elk fears that we will miss Crazy Horse if we don't move faster."

This, Thad thought to himself, is where Black Elk and I part ways, where the sharing stops. For he had no fear of missing Crazy Horse but quite the opposite. "Too bad," said Thad, only for the sake of being polite.

He then turned to Standing Eagle. "Where did you learn English so good?"

"At the agency."

"Agency?"

"Red Cloud agency, on the White River. My mother is cousin of Red Cloud. She say we must go with the great chief. But agency cheats chief like everyone else—bad meat, bad grain."

Thad recollected that he had heard of a big Sioux reservation on the White River up in Nebraska.

He knew that this was to be a test. It had been dawn when Black Elk had awakened him and motioned for him to follow. As they went out of the tipi, he crammed some dried meat into Thad's hand, which Thad guessed was supposed to do for breakfast. Black Elk led Thad a quarter mile or more out of the camp where some boys were mounted on their ponies. Another boy stood apart on his own pony and holding the reins of two others. Black Elk mounted one and signaled for Thad to wait with the other boy and watch.

Sixteen of the boys, including Black Elk, lined up in two rows facing each other with a distance of fifty yards or more between them. They looked toward the boy sitting on his pony next to Thad and he suddenly thrust his arm into the air and cried, *"Hoka hey!"* The two rows of mounted boys leaped forward furiously, charging their ponies. As the rows closed upon one another, the ponies reared and snorted while the boys whooped and screamed war cries.

Thaddeus stood transfixed. As the hooves flew and the manes danced, the boys grappled and wrestled with one another. The first young boy fell and quickly scrambled clear of the ponies' legs. The fight went on for several minutes until all of one team had been thrown or wrestled from their ponies. Black Elk trotted over to Thad, grinning despite a trickle of blood coming from his nose. He looked at Thad and nodded toward the group, as if to invite him into the game. Thad knew he was scared but he did not even let himself think. He automatically mounted the pony the boy had been holding for him. It was a game, their game, and it was a very dangerous kind of fun. The seventeenth boy followed. He, Thad, would be the eighteenth.

They lined up into rows, nine and nine. Black Elk was next to him on the left but he did not dare to steal a glance. He only looked forward. He did not find it one bit comforting that there were no real weapons and that these were boys still and not warriors, that they were but two-thirds the height and weight of a full-grown man. He found that he had a full-grown fear and not much time to think about it.

"Hoka hey!" The cry split the air. Thad's pony shot out. He felt swept up in the rumbling thunder. The lines crashed into one another. There was an eruption of hooves, then shrill whinnies and whoops, but the boys did not back off, nor did the ponies. To Thad's right, two riders were locked, their arms wrapped around each other. Black Elk had tried to block an attack on Thad, but was soon being attacked himself by the biggest boy of the lot. The next time I see Black Elk, Thad thought, he'll be on the ground. But it was Thad who was on the ground. Someone had ridden full steam into his right side, leaned over, and in one swift movement swept him off his pony. Thad was on the ground staring up at a calico belly and teats. He covered his head and rolled out from under the dancing hooves. Safe on the sidelines now and officially "dead" according to the rules of the game, he watched the finish of the round. It became more interesting to watch as the participants were thinned out. The game became more one of strategy and timing and intuition. Black Elk was the fourth out, but when they played again, he lasted to fifth and then sixth place. He was an incredible fighter. Scrappy, with the quickest reflexes and a bag of tricks to match, by the last round he had become unbeatable.

They played five rounds in all. By the end, they were all scratched and bleeding. They went down to the creek to wash off. Black Elk led Thad to a bend a short distance away from the other boys. The cool water felt good on Thad's face. After they had splashed the first handful, they both caught sight of the reflections of their blood-streaked faces floating on the water's surface. They looked at each other's faces in the water and laughed. Black Elk, his hands still bloody, scooped up some water from just the place where his image floated and offered it to Thad. He spoke softly and Thad drank the water from his hands. Then Thad did the same with the water from his own image that floated on the black surface. Then they both got up. Their images slid from the surface; their blood ran down the creek, and the two boys turned toward the encampment.

Thad rode with Black Elk for another half-day. At the point where the South Platte River joined Lodgepole Creek, they parted ways. He had spent little more than a day with the Sioux, but within that short span, it was as if he had packed an entire life. Time spent on the cattle drive had been one kind of life, but this was another. Although Black Elk was only eleven, he had seemed to be one of those ageless people for whom the actual number of years was unimportant. He seemed to share a part of himself with everyone, regardless of their age or his. It was not easy for Thad to say goodbye.

The Platte River, with its many strands of shallow waters, braided its way across the flat, nearly treeless landscape. There was barely a rise in the terrain from which Thad could gain a better and longer view of his friends who were riding north. But the day was clear, which made the distances in many ways deceptive, and although in his mind he knew that their ponies carried the Sioux farther with each step, he did not quite feel it yet in his heart. He could still make out the small figure of Black Elk, who rode alongside the travois that dragged his family's tipi with its pictures of battles won and lost, of hunts celebrated and droughts endured, of people broken and spirits made whole.

CHAPTER

6

Thad had been following the railroad tracks for some time. Just outside of Ogallala he came to a steep rise. From the opposite direction, he could see a train chugging from the east. It slowed down considerably when it hit the sharp upgrade, and Thad waited on the embankment to catch a closer look. He had heard Mr. Jim talk about these trains with their fancy new Pullman sleepers, and sure enough, there was one, sliding by as slow as molasses on a cold day. The car was dusty but he could see the gold lettering on the side, and, what was more, the windows had fancy curtains hanging inside with fringe jiggling all around their edges and looped back with what looked to be shiny ribbons. He wondered what the inside was like. Thad thought he saw some movement behind the window and a hand pull the curtain back farther. It took almost fifteen minutes for the entire length of the train to pass. Just after the caboose rolled by, he crossed the tracks and continued into Ogallala, where he stopped at the depot to ask directions for the Codys' place.

Thad heard the racket when he was still down the road a piece from the house. As he approached, there issued forth a variety of shrieks and snorts that could have belonged in a barnyard uproar—a coyote in the hen house or a bull wandered in with the pigs. But as he walked up the path to the house, he knew no animal had ever screamed the word *temporary!* A high-pitched voice pealed out from the open windows.

"Temporary! I'm sick of temporary, Will Cody. We got land to the north. We got land right here, not more than two miles away. It's time you built me and your young 'uns a proper home. I am not *temporary.* I am your wife. Maybe all *you* need is a bed in some fancy hotel—"

"Goldarn it, woman, you are the—"

"Don't say it, Cody!"

Warily, Thad climbed the porch steps. Just as he was approaching the front door, it opened. First came a man in buckskin britches and a dirty undershirt. His blond hair flowed down to his shoulders, and his handlebar mustache dipped into a small pointed beard. He looked at Thad quickly as he swept by. "Never get married, boy! Never!"

Thad, thoroughly bewildered, stepped forward as a white missile came hurtling out the door and smacked him square in the jaw. It felt soft, and the impact was not that great. Something splattered on his shirt. "I'll be!" he muttered softly. An unplucked headless chicken was lying at his feet.

"Louisa! What in tarnation have you done?" Cody was back up the steps of the front porch.

Then a square-faced woman with frank brown eyes and a no-nonsense brow came out from the house.

"Oh, for heaven's sake, Will. I hit a child!"

"Didn't you bleed that chicken before you threw it, Louisa? The kid's got blood all over him!"

Three minutes later, Thad was standing half-naked in the Codys' kitchen. Louisa had stripped off his duds, taking them to the laundry tub out back. He was wearing his short drawers, the ones that reached only to his knees, as his long ones had given up the ghost a hundred miles out of Greeley.

"Well," Cody said, lighting a long pipe and rocking back on the hind legs of a spindly kitchen chair. "Quite an entrance you made, kid. Couldn't have come at a better time—smack dab in the middle of connubial conniptions. Sorry about the chicken. Louisa's a wonderful gal, but she does have a temper. Guess we should be happy it was a chicken and not a meat cleaver."

"Guess so."

"Don't worry. She's not really the murdering kind,"

Cody said, removing the pipe from his mouth. "Chickens, the occasional pot, a ladle full of mush once—but it had cooled off. Nothin' real dangerous." He leaned far back in the chair and stretched his arms out until his shirt hiked up and Thad could see his belly button. "So, what brings you to these parts, Thaddeus Longsworth?"

Thad did not register the question immediately. He was thinking instead how he could not quite believe that he was standing here in this kitchen staring at Buffalo Bill's belly button.

"Hey, kid, you still got a chicken feather stuck in your hair beside your ear there." Thad reached up for the feather. "Other side. That's it."

"Well, sir, about why I'm here . . ."

He felt funny standing there in his drawers talking about his dream of being a scout, but what else was he to do? Just at that moment, he thought he heard a tinkly sound like laughter. He turned toward the staircase. Two little faces jerked back into the shadows and there were squeals. Cody was up out of his chair.

"Arta! Kit! You git on up there! Haven't you ever seen a fellow in his underwear?"

Louisa bustled in with an armful of laundry. "Are those children misbehavin'? And here you are still half-naked! Mercy, your clothes won't be dry till evening." She put the clean clothes on the kitchen table and rummaged through them. "Listen. For now, why don't you just wrap this around you? I know it's a petticoat but you don't have to wear it like one. Just wrap it around you and hitch it to your middle."

"Louisa, you cannot give this fine young man a petticoat to wear."

"It's only temporary," Louisa said, emphasizing the last word.

"Louisa, this could be an emasculating experience."

"You and your big words! If you had not left your other pair of buckskins at a certain hotel in Fort McPherson while visiting certain people who shall remain unnamed—"

"They were old, and you were supposed to make me a new pair!"

They were going at it again! "I'll wear the petticoat, ma'am," Thad interrupted hastily. "It's all right."

"That's a good child. I'll make you a pair of buckskins before I will that ole critter." She nodded toward Cody. "Now, what brings you to these parts?"

"I was just askin' that before you broke in with your freshly laundered petticoats."

"Well," said Thad. He had wrapped the muslin underskirt around him so that he was covered from his knees to his ankles.

"He looks like a bride!" a little girl's voice shrieked from upstairs.

"Arta!" Louisa Cody roared. She grabbed a broom and ran for the stairs. There was a scampering of feet.

"Go on, boy," Cody urged. "Don't give it no mind. This place is always like this."

Clutching the ruffled hem of his petticoat, which was wrapped around his waist, Thad leaned forward and tried to be as earnest as possible under the circumstances.

"I want to be a scout, Mr. Cody. I *am* a scout. I came up with Jim Dundee on a cattle drive."

"Jim Dundee. I know him from a while back. Good man. Good Comanche hunter."

"Well, he's dead now."

"No! What happened?"

"Took a heart seizure at the end of the drive."

"You don't say! So now you want to keep scoutin'."

"Yes, sir. I met a man in Greeley who said you scouted for some professor fellow. Dr. Babcock, from the east."

"Ah, yes! The professor and I became quite good friends. I'm not a Harvard man, but then again, he is not a scout. We appreciated the finer qualities in each other."

Sunlight seemed to pour out of Cody's face as he basked in his memories. "So you'd like to scout for Babcock?"

"Yes, sir." Thad then told Cody about the drive from No Creek, Texas, to Greeley, Colorado—his scouting and his adventuring.

"So, sir," he continued, "if you're fixin' to go scoutin' again for this professor, I would be interested in joining you."

"Would you be interested in doin' it on your own? You see . . ." Cody paused. "I've passed beyond that."

"What d'ya mean?" Thad asked.

"Make more money with the show. Got a family to support and, as you can see, Louisa's got her mind set on a certain style of living."

"It's not fancy. It's just permanent, as I said." Louisa had quietly come back downstairs. She held a sleeping baby in her arms.

"Our young friend here wants to scout for George Babcock. It's peculiar work, you know, Thaddeus, takin' them out to look for these fossil bones."

"I expect so."

"Don't fret," Louisa chimed in. "Mr. Cody will write you a nice letter of introduction. Anybody Buffalo Bill sends, Dr. Babcock will hire."

"It is the least we can do after the indignities you have suffered here," Cody added. "He's up at Fort Abe Lincoln now with General George Armstrong Custer."

"They really fixin' on going into the Black Hills?" Thad asked.

"Yep. It's the Sioux's sacred land, you know. But Babcock won't have any trouble with them. All the time I rode scoutin' for Babcock and for some of those other bone fellows, well, the Indians just left them alone. It was probably General Sheridan's idea that Custer take a bone man like Babcock with him."

"Sheridan?" Thad asked.

"Custer's boss. He's the one who wants to put all the Indians on reservations, keep them all in one place."

Thad tried to imagine Black Elk and his family on a

reservation. "But that's not what this expedition is about, is it—getting them to go into reservations?"

"Oh, no! No!" Cody answered quickly. "This is just exploring a bit." There was a brief silence. "But Fort Lincoln's a good piece from here, way up north in the Dakota territory. It'll take you four or five days. And you'll be sure to see some Indians. All you got is that single-shot Winchester?"

"Yes, sir. But I'll be fine. Indians don't bother me none. I get on with them well enough." Cody gave him a peculiar look but said nothing more.

"You stay here for the night," Louisa offered. "And we'll give you a good meal and a nice bed."

They were going to have chicken for supper, the same one that Louisa Cody had thrown at her husband and that had been intercepted by Thad's jaw. He thought he would have to wear the petticoat to the table but later in the afternoon there was a knock on the door of the spare room where he was staying. It was Louisa Cody. She was holding something wrapped in brown paper; on top there was also an envelope.

"What's all this?" Thad asked.

"You don't want to go around in that petticoat forever, do you?" She thrust the package into his arms. It felt soft under the paper. "Go on, open it." Thad opened it and saw the soft tawny colors of buckskin, buckskin britches.

"Mrs. Cody! These are too good."

"No, they're not too good. Had the buckskin all prepared. You look like a fine boy, and now you'll look like the scout you are. I wish I had had more time to make you a fringed shirt, but I'll get it to you one day."

"They look just my size," Thad said, holding up the britches.

"I just measured the old ones. Aren't you going to read the letter Will wrote for you?"

Something curled up deep inside of Thad. "Yeah, sure," he whispered. He took the envelope and looked at it for a moment. There were words on the outside, probably Babcock's name. Maybe he would try to fake reading it. "Uh . . . George Babcock," he said.

Louisa Cody had sat down on the bed next to him. "Doctor," she said, pointing to the word. She looked out of the corner of her eye at him.

"Yeah," he said.

"Fort Abraham Lincoln." She pointed to the words as she spoke. "Dakota territory." She paused. "Go on, open it."

His hands were trembling as he held the thin paper. He looked at the markings. " 'Dear George.' " Louisa Cody's voice was very soft. She looked up at Thad. "He and Will are on first-name terms. 'Dear George,' " she began again. " 'This letter is to introduce Thaddeus Longsworth, an experienced and intrepid scout. Mr. Longsworth has most recently been in the employ of the late James Dundee, cattle owner, on a drive north from Texas to Colorado, during which two thousand head of cattle were delivered in record time without serious mishap. This man knows the land. He can track, and he told me the remarkable story of how he spotted horse thieves by picking out the glint of the sun off one bandit's silver hatband. He has young eyes, a strong heart, and a very tolerant disposition. He will be an asset to the Harvard expedition.

" 'Louisa joins me in sending you our kindest regards. Sincerely, William F. Cody.' "

The words were most likely William Cody's, but the hand that wrote them had also stitched so beautifully the fringed buckskin britches Thad was now wearing. Of this he was sure. Just as he was sure that the thick pencil he found in his saddlebag had been put there by Louisa Cody. She hadn't embarrassed him by asking him how he had never learned to read or write. She had simply given him a tool to help him along, just as she had made the buckskins to help him look like the scout he was.

He had discovered the pencil the first night out from Ogallala as he made his camp near the North Loup River. Mrs. Cody had wrapped it up with several big slabs of johnnycake. In a tin box, she had packed a hunk of bacon on saleratus, or salt bread, and a small tin of coffee. He was so excited that he bolted down his supper and skipped the coffee altogether for fear of spilling on his paper, which had been used to wrap his clothes. He got out the letter to Babcock. He remembered a lot of the words and phrases she had read from the letter. So it was with these that he began his first lesson in reading and writing. Some words he already knew, such as his own name and Jim Dundee's. He had stared at that one long enough, seeing as all the equipment on the drive was stamped with it. He had a system all worked out. He would make a list of all the names or words in the letter that he knew how to read and then figure out which of those letters and sounds cropped up again. It was a fairly good system. He hit snags when he discovered that a single letter could have two different sounds or that one sound could be made by two different letters. The campfire had gone out when Thad finally put away the pencil and paper.

CHAPTER

7

It was not as green as England. That was Julian's first impression of the landscape as it started to open up outside of New York City. But then he forgot about the greenness as he began to perceive the real difference, which was one of scale. The geography seemed to explode in much grander dimensions even though the train had not yet reached the broad rivers, the prairies, and the mountains of the west. He had read about this fantastic landscape in a book his father had given him about the explorations of Lewis and Clark. This country that the train sped through at twenty-two miles an hour, the middle route through Pennsylvania and into

Ohio, would be dwarfed by what awaited them on the plains and beyond.

The DeMott party would disembark in Carbon Station, Wyoming, a few days after the Sheridan party, which was bound for western Nebraska, left the train. The trip from New York to Chicago took four days. In Chicago, they transferred to the Rock Island line, which took them to Omaha, the muddiest place Julian had ever seen. In Omaha, they boarded the Union Pacific. Throngs of people were headed west. The station in Omaha was thick with rumors of Indian attacks, which helped to promote the sale of insurance policies. The DeMott party had, of course, the best insurance policy of all—General Philip H. Sheridan.

Julian had never seen a train to compare to the Union Pacific. Its elegant sleeping carriages and dining cars were known as palace cars and were designed by George Pullman. Julian found himself in a private compartment with a sofa that opened into a wide berth. There were a table and a lamp beside it. He had two windows with dark brown velvet curtains fringed with golden tassels, and from this cozy, vibrating nest, he could look out into the unfolding vastness of this new country. He could not imagine how his father could tear himself from the window, but he did do just that.

For the better part of each day, Algernon DeMott conferred with his colleagues. There were long sessions. Every topic from equipment and camp supplies to strategies of excavation and preservation was discussed with an intensity that would have withered

most. When not in group discussion, they often retreated to their compartments to pore over various geological maps, trying to second-guess a terrain they had
never seen and plotting out private strategies tinged
with dreams of glory. For DeMott had promised that if
one of them should be so lucky as to discover a new
species of dinosaur, that species would bear the discov-
erer's name.

Sheridan's party kept its distance, but there was an
abundance of jokes freely circulated among the other
passengers about "fossils," those yet to be discovered
and those already excavated and riding the rails.

For a short time after Omaha, the train passed
through a region of bluffs, but then the prairie unrolled
like an endless sea of gray-green grass. There were
occasional trees. Ian Hamilton-Phipps and Bertie
Blanchford had just been complaining of the monotony
of the prairie after so many hours when Charles
Ormsby suddenly exclaimed, "By Jove! It appears almost as if we are standing still. I can feel us move, but
look out the window. Is there not an odd sensation of
being stationary?"

"He's right! Absolutely right!" Hamilton-Phipps
cried. "Look, Bertie, wouldn't you say we were still if
you could somehow obliterate the noise and vibration
of the train?"

"Precisely!" Blanchford agreed. "Still in a field of
endless grass."

But to Julian nothing seemed still at all. Such sensations of immobility were squelched by a sense of over-

whelming possibility, of infinite chance. Until that moment in the dining room of their house on Eaton Square, his life had seemed so set, so austerely predictable, and so rigidly controlled. He had never actively protested against his father's domineering manner. He was never even aware of chafing under the iron grip, but suddenly he knew that in this land the grip would loosen. His father might be able to maintain a semblance of power over him, but Julian knew it would be only an illusory thing. Life would change for him in a landscape of such scale and dimension. Until this moment, he had never questioned his father's power. He was not really questioning it now. He had just felt the first stirrings within himself of his own power. It was a quality within him that this landscape seemed to address, to challenge.

There had been talk of Indians—constant talk—but none were seen until the approach to Loup Fork, Nebraska. These were Pawnee.

"Note the bloodthirsty appearance." General Sheridan had begun a running commentary in the dining car, where they had just finished a luncheon of roast woodcock served with wild rice and plum sauce. The train had slowed on a slight upgrade and, along the track on both sides, a scattering of Indians had appeared. Most were men, their heads shaved except for a tuft of hair on top of which feathers had been attached. Their faces were painted and they stood solemnly wrapped in their blankets.

"Is it true, General," someone asked, "that from their tipis they have scalps waving?"

"First of all, these are Pawnee and they do not have tipis. They live in earth lodges, or used to. The ones you see here are reservation Indians. We've taken all the Pawnee in. So, I daresay, there are few lodges left with scalps flying from their lodge poles!" There was a ripple of laughter. "Our intention is to see that all Indians are taken to reservations within two years. If it takes any longer, the entire stability of the reservation system will be in jeopardy."

"Is that a dream, General?" Samuel Wilbur asked. "Expecting them to come docilely like children into the embrace of the Great White Father's reservation system?"

"It is a dream that will come true. The other side of it will be a nightmare for them. For we shall not treat them like children if they resist. When Black Kettle asked for ammunition, sir, do you know what I said?" He did not give Wilbur a chance to answer but boomed above the rumble of the train. "I said give them arms, and if they go to war my men will kill them like men!"

As they pulled into the station at Loup Fork, they saw more Indians—Sioux, some Cheyenne, a few Crow. The train stopped for half an hour and the passengers were permitted to get off and have a closer look. Even Algernon DeMott disengaged himself from a stratigraphic map long enough to observe at closer range the physique and bearing of the "savages." The women of the train were particularly interested in the tightly swaddled babies carried on their mothers' backs.

"Gentlemen!" General Sheridan called out from the platform. "A dime will buy your ladies a look at a papoose." The Indian women began unwrapping their babies while the gentlemen reached into their pockets. Julian glanced into one of the cradles. A baby's face appeared like a shining dark-red moon. He stood looking about the platform. There were clutches of well-dressed travelers observing the Indians, watching six Indian men load wood into the locomotive tender, peering at papooses and staring unabashedly at three vacant-eyed Indian women who squatted on blankets by the station door. The grand scale that had impressed Julian so much before suddenly contracted. The world seemed to shrink. The sensations of infinite possibility evaporated, and America seemed reduced to this dusty little train platform frozen in time.

First there was a sharp crack that split through the rumble of the train. Then Julian could hear feet running through the corridor, punctuated by whoops and hollers. He opened the door of his compartment. The corridor seemed to swirl with dust. "Buffalo!" someone shouted, and then he heard the cry repeated. Windows were being raised and dust seemed to pour into the train. Julian took out his handkerchief, the one Mrs. Oliver had given him as a present before he left, and tied it around his mouth. Unexpected and very rare, a sea of buffalo with swells of shaggy fur rolled alongside

the train. The great herds had disappeared from the
region and it was only on the Union Pacific line in
southern Nebraska that one could expect to indulge in
that singular joy of western travel—potshotting from
close range at the hugest of targets, the American buffalo.

The gentlemen travelers were in a frenzy of excitement, their eyes gleaming as they unpacked their
heaviest rifles. Conductors and dining-car waiters became loaders as the gentlemen unleashed rains of large-
caliber bullets into the lumbering "monarchs of the
plains." The beasts fell in heaps by the side of the
tracks, left to rot as the train hurtled on, carrying the
dreamers west.

It was late afternoon, several hours after the last of
the buffalo carcasses had disappeared into the darkening east behind them. The train slowed outside of
Ogallala in the grip of the steepest upgrade yet. They
were not moving more than eight miles an hour when
there appeared within the frame of Julian's window a
boy on a pinto horse. The boy seemed to be about his
age. The train shuddered to a halt. The boy was framed
in the center of the glass pane. The velvet curtains of
the train window could have been those of a stage, and
the boy could have been a figure on the stage, an actor,
except that he seemed too real. He wore a cowboy hat
and his dark blond hair fell down over his ears. He was
not big, certainly not as heavy as Julian.

He moved his horse closer to the track and pushed
up his hat slightly. Julian could see his face better as he

looked straight into the window, directly at Julian. His skin was burnished a deep coppery bronze. His eyes were gray-green, the color of the prairie grass, and they did not have the vacant stare of the station-platform Indians, nor the frenzied ecstasy of the gentlemen travelers. They were clear eyes, and Julian felt relief. To Julian, the eyes seemed to reveal a spirit with a depth that matched the scale and dimensions of the land. As the train started up, he wondered whether he would see such eyes again in this strange new land.

CHAPTER

8

If anyone had told Thad six months before that there was a place hotter than Texas, he would have thought them stark raving mad. But the Dakota territory was hotter than a greased skillet. By the end of the second day, he had crossed out of Nebraska and caught his first sight of the Big Muddy—the Missouri, which looked thick as molasses and moved a lot slower. He decided then that he would travel by night and into the early morning, then rest during the day. He camped on a high bluff and before dawn pushed on toward the river. He had the notion that if he got close enough maybe there would be a breeze. But there wasn't.

It was too hot to ride. Thad camped under a big cottonwood and tried to get to sleep. The tree shaded him fairly well, but he could look up through the branches at the white heat of the day. The sun never seemed to give up. It broiled the thick old river and fried up the air until everything around him danced with spots of sun. The heat was so bad that it pressed him down like a hot iron. It was so hot, it was hard to breathe. He watched the spots of sun over his face and he could see the smallest particles of dust and straw in their own frantic dance, all suspended in the thick air over his face. The air, still hot and spinning, suddenly turned rank with a low sharp smell that weaseled into his nostrils. He felt his tongue swell thick and dark in his mouth. There was a scream but he couldn't push it past his tongue. His tongue had become this monstrous dark thing swallowing all sound, choking all cries, strangling all life. *For God's sake, stick it back in!* a voice cried out. And then he woke up. His chest heaved as he inhaled the hot air, and a hoarse noise escaped from his throat as he looked toward the river and saw the small herd of buffalo drinking. There was a ripple of a breeze blowing toward him. The spots of sun began to dissolve. He reached for his canteen, uncapped it, and gently touched the rim of it to his tongue.

The water was almost hot. But it still felt good. He felt his tongue shrink up. But he wanted to check to make sure it was normal. He had always imagined that when Mr. Jim had told Ditty to stick his mother's tongue back in, that it was black. He stuck his own tongue out as far as he could. He got cross-eyes looking at it, but it was pink and glisteny. He looked down toward the river. It made him mad, dang mad, to think he was destined to dream this horror for the rest of his life. If he killed the buffalo hunter, the one called Hutch, would that kill the dream? He would kill him— he knew that—if he ever got the chance, but there were no guarantees that the nightmare would end.

In half an hour, the sun would be low enough to start traveling again. A heat-dazed jackrabbit perched on a rock not twenty feet away. He could kill it easy as pie. He was hungry. He reached quickly for the Winchester and brought it down. The buffalo bellowed and swung from the river and ran. Thad skinned out the rabbit quickly, built a fire, and roasted it. It was tough and stringy but he was no longer hungry when he finished.

The next day, he was following a trail that hugged the river. As the sky began to lighten, he picked out some marks wavering on the horizon. It had to be the fort, still several hours away. He rode until it was too hot, then rested and waited for the sun to slip down.

He started off again in the late afternoon. By twilight, he could clearly see two wooden blockhouses. They were tall and gloomy. As he drew nearer, he could see on the slope above him soft billows of color. He could not for the life of him figure out what they were. They looked like gigantic flower blossoms and, although there was no wind, they seemed to sway to a breeze of their own. Above the puffs of pinks, lavenders, whites, and pale blues were soldiers patrolling with rifles. Then a pink puff rose from the ground and Thad realized it was a woman, a woman with a basket, her sunbonnet slipped back off her head and tethered with ribbons. These were all women, out picking the wild flowers that grew below the rifle pits and the Gatling emplacements that were dug out at the top of the slope. Above them rose the blockhouses. The women were under the constant vigilance of members of the Seventh Cavalry, the command of General George Armstrong Custer.

Fort Abraham Lincoln was made up of sprawling wooden buildings sheltered by the towering blockhouses. At each corner, like dark eyes, their small watch windows and gun slots gazed out on the flat plain below the bluff.

Thad rode across the flats toward the bluff. He ascended toward the fort and at the gates stated his business. He was told that Dr. Babcock was staying in "officers' row," and was then directed to the stables, where Jasper was lodged in a stall, his first ever as far as Thad knew. He hoped that Jasper wouldn't get spoiled. Inside the fort, Thad found a teeming city. On his way to Babcock's quarters, he passed a granary where half a dozen men were unloading huge burlap sacks from a line of wagons, then—from what he could smell—the kitchen, and not far from it, a barber shop. After asking directions for the third time, he cut behind a laundry house to reach "officers' row" and was startled to come across a thickset person with sleeves rolled up, arms bright pink and a face to match, scrubbing away in a lather of soapsuds and cuss words. The curses had carried a good distance away. The person who was scrubbing stopped, looked straight at him, took a swig from a bottle, then picked up a wet garment and began beating it against the stone slab with a violence that a cruel master would reserve for a stubborn mule. The laundress looked like a woman but was dressed in men's clothes.

Dr. Babcock and his team from Harvard were occupying a large section of the barracks on the side of the parade grounds nearest the river. It was distinguished by a pretty garden that ran the length of the building. Thad rapped on the second door from the end. A young blotchy-faced boy with a shock of pale-red hair falling over his brow opened the door.

"Yes?"

"I would like to see Dr. Babcock."

"Well, if you're from General Custer's household, I have already sent a message with his aide that Professor Babcock prefers to stay here in 'officers' row' and he will give him his answer tomorrow in regard to the expedition."

For a moment, Thad could hardly understand what the young man was saying, for he had the strangest accent he had ever heard. Half the words sounded as if they got squashed flat as a flapjack way back in his gullet. "Is that clear?"

"Who is it, Oliver—not from Custer again? Tell him his wife's cakes were delectable."

"Who are you?" the young man asked.

"I'm Thaddeus Longsworth and I'm not from Custer. I'm coming from Cody, Will Cody."

"Buffalo Bill!" A portly man with thin graying hair and a neatly trimmed beard suddenly was at the door and pulled Thad in as he shook his hand vigorously.

CHAPTER

❧ 9

"So you haven't even seen the great general himself yet?" Oliver Perkins looked up from the list he was checking as he put supplies into one of the numerous trunks in a storage area that was part of the stables. He wiped his brow and smoothed back his pale-red hair.

"Nope," replied Thad. "Do these go in the book trunk?" He held up a stack of blank ledgers.

"Yes, I suppose that's where they'd fit best. And by the way, let Nat Forbes pack all the art supplies. He's rather finicky about how his various papers and pencils are arranged."

Thad had been at Fort Lincoln for two days. Babcock

had hired him immediately on Bill Cody's recommendation. The expedition was ready to move, waiting only for word from Custer, and in the meantime they were double-checking and repacking their supplies.

"Custer's pleased as can be about your being here."

"Why's that?" asked Thad. "He doesn't even know me."

"That's right. I should say that indirectly he is pleased with you. The fact is, the professor was unwilling to go until he had a good scout. And till the professor moved, you can bet Custer wouldn't budge."

"Because he's a bone man?" Thad set down a carton full of burlap strips wound up into rolls like bandages. These Harvard scientists, he thought, brought the strangest bunch of stuff with them—books, colored pencils, rags, bags of something called plaster of paris, picks, shovels, and every kind of spade and utensil to dig with imaginable.

Oliver now stood up straight and grinned. "Precisely. Some, my dear fellow, might call us paleontologists, but to the Indians we are Men-Who-Pick-Up-Bones, to be regarded with awe. We dig for holy things. And Custer needs us as his good-luck charm against Indian attack, as the government, contrary to all previous agreements with the Sioux, is invading their sacred land."

"But we are going to pick up bones, aren't we?"

"*We* are," Oliver replied. "But I'm not so sure if they are. There're rumors of gold, you know."

"Oh."

"But, of course, they are billing this as a scientific expedition. Custer's always telling the newspaper chaps about his Harvard paleontologists and his botanist, and the geologists who are going."

"His whats?"

"Botanist—A. B. Donaldson—studies flowers."

"And what did you call the other fellows?"

"Geologists. They study the earth—rocks, minerals, and gold among other things. Very handy on an expedition like this. No one will even mention the word *gold*, of course. No, they have an official purpose." Oliver spoke now in a singsong voice. "Information in regard to the character of the country and investigation into the practicalities of establishing a military post in the Black Hills in order to better control the Indians."

"Is that what Custer said?" Thad asked.

"No, General Sheridan. Custer just mouths him. I doubt if Custer has ever had an original thought in his life." Oliver sighed. "But I fear it's basically a gold hunt. If we're lucky, we might find some good bones along the way."

Thad plunked down on an enormous trunk. "And who's this Cunningham fella Professor Babcock was so het up about last night?"

"Not just last night. The professor has been het up about Cunningham for years. Oh, he's coming, too."

"Another bone man?"

"Yes. At least, if Cunningham ever arrives, we'll be able to keep an eye on him. Cunningham has a way of sneaking in on good bone sites that Professor Babcock has gone to great trouble to find. Would you believe that last summer Professor Babcock went all the way out to the Judith River Badlands in the Montana territory in *disguise?* He'd been told the terrain there was promising and he wanted to make sure Cunningham didn't find out."

"Disguised himself!"

"Yes. The competition is very fierce."

"Must be," Thad replied.

On their way back to the officers' quarters, a young soldier came up to them.

"Ah, Private Ewert!" Oliver said. "You know Longsworth, don't you?"

He nodded at Thad. "Are you and the rest of the gentlemen from Harvard going to the party tonight that Mrs. Custer is planning?"

"Another party! Why, I believe that's all you do out here, Ewert."

"Starting to think so myself, but Mrs. Custer feels it's good for us boys away from home to be exposed to the nicer things of life."

"Yes, well, I shall tell Professor Babcock about it."

When they arrived at the professor's quarters, however, Babcock was in no mood to discuss parties.

"He's not coming!" the professor said coldly, with a steely edge in his voice, as Thad and Oliver entered the room.

"You mean, sir, that Cunningham is not coming?"

"Exactly!" He began to pace up and down the room

furiously. "We were assured that he was. Needless to say, it would have been strained, keeping such close company, but I'd rather have him where I can keep my eye on him." Babcock stopped and looked directly at Oliver, his eyes brimming with fury. His voice became low and hoarse. "Now, can you guess, Oliver, where he is?"

"Not the Montana territory, sir?" Oliver replied.

"Precisely. We were informed, just minutes ago. To think of the pains I went to with that fool disguise."

"How did he find out?" Oliver asked.

"Spies. He's rich. He can spend inordinate amounts of money on anything he wants. He could buy all of Yale!"

Babcock looked at Thad's blank expression. "Yale is the other place in the east. The one Cunningham works out of." Babcock heaved his large form partway onto the corner of a table and ran his fingers through the few strands of hair on top of his head. "While we sit here waiting for this damned 'scientific expedition' to get under way, to a region that hardly promises fossil riches compared to what I discovered last summer, Cunningham is out there excavating!" Babcock jumped up from the table, which creaked loudly, and began pacing again. He was quite agile and quick for a man of his size. "And believe me, gold and dinosaur bones don't mix that often."

"What do you mean, sir?" Thad asked.

"They're in different strata." He again caught the confusion in Thad's eyes. "Layers of soil, you know, rock and sand. In certain kinds of strata, we find fossils. It is rarely the kind that gold is found in." He paused and looked at Thad. "And do you know what we must endure on top of everything? These endless socials staged by the general and his wife. It's driving me mad. You haven't been here long enough, Longsworth, but you'll get your first chance this evening."

"Yes," Oliver interjected. "We ran into Private Ewert on our way here."

"Wouldn't you say, Oliver, that the general's wife, although quite pretty, is about the silliest thing ever encountered?" He paused. "I mean, we're all used to silly women, but Elizabeth Custer really takes the prize."

"Well, actually, sir, not to disagree, but her husband is equally silly."

"I suppose you're right. His uniform covers a lot. You know he keeps a pet mouse in his inkwell?"

"He does, sir?" Thad exclaimed.

"Yes, it's quite distracting when you go into the office to talk with him. It crawls all over him—nestles in his epaulets."

"A pet mouse in an inkwell!" Thad whispered to himself in disbelief.

"Yes. Apparently, 'the General,' as Mrs. Custer calls him, is, and I quote, a 'gentle, gentle soul who adores animals.'"

"A few problems with Indians," Oliver chimed in. "But a friend to the little furry fellows."

"Yes," Babcock continued. He seemed less agitated

talking about the Custers than about Nathaniel Cunningham. "Over the course of their time at Fort Lincoln, they've had a pet badger, a porcupine, a raccoon, and even a wild turkey. This is one of Mrs. Custer's favorite subjects of discourse—the general's affection for animals."

"There's also the fire and her wig," Oliver said judiciously.

"The fire and her wig?" Thad asked.

"Oh yes, how could I have forgotten? Another favorite topic of Mrs. Custer's. It seems that shortly after the Custers came to Fort Lincoln, a fire destroyed the wig that Mrs. Custer had fashioned for herself out of the general's blond curls."

"Golden curls," Oliver interrupted.

"Ah yes! Golden curls cut from her husband's head."

CHAPTER
10

She was very small, with dark wavy hair, and despite the fairness of her complexion, it was difficult to imagine her in golden curls. When Thad first saw Elizabeth Custer, she was greeting guests on the porch, which he later learned was called the piazza. She stood like a beautiful doll in her soft peach-colored gown with a bunch of fresh flowers pinned to the bodice. They were the same kinds of flowers that Thad had seen growing on the slope out in front of the fort. She leaned delicately toward the group of young officers in full-dress uniform who had just arrived from West Point. Thad stood to one side, feeling awkward and trying to look as interested as he possibly could in the glass of lemonade he was holding. But he could not escape the sweet tinkle of Libbie Custer's voice.

"Oh! I fear for you young officers facing the sameness of garrison life!"

"Ma'am, your lovely parties vary any sameness."

"Well, we do try, and we have our musicales, too, in the autumn. I hope you shall not succumb to temptation, though. You do not smoke or drink?"

"Oh no!" they chorused.

Thaddeus wandered away from the porch into the house. In one corner, a group of ladies and officers sat at a table playing cards. Thad got another glass of lemonade and a sugar cookie, then stood at a discreet distance while he watched the cardplayers. Suddenly, he was aware of a delicate scent that engulfed him as completely as a dust cloud does drag riders who follow at the tail end of a cattle drive. A bare white arm slipped through his.

"I have not the mental organization for cards. I have been playing close to ten years and I have yet to trump a partner." Thad froze. "Mr. Longsworth." Libbie Custer was gently leading him away to a quieter corner. She let his arm go and faced him. "So you are the young man to whom we are indebted."

"Me?"

Her earnest eyes opened wide, as if she was explaining something to a young child. "It is because of you, Mr. Longsworth, that the general's great scientific expedition will be able to proceed. When William Cody refused to scout for Professor Babcock, and Professor Babcock refused any of the regiment's scouts, the expedition fell into grave jeopardy. But now that you have come on Mr. Cody's own recommendation, the professor seems much more inclined. Indeed, he is in with the general now at this very moment as they finalize plans. And this expedition, do not doubt it for one moment, is a vital one." The soft light in her eyes suddenly took on a glare of passion. "It's a sacred mission, Mr. Longsworth."

Thaddeus was confused. He thought the hills were sacred but that General Custer was aiming for gold. As if reading his mind, Libbie Custer said suddenly, "Oh, you'll hear talk of baser reasons for this expedition. But don't you believe it. No, the real mission is to discover the true character of the country. That is why all of these eminent scientists are here. And at the same time, the mission is to make the Black Hills safe—to control the Indians. Their savagery is boundless." Her voice became tight and dark, as if it had slipped into a cellar or some narrow, dimly lit passageway. "Their depredations are imaginable only to those who have witnessed them." Her voice dropped even lower and her long eyelashes cast spiky shadows across her delicate round cheeks.

"You've witnessed their dep-depredations?"

"Oh yes! Yes! Why, only this spring, the general and I were out for a ride along the river. We had followed a magnificent black-tailed deer. They are so beautiful. My husband, you know, is a great lover of animals.

Well, we had only gone a bit when we came upon a detachment of cavalry that had just arrived upon a horrible sight—the body of a white man . . . oh dear!" She took out a lace-trimmed handkerchief and held it to her nose. "Staked . . . Well, Mr. Longsworth, I suppose you have heard of the method that is often employed by the Indians in torturing a victim. I need not go into precise detail." But she did just that, even though Thad had nodded to indicate he had heard of such methods. "Now," Mrs. Custer continued, "when the Indians run short of time after they have disemboweled their victims, as was the case, they often pinion the captive to the ground and build a fire and collect the hot coals to . . .

"But really," she said, with a new perkiness in her voice, "I shouldn't even speak poorly of Indians here. The general always says 'a party's a party,' and he will not tolerate any kind of negativism or criticism. At a gathering, I once was cool toward someone who had treated my husband most unfairly and the general felt obliged to scold me for my behavior afterward. Have you met him yet, Mr. Longsworth?"

"No, ma'am, I haven't."

"He is the most wonderful man alive!" There was that momentary glare of bright passion, then a soft light stole into her eyes. "He has been called many things, you know—*Ouchess* is one."

"Ouchess?" Thad asked.

"Yes. Creeping Panther by the Kiowa and Cheyenne. Longhair by the Sioux, or Ringlets by jealous officers."

Mrs. Custer laughed. "But do you know what the Arikaras call him?" Arikaras was what white people called the Ree Indians.

"No, ma'am."

"Son of the Morning Star . . ."

"Ah, madame." A small gentleman in civilian dress had come up to them. *"Rosa suffulta* and *Solidago scrotina!"* He was looking at the cluster of flowers pinned to the bodice of Mrs. Custer's dress. "A stunning combination."

Thaddeus guessed that the man was talking about the flowers, which looked like roses and goldenrod to him.

"Professor Donaldson, have you met Mr. Longsworth?"

"Why, no. But I have heard about you, young man. We are in your debt."

"I was just saying the same thing," Mrs. Custer said.

This feeling of indebtedness was making Thad uncomfortable. Suppose the charm of being Men-Who-Pick-Up-Bones failed? Suppose they all got scalped? It was the *Paha Sapa,* and the Indians might well forget the so-called medicine of the dinosaur bones when their sacred country was violated. But Thad murmured politely. After all, as General Custer had said, "a party's a party." At the first possible moment, however, he excused himself.

The regimental band had started to tune up, and as the furniture had already been pushed back, Thad realized that the most likely next event would be dancing, something that he knew nothing about. He quickly left the room and began to wander down a corridor. George Babcock's voice was coming from an open door. He slowed his steps, and peered into a room hung with maps and all kinds of firearms and swords. Babcock wasn't visible but Thad could still hear his voice. That, however, was not what drew his attention. The room was steeped in thick shadows that dissolved into soft pools of kerosene light. But there was a yellow blaze brighter than the lamps or the gleam on the scabbards of the swords or the polished hardware of the mounted pistols. It was a fire unto itself and it seemed to consume the air around it. A fringe of gold epaulets, stars and braid, then a thick cascade of curls—this was Thad's first view of George Armstrong Custer, from the back. The blue of the dress uniform and the figure of the man seemed to dissolve into the shadows, leaving the curls and golden fringe to hang in a kind of mysterious suspension. But then, a hand reached out from the twists of gold braid on the cuff to scratch a hound's head. The hand was long and white and delicate. The thumb was slightly splayed.

"I do not see, Professor Babcock, that we are at cross-purposes at all," the voice drawled. It was a high-pitched voice, with a raspy edge that had been softened slightly, filed down by the lateness of the hour, or perhaps by some spirits consumed. There was a quick silky movement on the extended arm. Thad squinted, trying to see what it was. Something furry rippled across the thin white hand, then curled back and settled into the labyrinth of gold braid on the cuff. It was a mouse!

"I just want it clear that my scout looks for fossil-bearing strata and not gold-bearing strata."

"It's all the Good Lord's strata." The words erupted like buckshot in the shadows.

Thad turned quickly. In the large parlor, the ladies and gentlemen were dancing. But there were a few clutches of young officers who apparently had been unable to find partners and were standing about the food table, which had fresh platters of sandwiches and the huge bowl of lemonade.

"Did you hear the one about the Oglala out hunting eagles in the *Paha Sapa?*" an officer asked a fellow not in uniform, who Thad recognized as one of Babcock's team.

"Now, is that the one with the gold-tipped arrows?"

"No. No. That's another story. This one's true. You see . . ." The young officer moved closer, his face animated. "The Oglala boy was out catching an eagle. They use them for their ceremonies, something to do with becoming a man. Anyhow, the Indian sees a badger digging a hole and decides to shoot it, which he does. When he goes to retrieve the carcass, he sees that the ground all around the hole is covered with gold nuggets. So he fills his pouch."

"But that pouch was nothing," interrupted another officer, "compared to those coffeepots filled with gold that—"

"Oh, those coffeepots and the goose-quill pens with the gold dust—they were from the Montana territory," said a third. "Those are old stories. Now, I don't doubt for one minute that there's gold in the Black Hills."

The young man who was not in uniform stepped back from the group. He was clearly forgotten as the three officers seemed drawn into a web of their own gold-spun agitation. He acknowledged Thad with a wink and began talking. "My sister back east would laugh if she could see this. She wanted so badly to come out to the west. But it was deemed unsuitable for a young lady. Permit me to introduce myself—Jonathan Cabot. I'm with Professor Babcock."

"Pleased to meet you. I'm Thaddeus Longsworth."

The fellow had an open and friendly face, quite handsome, with deep dark-brown eyes and thick dark hair. "In any case, so far not much unsuitable has occurred, and I doubt if Abigail would have found these parties any less boring than the ones she attends in Boston. As for myself, the west I have viewed so far has been that from the window of a train. And although this is supposed to be part of my education, marching in lockstep with Custer, whose purposes we now find out are dubious ones indeed, hardly seems to justify leaving my classes at Harvard for the fall semester."

Thad was drawn to this young easterner. They spoke for a few more minutes and then the band struck up a waltz. Jonathan Cabot excused himself to find a partner and was soon leading her gracefully around the floor. The woman's hoopskirt swung in time to the music.

Thad wandered away. Out of the corner of his eye, he caught a swirl of peach from another door as another hoopskirt dipped and swooped like a great bird in flight. Thad stopped short. Alone in a parlor, the general led his lady around the room. Their eyes were locked. Perhaps, he thought, he should not be watching, but he realized they would never see him. They seemed to exist within a bubble of golden light, apart and distant from everything else.

CHAPTER

11

They left three days later, and Thad never in his wildest imaginings could have ever envisioned such an event. Over one thousand troops—twelve companies of infantry and cavalry—had formed into four columns on the bluffs outside the fort. There were one hundred or more covered wagons, a cannon, three Gatling guns, and over five thousand hand weapons. There were one thousand cavalry horses, three hundred "beeves," or beef cattle, one hundred Indian scouts, mostly Rees. In addition to the scouts, there were teamsters, interpreters, and reporters from newspapers back east. In all, there were over two thousand animals and fourteen hundred people.

It was the largest and best-equipped expedition ever to set out on the plains. The formation that held for most of the expedition had the wagon train in the center of a square formed by an advance guard. There were then a column of cavalry on each side and a battalion of infantry in the rear. General Custer rode out front with his guides and Indian scouts. Thad rode with Professor Babcock and his team, somewhere toward the middle of the left flank.

The day had been cloudy, but then the sun burst through and the air seemed to clang with shards of sunlight and sounds of brass instruments. The band had begun to play. Thad saw Custer galloping back toward the rear of the column, his curls streaming out, his drooping mustache as bright as his yellow hair. He wore two ivory-handled pistols in his belt, as well as a hunting knife sheathed in a beaded scabbard. Jammed into a saddle holster was a Remington sporting rifle.

"What's that music?" Thad asked Oliver, who sat uneasily in his saddle on the horse next to him. But before Oliver could answer, an older man, Luther North, one of Custer's guides, responded, " 'Garry Owen'—the general's favorite. And the one before that was 'The Girl He Left Behind.' "

They played "Garry Owen" for the first two miles of their march every single day into the Black Hills. The music wrapped the troops in a shield of invincibility,

welding the people, horses, pack mules, and gear into
one huge machine rumbling across the plains.

Thad did not officially start to scout until the third
day. Before then, he received a geology lesson on
horseback from Professor Babcock, in which the professor pointed out various types of geological formations and rock strata that could contain fossils.

Late in the afternoon of the second day, Thad noticed
a strange person trailing the regiment. The person wore
what appeared to be parts of a cavalry uniform—the
pants and a cap, mixed with other civilian clothes.

She fell in alongside Thaddeus. "You're just a kid!
Ya gotta drink? I need one real bad."

"No, ma'am."

"Ya think yer fancy pre-fessor friend's got one?"

"No, ma'am, I don't think so." Thaddeus said this
while trying to keep his eyes straight forward.

"Calamity! Git out of here!" A lieutenant came riding
up. "You do the laundry tonight for E company and
you'll git your likker. Don't go botherin' the scientists."

The woman muttered an obscenity under her breath
and turned her horse away.

"Who is she?" Thad asked.

"Calamity Jane," the lieutenant replied.

Their route had been southwesterly out from Fort
Lincoln. They were heading toward a bend in the Heart
River, and then across its south fork. By the next day,
Thad was riding scout. He had reached a canyon well
in advance of even the Ree scouts and was now taking

a detour down what appeared to have once been a tributary of the river. He was looking for white sandstone blocks—Dakota sandstone, the professor called it—and for outcrops of the sandstone covered in a black mass of mudstone or shale. The way Babcock had described the strata to Thad, he had made the rock sound like sandwiches, stone sandwiches—all layered up and pressed together by time and the upheavals of the earth.

Thad had found it challenging to look for these formations. In fact, it was so much fun that he sometimes wondered why he was getting paid to do it. What value did rock have or, supposing they found them, fossil bones? They weren't like big game. You couldn't eat them and you couldn't hang them on a wall like a hunting trophy and point to the ferocious critter you had shot down. Thad could not quite understand why these fossils were so important that people spent money trying to find them and that young men like Oliver Perkins and Jonathan Cabot spent years studying them in school. One morning when he was riding with Cabot, who was a most open and agreeable fellow, Thad decided to ask him just that.

"Don't mistake my meaning, Jonathan," Thad began.

Jonathan looked over at him and raised an eyebrow. "Why should I?"

"Well, I got a question that might seem funny-sounding to you."

"Let me hear it."

"All right." Thad paused. "I don't quite see what it

is we're looking for out here. I mean, I understand *how* to look for it, the kind of rock and all that, and I think I'll know a fossil when I see one. But what do these old fossils mean?" He pushed his hat back on his head and looked harder at the horizon as he tried to put his thoughts into words. "If I told my old trail mates what I was up to, they'd think I'd gone crazy or something. I know the professor isn't crazy but . . ." Thad reined Jasper to a halt. He turned in the saddle and spoke directly to Cabot, who had also stopped his horse. "Jonathan, you're about the only one I feel real comfortable asking this. Why in tarnation are these bones so important?"

Jonathan waited several seconds before he answered. "Well, I can tell you why they're important to me and why I choose to learn about them. The truth is, I've thought a lot about this myself. I come from a world of . . . well . . . a world of things and a world of . . ." He paused as if searching for the right words. "A world of very set rules about how you can behave and what you can do. My family has been in Boston since there was a Boston. My life has been decided for me since the time I was born—where I would go to school, who would be my friends, even who I might marry. I suppose someday I'll go to work in the family business. It's a *little* world, Thad. People there couldn't even imagine anything like this." He gestured with his arm toward the vast expanse of prairie that seemed to roll west endlessly. "And," he continued, "in their wildest dreams, they could never imagine a time before there was human life, let alone Bostonians."

"What do you mean, before human life?"

"Don't you realize, Thad, that the creatures we are looking for lived long before people, probably millions of years ago? Where we are right now was a kind of vast swamp left over from the Cretaceous sea."

"Right here?" Thad whispered in disbelief.

"Right here." Jonathan nodded. "There were no mountains, no Black Hills with their gold. Just these immense lizards, some towering as tall as the biggest trees! Some slithered through the mud and shallow waters like the huge sea crocodiles. There were giant turtles and huge fish. We are just a little speck at the most recent point of a most ancient history. And now, don't mistake me, Thad, for I dearly love my family, but that tiny world they believe is the hub of the universe, that Boston, seems rather trivial in comparison to all this." Jonathan had been speaking with great intensity. Suddenly, he smiled at Thad and shrugged. "Some people are afraid to see history this way. It's unnerving, I guess, to think that we have not always prevailed. But I find it very exciting. To come out here and look for gold seems so futile to me, but to look for bones of some ancient creature who walked the earth millions of years before man, well . . ." Jonathan's words dwindled off.

Thad squinted his eyes in the low-angled light. Waves of heat rose from the plains, and he tried to imagine the rippled air as water. He had never seen an ocean or a *crocodile,* whatever that was, or a fish as huge as the ones Jonathan had described. But he was beginning to understand the excitement of searching for the clues, the evidence from this vanished world before man.

The particular kinds of stone sandwiches that the professor was keen on finding were few and far between, but Thad knew exactly what to look for. He had been riding due north in the early afternoon when he had spotted one. Within less than five minutes of scraping away the mudstone surface with his hunting knife, he had begun to notice the unusual markings. The rock had been inscribed with a radiation of straight lines that fanned out as wide as the palm of his hand. Between the spray of the lines, the stone curved into narrow rounded ridges. It was beautiful. Was it some kind of flower, or the paw of an animal? Thad had no idea. He knew that his were probably the first human eyes to see it. He had brought sunlight to this fragile and lovely picture printed in stone millions of years ago, and to him it seemed to bring a whisper of beauty and order from a dim past.

Babcock was impressed with his young scout.

"You catch on faster than Buffalo Bill, I believe, Thad."

"But what is it?" Thad asked.

"It's the imprint of a clam—a shallow-water clam."

"Clam?"

"Mollusk, shellfish. There were once two shells attached at the base. A little fleshy creature lived inside. There are still clams today. Descendants of this one, I dare say, but this is one of the more ancient species of the great Cretaceous sea."

"But I've never seen any seas," Thad said wonderingly.

"Well, you have now," said Babcock, laughing. "You've just time-traveled over the millennia to see a most ancient one. Now let's think about getting this clam fossil out."

Babcock had brought a kit of tools for extracting small finds, which included hammers, chisels, and picks, as well as flour paste and varnishes. The clam shell proved a delicate but instructive exercise in demonstrating the basic techniques for excavating a fossil.

Thad worked with care and patience, and seemed to know just where to begin a cut that would be least risky to the fossil. Babcock praised him for having a good eye for the tiniest hairline cracks in the rock surface that could either help or threaten the delicate excavation work. A few feet above where they had dug out the clam-shell print, in the overhanging crust of the stone sandwich, they found some fossilized teeth.

"Are these dinosaur teeth?" Thad asked. They were not as large as he might have imagined a dinosaur's tooth to be, but they looked as if they had at one time been longer and sharper.

"No, these are more modern," Babcock said, turning over the teeth in his hand.

"Modern?" Thad asked.

"Yes. Probably just a few million years old. We have no way of knowing the exact number of years, only the relative age depending on where it is found in the strata."

Thad was quickly learning to adjust his notions of time. A thousand years in geological time was hardly worth talking about. Ten thousand or even one hundred thousand years were just the blink of an eye. Paleontologists kept time according to their own notions and definitely not by the clock of George Armstrong Custer.

They were camped on a flat grassy plain. Behind them, a bluff rose steeply, the top of which was crowned with a thick cluster of trees. A clear cold stream called Hidden Wood Creek ran out of the base of the bluff.

"I think we are in for something more than science," Oliver said, unmolding the casting he had made of Thad's clam shell. He had just looked up and seen Private Noonan, Custer's aide, making his way toward their camp. The camp stretched for more than a mile. The bivouac fires were scattered about like embers across the plains. There were corrals of wagons and herds of cavalry horses under guard as they cropped the grass. Toward the center of the camp, a band played airs—"The Blue Danube," selections from *Il Trovatore,* "The Mockingbird," and other tunes.

Private Noonan arrived and abruptly demanded that Thad follow him to the general's tent. He spoke with all the cheap authority that comes to some who have been bullied. Thad followed him reluctantly.

The general's quarters were an elaborate construction of several tents. Outside it, Bloody Knife, Custer's head scout, was smoking with another Ree. Inside the first tent, the general's brother, Colonel Tom Custer, pored over a map. The buckskin trousers and shirt favored by the general for expeditions in lieu of the regimental uniform lay draped over a rope stretched between the tent poles. Through a flap that opened into an adjoining tent, Thad could see shadows moving, and then he heard the high-pitched voice calling out, "My *robe de nuit.*" An orderly who had been standing behind the colonel and looking at maps quickly reached for a red garment hanging next to the buckskins and went into the adjoining tent. When the orderly returned, he told Thad that the general would see him now.

"Do you know, Mr. Longsworth, what they do if they capture you?"

That was how he began.

"You mean Indians, sir?"

"I mean Sioux and Cheyenne."

"Well . . . well, yes, sir, I have heard rumors."

"If you've heard rumors, I need not elaborate on their methods of torturing and killing. Perhaps you can pass along the details to Professor Babcock and his Harvard boys. I believe their school colors are crimson, the same as the inside of their scalps and their guts, the latter of which will not look so pretty when drawn out of a tiny hole bored in the stomach and staked to the ground by an Indian. Do you understand my meaning?"

But Thad didn't understand anything.

"I thought the Indians wouldn't touch them because they pick up bones."

Custer's face drained of color. His eyes turned icy. "That is precisely why they've got to pick up the bones near us! We need their medicine. We are coming into the territory of hostile Indians. Another excursion like the one today and they shall be made an example of."

"What do you mean?" Thad was more confused than ever.

Custer's voice grew smooth and low. He came up so close to him that Thad could feel his hot breath in his face. "Did you see those two Ree scouts in front of my tent, boy?"

"Yes, sir."

"Son, they are thirstin' for blood, any blood. I keep 'em hungry for it. Makes 'em good when I need 'em." His words had begun to slur a bit, but now he started to speak more precisely, as if he wanted every syllable of his intention to become perfectly clear. "I am not loath to offer up one of those fool scientists."

Thad's mouth was dry. He swallowed. "But, sir, you need the protection of the Men-Who-Pick-Up-Bones."

"Not if they're off eight hours a day, twenty miles away. I've watched these fellows for nearly a week now. They could be any man out of uniform—any Tom, Dick, or Harry who looks at the ground and occasionally picks up a bone. I can train any of my men to do the same thing and pass them off as fancy Harvard gents. Understand, Longsworth?"

"Yes, sir."

"Dismissed."

CHAPTER

12

They had been out just two weeks, Thad scouting in strict accordance with the general's orders, when he saw for the first time a dark smudge on the horizon. Luther North came riding back. "There they be," the scout said. By late afternoon, the smudge had heaved itself up from the plains like the humped back of an enormous black buffalo—the Black Hills. Thad had ridden back to rejoin Babcock and the rest of the expedition, which was following the Little Missouri River. "They certainly look black," commented Alban Mallory, another one of Babcock's students.

They had camped out that night near the headwaters

of Owl Creek. The following day, they had veered to the west and descended to the banks of the Belle Fourche River that bordered the Black Hills on the north. The hills were clad in lush forests of pine and spruce but at their base and extending toward the expedition was a velvety green meadow splashed with the colors of hundreds of different wild flowers. Stands of elk and buffalo grazed in the distance. Thad turned Jasper and headed for some higher ground for a better view. The hills did look black, and they thrust out of the earth like a huge shadow against the sky.

"Once, of course, there was the Cretaceous sea—a vast, shallow inland ocean." Babcock had followed Thad on his horse for a better view. "But that was before the hills. Look for the ripple marks in the sandstone."

"But what about the hills?"

"Long before the creation of the Rocky Mountains, a flood of hot liquid rock formed deep within the earth. It was thrust up like a dome, a granitic core. It cooled and warped over time, folding and buckling through millennia to make the ridges and valleys and hills you now see."

Thad looked across. His eyes adjusted. Just as his vision grew accustomed to the night, so that he could see the shadows within the blackness, the grays within the dense pitch, he now began to see the crinkled ridges and wind-whipped crests, the myriad of streams that threaded and mingled easterly toward the Cheyenne River, which were all part of the Black Hills.

* * *

The next morning, well before noon, the Ree scouts galloped back to report Sioux lodges, a few miles ahead. Custer sent his aide to fetch Thad, Professor Babcock, and two other members of the Harvard team—Jonathan Cabot and Oliver Perkins. Then Custer rode off with an interpreter, Lieutenant Wesley, under a flag of truce, while the rest of the company and Babcock's party waited a short distance from the village.

About an hour passed and then Custer returned at a gallop. "Gentlemen!" he said. "It seems there is a celebrated person in this village—Red Cloud's daughter. She is married to the headman. I propose we go in, give them our assurances of peace, offer a few trinkets, perhaps some food, and introduce our expedition scholars."

There were several tipis, many more than in Black Elk's encampment near the North Platte. The tipis were of varying sizes and one was extremely large, which the interpreter called the medicine lodge, and to which they were led. Thad guessed that at least forty hides must have been stretched over an equal number of poles to erect this tent. Around this tipi were a number of other poles hung with roots and herbs to ward off evil spirits. Thad had learned this from the time he had spent with Black Elk. Standing in front of the lodge was a group of five or six Indians. One was a woman, presumably Red Cloud's daughter, standing next to a man who carried the authority of a chief.

Custer nodded a greeting to each person and spoke through his interpreter.

"The Great White Father in Washington sends his greetings of peace . . . we come as friends into—" He stopped abruptly and turned to Lieutenant Wesley. "Just say we come as friends."

Thad looked at Custer closely. He would never say the words *Paha Sapa*. To use the Indian name for the Black Hills would mean he recognized the land as their own. "Are they going to invite us into the lodge, Lieutenant, to smoke a pipe?"

"I doubt it, sir."

"Can you ask?"

"It's a rather delicate business, sir. . . . Er . . . uh . . ." Lieutenant Wesley hesitated. "Given their peculiar feelings about the hills."

"Well, good Christ, Lieutenant, I've smoked pipes with Sioux all over the Dakota territory and down into Nebraska."

"Yes, sir. I understand, sir."

The headman spoke next. Lieutenant Wesley translated.

"He wants to know why we fly flags of the Great White Father over our camps here in the hills."

The general looked at his feet and put a hand casually over his mouth as if to smooth his mustache. "Good Lord," he muttered. "This *is* getting delicate." He cleared his throat. "Tell him, Lieutenant, that . . . er . . . it's just a harmless custom to keep off evil spirits.

Just like those herbs and roots hanging off their tipi poles."

The lieutenant translated. The Indians did not respond.

"Did you tell them?" Custer asked.

"Yes, sir."

"Tell them now that I would like to introduce the Men-Who-Pick-Up-Bones—Professor Babcock, Mr. Longsworth, Mr. Oliver, and Mr. Cabot."

The lieutenant translated.

Again the Indians remained stolidly silent. Custer waited, then coughed to fill up the awkward silence. "They aren't buying much, are they?" he said. "How 'bout we offer them some food, and maybe they'd like to visit our camp."

Lieutenant Wesley translated once more. The headman responded this time.

"He says they have no need of the food. They cannot visit a camp that flies the flag of the Great White Father in the sacred hills."

"Well, I'll be! All right, if that's the way they want it . . ." Custer clicked his boots together and made a stiff little bow from the waist. "Thank them for honoring us with this meeting and tell them that we come with peace in our hearts and minds."

The lieutenant told this to the headman, who then replied.

"What'd he say?" Custer asked.

"He wants to know: When do the Bluecoats leave the sacred hills?"

Custer looked straight at the headman, nodded quickly, and walked away.

A few days later, the expedition crossed a beautiful floral valley and camped near Harney Peak. It reached nearly eight thousand feet into the sky. From the mule packers to the cavalry officers, men began picking bouquets of flowers. The flowers grew so thick and high that the men did not even have to dismount to pick them. Professor Donaldson, the botanist, came rushing up to Babcock. "George!" he exclaimed. "Three varieties of primrose within fifty feet of each other, and look at the mariposa lily!" He held forth for inspection a pale pinkish-gold blossom.

Several of the officers, including Custer, and a few of the scientists and journalists could not resist the challenge of climbing the peak in this valley.

"We shall be the first human beings to climb this peak," Dr. Donaldson said. Thad was standing nearby trying to decide whether to go or not. He wondered if Indians had ever climbed it. Calamity Jane, already weaving from drink, seemed to read his thoughts. "What about Injuns?" she asked. Thad turned toward her. Her face was bloated. The peak was reflected in the bleary pools of her eyes.

"My dear Calamity," Professor Donaldson said, "it is well known that the noble, the royal, the genuine North American Indian is one of the laziest mortals on earth. I doubt one would ever take on a peak like this."

"Dat so?" said Calamity. Her words and the shape of

the peak were making an impression on Thad. He had
seen that peak before, and it suddenly struck him
where—down in Nebraska when he was traveling with
the Sioux. Indians *had* climbed it—Black Elk, for one.
This was the peak drawn on the tipi, the one that
showed Black Elk standing on the flat top of a mountain with the birds overhead. He remembered the decorated stick that the boy had carried, and wondering
whether it was a weapon or not. He might never know,
but here was his chance—to climb to the peak and see
with the eyes of his friend, the spirit traveler Black Elk.
To share a view from the top of the world. Perhaps to
see through time, to long before now, before there were
people and everything was different.

The air was thin and still, the day cloudless. Thad
gazed out at the distant cliffs. There was a startling
clarity to the atmosphere, and Thad, with his keen
eyes, could see the people of the expedition and the
horses and the wagons, and he knew that it was wrong
that they were here. There was a timelessness to the
land and it would soon be changed. He could now
imagine that the stick was a weapon. He felt trapped
between two visions—the ageless vision of an ancient
people, and that of his companions, hard, bright, and
new. He could hear the others coming up the winding
trail to the summit now. He would only have a few
more minutes alone.

On a day like this, he could imagine deep into the
past, when the Black Hills had first risen from the Cre-

taceous sea. He looked at the surrounding spires and pinnacles carved by the tributaries of the streams and imagined the soft ooze of the ocean floor from which they had risen and into which life had sunk. He thought of the creatures that had become fossilized in the accumulating silt as the sedimentary rock began its journey to the top, to form the spires and peaks that pierced the sky, eventually thousands of feet above sea level. He thought of this raising up of the hills, the quickening of the once slow-moving streams that began to scour channels down the mountainsides.

In the short time they had been in the Black Hills, they had found hundreds of examples of this fossilized life, nothing as big as a dinosaur yet, but shells, leaves, crabs, snails, and bones of small mammals. Babcock was longing for something larger—"at least a great turtle," he had said, just that very morning.

Although nothing grand had been found, Thaddeus had enjoyed, more than he had ever imagined, the adventure of it all, the surprise of seeing the print of ancient life emblazoned on a rock. He, too, of course, wanted to find something big, but his dreams of big game hunting, of bringing living animals to death, seemed far away. Now the real thrill was that of bringing extinct animals nearer to life. Gunfire interrupted his thinking. The air was laced with bullets. The combination of their physical exertion, of their achievement, of the thin air and the rare beauty seemed to fill the climbers with a kind of mad ecstasy as they shot at the sky with their carbines to celebrate their ascent.

"Thaddeus, my boy!" Donaldson came over and clapped him on the shoulder. "How'd you get here so fast?"

"An Indian showed me the way."

"Oh!" said the professor abruptly. "Indians? They've made this climb?"

"Yes."

"They're here now?" There was a note of agitation in his voice.

"No."

This seemed good enough for the professor. A few minutes later, he scribbled a note that he and five others signed, including Generals Custer and G. A. Forsyth, attesting to the fact that they had climbed the peak. They rolled up the paper and inserted it into a cartridge that they then hammered shut and pushed into a crevice.

Everyone had tethered their horses at a midpoint up the peak as the going became very rough, everyone except General Custer, who forced his horse to the summit. On the descent, Custer's horse had a very hard time of it, and by late afternoon, when Thad saw the general coming into camp, his horse was in sad shape with heavily bleeding knees.

CHAPTER

➤ 13

It was near Harney Peak that Custer made a permanent base camp from which he would strike out for further explorations of the Black Hills. On his first major reconnaissance mission, he took five companies of cavalry and headed toward the southernmost extension of the Cheyenne River, with high hopes of finding gold. In the meantime, Thad, with an increasingly anxious Babcock now accompanying him, scouted for good strata. Babcock had given orders that they would not stop for any fossils that were not within the time margins of the dinosaurs. For one thing, they did not want to waste precious wagon space. The team had three wagons—one for gear and two for fossils. Thad wondered how he would know the difference between an ordinary bone and a fossilized one. The very next day, he found out there was no mistaking one for the other.

At the first pink streaks of dawn, Thad was on Jasper, heading back over the land they had explored the day before. In the distance, he had seen a very steep cliff, an escarpment. There had been something about it that called to him, demanded a closer look. Perhaps it was the taluses, the rocky fragments that accumulate at the bottom of a cliff—something about their color or the very fact that they were so thick that suggested heavy erosion. Jonathan Cabot had compared the action of erosion, the wearing away of rock, soil, or sand that exposed older sediments, to the drawing open of the curtains on the window of ancient life. So if the escarpment had been eroded, there was the chance of a window into the geological past. As the dawn peeled off the night, Thad, riding in an easterly direction, felt himself inexorably drawn forward. Here, for sure, would be the old sediments, exposed.

The escarpment curved in deeply. At the top was the same old stuff they had been seeing for days. But then the color changed to a grayish-green sandstone that seemed to extend vertically for fifteen feet or more from just above the middle of the escarpment to the ground. When Thad was ten feet away, he saw lighter-colored fragments mixed in with the talus. He picked several up and they were very smooth. He then walked over to the base of the escarpment, stuck in his hand spade, and began digging out small scoops of dirt. On his fifth scoop, the spade hit something hard. He knew in an instant that it was fossilized bone, not rock. For there was not the sharp, quick noise of metal on rock but, instead, a thick dull sound, a *clunk*. He began scraping away the dirt, and within a quarter of an hour, he had exposed a patch of bone.

The sun had just climbed onto the horizon. In the moist early-morning air, it appeared huge and shimmered briefly, like a ball of fire ready to spill its flames over the land. As Thad scraped, exposing more of the bone, he was again struck by the extraordinary realization that this was the first sunlight to shine on this bone in millions of years.

The exposed patch was big enough for Thad to realize that this fossil belonged to a larger animal than any they had found thus far. Within two hours, he knew that he was looking at the very small part of a backbone. What had Babcock called these? Vertebrates! Of course. They looked fragile, too. Thad could discern some hairline cracks. It was time to go back and get the professor.

"Astonishing! Beautiful!" Babcock had exposed several more square inches. "I doubt it's a dinosaur."

"Oh!" said Thad, disappointed.

"Don't fret, Thad. I have a hunch it's something that many would give their eyeteeth for, especially if it is intact and articulate."

"What is it, sir?" Thad asked.

"A fish," Jonathan Cabot interjected. "Do you think it's one of the portheians?"

"Very possibly a *Portheus molossus.* Or perhaps a new species of portheus."

"It's going to be difficult to excavate." Nat Forbes was studying the cliff face. "Gravity is not on our side in a situation like this." Nat was the expedition's artist. It was his job to diagram just how the bones lay after they were revealed in the initial exposure. His drawings helped determine the plan of the excavation. "This one's going to take some real strategy to get out."

It was going to be the first significant find. Before the excavation could commence, the entire company would have to halt so that there would be time to dig. It was Babcock's notion that the fossil might give the Black Hills Expedition some real historical importance. He was counting on this to convince Custer that it was worth the delay. And he sent Jonathan Cabot to do the convincing. Jonathan's blend of diplomacy, natural superiority without arrogance, and cleverness would stand him in good stead with Custer.

Jonathan shrewdly took to the meeting two reporters from the east, thus turning it into a press conference to announce that the Harvard team was on the brink of a fossil discovery of "great antiquity" and "unequaled significance." As Jonathan reported back to the team, his speech was laced with superlatives. The finishing touch was when he suggested that Custer's name might be included in the formal Latin nomenclature of the species—*Portheus custerus.* That did it. Custer announced that the Harvard team should have all the time that was necessary.

And it took a great deal of time to tool out the sandstone and shale. The fossil lay horizontally in an exposed bed of sediments. As they dug, the remaining sandstone above the fossil hung out farther and farther, becoming an increasing threat to the bones being exposed below.

"We are going to have to start making some support struts," Oliver said to Thad after they had been excavating for only a few hours. "Or that overhang will come crashing down on everything. One of the funny parts of this excavation business, especially with big bones like this, is that the closer you get to freeing them up, the more likely it becomes that they get broken in the process. That's why we have to harden the exposed parts with shellac and then put a cast of flour paste on them. And sometimes it's too difficult to free them up enough to even do that."

"So then what do you do?" Thad asked.

"We take the whole business—matrix rock and all. That's what the big chunks that the bones are embedded in are called—matrix rock. Better safe than sorry, although it's not very convenient lugging such big hunks around. And the thinner, more fragile bones can still come to harm even within the matrix rock."

Unexpectedly, it was Thad who came up with an innovative method for ensuring that the fragile fossil bones stayed intact. They had been excavating for almost ten days, and indeed it was a time to celebrate.

The creature they had been digging out lay before them, twisted slightly so its spine faced out.

They had succeeded in exposing most of the head. The trunk region, too, had been uncovered, although many of the ribs had vanished. And there had not yet been revealed any fins.

"Eons ago, this fellow swam in the vast Cretaceous sea," Babcock intoned. "I would imagine from looking at these sediments that this was once an ancient streambed running off from the sea, and his body came to rest here in death, covered by the sands of countless millennia, then eroded by the endless winds of eternity."

As Babcock spoke, Thad concentrated on the animal, not in life but in its position of death. Thad was unsure whether he sensed or actually saw the dim impression of a kind of forelimb frozen in an upward sweep, as if swimming toward the sky. But suddenly, he seemed to know exactly how the rest of the creature lay and where the unseen parts were.

"Oliver," he asked, "those fin things you were talking about—they're kind of like paddles, foot paddles for this critter?"

"Yes," Oliver said. "Why do you ask?"

"I think they might lie right over there."

He was right. The front fins lay at an angle off the head.

Babcock stood back in amazement. Later, members of the team would say that the boy was uncanny. He could barely read, yet he saw through stone. And not just saw through it but seemed to have an intuition for each pressure point, fault, and cleavage line.

The fins were extremely fragile and even with plastering and cutting deeply into the matrix rock, it would be delicate work.

"This is going to be very tough," Nat Forbes said, rubbing his jaw. "How do we work with something that flat and thin? That matrix sandstone isn't going to do beans for us here."

"What about splinting it up?" Thad said.

"What do you mean?" Oliver asked.

"If the sandstone hunk isn't enough protection, let's splint the whole thing up like you would a broken arm. Only we'll do it before the thing breaks."

"It might work," said Nat. "Let's think about it. Too late now to get started."

But Thad returned later that evening. Even with the splinting, it would be risky. He looked at the thin, flat, exposed surface of the fossilized fin and imagined it splintering into a thousand tiny little cracks. What it needs, Thad thought, is the protection of a strong skin. If only I could glue one down. That was it, he suddenly realized—a skin! Now, what could be used as a substitute skin?

Paper turned out to be the second skin, a special kind of thin paper that Nat Forbes used for drawing and tracing. The team watched the next morning as Thad tried out his idea.

He held the paper against the fin, three-quarters of

which stood out in relief from the rock matrix, and carefully traced its outline. He cut out the shapes and then cut these shapes into smaller pieces that appeared like parts of a paper jigsaw puzzle. He thinned out shellac with some preservative alcohol and then proceeded to dip each piece into the solution. The pieces of paper clung to the fractured fossil like a skin. A splint was then put around the bone. Then strips of burlap dipped in flour paste encased the splint. They were now ready to dig the rest of the bone all the way out from the matrix.

The portheus fin came out beautifully, without a fracture. Thad's new technique was immediately applied to other fragile parts of the fossil. Babcock was greatly pleased, but he was beginning to speak longingly of the fossil-rich Judith River Badlands of Montana. The team had been completely immersed in the excavation, which had taken over two weeks. They had become quite removed from the rest of the expedition, which, they now realized, was in the throes of excitement over numerous rumors of gold. Custer himself could barely maintain the dignity required of an expedition supposedly dedicated to science. He was as infected with dreams of gold as the most common foot soldier. He had almost entirely forgotten about Jonathan Cabot's suggestion that the fossil be named after him.

Thad rode ahead, now scouting for any "extraordinary Cretaceous or Jurassic" sediments that might yield a dinosaur. Professor Babcock had drawn diagrams of the sedimentary sequences, stippling the paper to show the shift in textures of the rock strata through the years.

But if the "great ones"—as Babcock sometimes referred to the dinosaurs—were present, the natural machinery of erosion, wind, water, ice, and gravity, the agents of change, had not yet pulled back the earth's skin to the point of revealing these ancient creatures.

At night, Thad pored over a copy of a translation of a book by Carolus Linnaeus that he had borrowed from Jonathan Cabot. It was called *Systema naturae.*

"Musci?" he whispered to himself one evening as he studied in the flare of his kerosene lamp. He had not heard Jonathan enter his tent.

"What'd you say?"

"Oh, I'm just trying to sound out this word. It looks so simple but I never heard of the word."

"What's that?" Jonathan asked, going over to look. "Oh, *musci!* That's Latin for moss."

"Lordy! I don't want to read Latin. I want to learn how to read English!"

"Well, it looks like you have indeed mastered all the English names of the categories of living things. But he does list all the living things in Latin, doesn't he?" Jonathan picked up the book and flipped through it. "Ah ha! I knew there had to be a translation of this table. See, right here in the appendix, both Latin and English names given—*Zea mays!"*

"What's that?" Thad asked.

"Corn."

Thad got up and looked over Jonathan's shoulder to where he was pointing. "Yep. Now that's spelled the way it should be. I'll stick to the English."

Despite such satisfactions, it was getting harder and harder for Thad to tolerate what he saw around him. There had been rumors of gold for weeks. Then one of the expedition miners took a bottle of gold dust with a few tiny nuggets in it from his pocket and showed it to the general. Even though it amounted to only ten cents' worth of gold, the dream was confirmed into a dime of reality. By the next day, every pick, pothook, tent pin, and shovel had been drafted into service as people swarmed over the discovery site. Babcock and his team occasionally ventured there, too, but Thad did not. He either stayed in the lab tent and tried his luck at drawing some of the specimens or, more often, went scouting for the stone sandwiches of the Jurassic or Cretaceous sediments. On some of these excursions, the young Private Ewert, whom he had first met back at Fort Lincoln, would accompany him. Ewert seemed to enjoy Thad's company and, even more so, loved sounding off to Thad about the general, whom he could not stand.

Each day brought an increasing sense of foreboding as the expedition advanced. With the discovery of the first traces of gold, it sharpened. Thad didn't sense danger as much as *violation*, and he realized he had felt it from his first sighting of the dark smudge that was the Black Hills. The power of the *Paha Sapa* could be felt even at that great distance.

Now he was sure that the land was indeed sacred, and that this expedition was a profanity. He had thought about getting out. The money was good, but no money was that good. He liked Babcock all right, but he did not have the kind of loyalty for him that he had felt for Mr. Jim. There was one simple reason why Thad did not leave: He didn't want to die, and he knew for certain that Custer would set the Ree scouts on him.

Thad, along with Private Ewert, had just ridden down a defile into the wash of a dry creek bed. He dismounted to sift through some rocky fragments. It was very hard, he now found, to pass up a place such as this.

"Stones and bones." Ewert sighed. "You never get tired of it, do you?"

"Guess not," Thad said. "Here, catch." He tossed him a small rock striped with ripple marks. "Touch a million-year-old piece of life."

"A million! No kidding."

"Yes. Maybe fifty million years old."

"You're joking. That's before Adam and Eve."

"Guess so. Before Custer, that's for sure."

"Why don't you get out, Thad?" Ewert suddenly asked. "You're not part of the army. You can quit."

"Well, quitting the professor wouldn't be right, and besides, Custer might set the Rees after me."

"Naw. They're all caught up with the gold now. They don't care. The scouts have done their job. Is it true that they named that thing you dug up after the general?"

"So I hear."

That evening just at sunset, Thad mounted Jasper again and headed to the dry creek bed. This time he was alone. He wanted to think about what Ewert had said, and the best way for him to think these days was to sift through the rocky soil. Touching the earth, he seemed to touch time, and he found a great comfort in this deep time that might be measured in millions of years.

But then there was no time to think. He felt something strike the side of his head and the sound was not unlike the one his spade had made at the escarpment, the dull *clunk* of metal against fossil. When he came to, he thought, Where are the Rees? He sensed that he was not in the dry streambed but on some kind of pallet. Then he thought of a little joke that Oliver and Jonathan would have liked. It was this: If he had died, which apparently he had not, he should try to select a place good for fossilization and convenient to excavate. The streambed would have been perfect.

CHAPTER
14

"I thought you were not a miner."

The face hung over him like a bronze sun—Standing Eagle. And behind him Thad could see Black Elk, frail, his eyes swimming with confusion.

"Pahuska must get out." The soft voice came from behind him. Thad was still lying down, so he craned his neck around. The warrior who spoke was wearing a buckskin shirt and the red feathers of a hawk in his flowing hair.

"The Men-Who-Pick-Up-Bones," he continued. "Their medicine no good for Pahuska Custer. Tell them that." Perhaps this was all the English he knew, for the warrior then spoke in his own language. His sense of command, his authority filled the tipi. All eyes were on him. Then Thad heard Black Elk say something, and within the rush of words, he caught the familiar ones, Tashunka Witko. The meaning exploded in his brain— Crazy Horse.

Thad slowly lifted himself up to a standing position. He felt shaky, but the dread that he had felt for days suddenly melted away. He was now face to face with that which he had feared and hoped against. And yet there was a feeling of lightness, as if the excuse of this expedition had finally been stripped away.

Next to Crazy Horse stood a smallish man. In the dim light of the tipi, his deep-copper skin glowed as bright as embers. He was silent but stared at Thad, his body and face taut. He looked at Crazy Horse occasionally, as if awaiting a signal to pounce. Thad wondered. It was as if the man were coiled in tension, ready to unleash himself at the slightest sign—as if he were the spring behind Crazy Horse.

"I will do what you ask, but . . ." Thad now turned to Standing Eagle and Black Elk. "I am not a miner. I am one of the ones who picks up bones." Standing Eagle translated what Thad had said. Crazy Horse responded in his own language, which Standing Eagle then translated for Thad.

"Crazy Horse says we know that, and we know you never carry the firearms when you dig the bones, only the pickaxes. But we all still feel great anger. You are still a part of Pahuska's march through our sacred country. And even for the Men-Who-Pick-Up-Bones, their medicine will thin when they serve men like Pahuska Custer."

The small man who had stood beside him handed Crazy Horse a blanket, which he draped around his shoulders. Then Crazy Horse's eyes narrowed to mere slits as he looked hard at Thad. Warriors stepped apart and Crazy Horse left the tipi. Others then left, too. And finally only Thad and Black Elk were left. Thad now knew with finality that he had let himself be used— used by Custer along with the rest of Babcock's team as a camouflage and a charm to fool the Indians.

Thad felt compelled to speak, even if Black Elk did not understand his words. He had to tell Black Elk what he had come to realize at Harney Peak. With the toe of his boot, he scratched an outline of the peak into the dirt floor. He looked around for something with a finer point and spotted a stick of wood. He used it to inscribe a human figure on top of the peak. The outline looked almost identical to the one drawn on the outside of Black Elk's tipi.

"When I climbed the peak, Black Elk, I knew that I was seeing through the eyes of the boy in the drawing. I knew then that we were all wrong, so wrong."

Black Elk seemed to understand what Thad was saying. He picked up the stick and stippled the dirt above the peak with short slashes. As he drew, he spoke. "Nothing left . . ." he said in English. Standing Eagle had reentered the tipi, and Black Elk continued in his own language. "Nothing left," Standing Eagle repeated.

"Black Elk is right. The bullets will rain from the sky and the gold will be ripped out of the earth and the people and the earth will die."

Thad looked at the slashing marks in the earthen floor of the tipi. As he stared at the marks, he felt Black Elk's hand lightly on his shoulder. "Come. Come," Black Elk was saying. "Come to tipi of my mother, White Cow Sees."

Sharing a somber nighttime meal with Black Elk's family, Thad asked about the small man in the lodge. "Little Big Man," Black Elk replied. In his hesitant English he conveyed that Little Big Man often acted as an envoy, or agent, between Crazy Horse and representatives of the government in Washington. Then Black Elk fell silent.

It was a clear night and the stars began to twinkle fiercely. Suddenly, there was a smear of white across the Big Dipper as a comet streaked through the Dakota sky. The camp tensed. A meeting of his closest counselors was called by Crazy Horse. Black Elk was called to join them.

When he returned from the meeting, he seemed particularly agitated as he and Thad and Standing Eagle sat by the dying embers of the campfire.

"It is a sign." Standing Eagle translated Black Elk's words.

But then Black Elk seized a stick and inscribed once more the picture that Thad had drawn in the tipi earlier. This time, he drew a comet's tail sailing over the peak. He looked up directly into Thad's eyes. "Wakan-Tanka," he said very clearly. "Wakan-Tanka angry . . . angry Bluecoats come. Wakan-Tanka angry with Sioux . . ." and then English words failed him and he continued in his own language.

Standing Eagle spoke. "Black Elk say comet is a sign of our Creator's anger. Wakan-Tanka not just angry with Bluecoats but with Sioux for allowing Bluecoats to continue in sacred land." Standing Eagle went on to explain that the counselors had agreed with Black Elk on the meaning of the comet, and they had decided on a course of action. It would not mean war—not yet. But their plan would include Thad.

"Black Elk now comes to tell you the words of Crazy Horse." Standing Eagle was translating as rapidly as he could. "The comet is the flash of Wakan-Tanka's anger. Crazy Horse say tonight we must act, to stop Wakan-Tanka anger with the Sioux." And then Standing Eagle's face split into a grin as he heard Black Elk's next words. "Black Elk say that you must know that Crazy Horse is cunning as he is brave. He know all tricks. He invent traps many times before this for Bluecoats." He paused a minute and listened to more of what Black Elk was saying. Black Elk never took his eyes off Thad. It was as if Thad was gradually beginning to understand his meaning without the words. . . .

The gist of it was that Wakan-Tanka was most angry with the Ree scouts who served as guides for Custer in leading the *Wasichu,* or white people, into the sacred hills. Pahuska Custer depended heavily on the Rees, and the Rees would be nervous tonight for they would have seen Wakan-Tanka's anger flash across the sky. Now, with Thad's help, a scout would be decoyed.

"A comet's a comet," Custer said testily the next morning to a Lieutenant Calhoun. "What are they so fidgety about?"

"They're Injuns, sir. Makes no difference they been with white men for weeks now. They want to get us all out of here."

"Well, I'm the commander-in-chief and I'm the one who gives orders. Send them in here. I'll deal with this."

There was, however, a slight commotion outside the tent.

"What's that?" Custer barked.

Calhoun looked out. "That kid from the Harvard team—Thaddeus Longsworth. He's back."

"Good Lord. Send him in. Thought he'd be dead."

Thad entered. There was a large blue-and-yellow bruise that had spread over his left temple and engulfed one whole eye to the bridge of his nose.

"Delivered from the jaws of a dinosaur?" Custer asked.

"No, Crazy Horse." Thad was sure to say the name loud and clear so Custer's two Ree scouts would hear. Then the news would travel like wildfire.

"Sssh!" Custer hissed. "I thought he was down on the Powder River." There had been rumors about Sitting Bull's presence in the Black Hills all along. But rumors of Crazy Horse were another thing, and Thad knew it.

"He's not," Thad answered in a voice only slightly lower.

"Well, you seem to have lived to tell about it," Custer said in a whisper. "You some kind of Injun lover?"

Thad ignored the remark. "Crazy Horse says you got to get out, and get out fast."

"So he does, does he? Well, boy, I can see you've been impressed by our Indian friends, but they are just no match for us."

Thad figured he would say that. Custer was hardly going to leave the Black Hills just because some two-bit Indian leader (in his opinion) had said "scat." If the comet had been taken as a bad omen by the Ree, Custer would regard it as a minor problem. Nevertheless, Thad's purpose had been accomplished. He knew that the Ree scouts outside the tent had overheard him say that Crazy Horse was near. That was enough. The rest would take care of itself.

That evening, Thad heard that the Ree had sought a meeting with Custer. He went looking for Private Ewert.

"Did you hear there was a meeting with the Ree scouts?" Thad asked Ewert when he found him.

"I heard the whole thing. I was right in the connecting tent sewing up the general's britches for him."

"The Ree don't want to go on, do they?" Thad asked.

"You can bet on that."

"So what'd he do?"

Ewert sighed. "Would you believe that he opened up a bottle of whiskey and poured a glass for each one of the scouts, then dropped in a gold nugget? He promised that there would be a glass waiting every day for each one of them as long as they continue."

"And they agreed?" Thad asked.

"Course they did. Show me an Indian that would turn down a glass of whiskey."

Thad thought he had indeed met a few.

The next day, the Ree scout Hard Bone had ridden down a defile to a gurgling creek. As Hard Bone moved his horse through the shallow waters of the creek, he was thinking about gold and comets and whiskey. He was thinking about how much he hated Long Hair Custer. But he hated Red Cloud, too, down at the agency, and he hated the headman in his village who told his mother, Yellow Hawk Woman, that he, Hard Bone, was a shame to his people, and then took Hard Bone's wife for his own. He wouldn't wait for the general's liquor that night.

He took a flask from his pocket and began swigging from it. As he drank, he began speaking aloud, mostly about those he hated. He heard a thrashing up in a stand of cottonwood trees. He looked in that direction. Were his eyes tricking him? Had the whiskey worked that quickly? It looked like an eagle in the cottonwoods. Maybe this was a sign. He headed his horse up the embankment toward the trees. He had just dismounted when two warriors stepped out. One held the eagle decoy. The other had white hailstones painted on his body and a red lightning bolt on his cheek.

"You hate me, too, Hard Bone?"

"Crazy Horse!"

Another Ree scout found Hard Bone's body the next day. He had been scalped, but the scalp had not been taken—a bad sign. It meant that whoever had killed him did not respect him enough to take his scalp. And there was little doubt who had killed him. A red bolt of lightning zigzagged across Hard Bone's chest, Crazy Horse's signature. And although Hard Bone's eyes were cloudy in death and stared sightless at the sky, the Ree scout could imagine that his last vision had been of painted hailstones.

Directly after reporting to Custer, Thad had gone to Babcock. He told him the situation, which Babcock and the rest of the team fully appreciated. Again, it was planned that Cabot would be dispatched on a mission of "reason" to Custer: to reason him out of the Black Hills as quickly as possible.

But there was no need. By that evening, the news about Hard Bone had hit the camp. The Ree scouts became fractious and drunk. In short, they were impossible. The main mission of verifying that there was gold in the hills had been accomplished. So the next morning, the message passed through the columns that the expedition would be departing the Black Hills soon.

Babcock's party began making their own final preparations, crating and packing the few fossils they had found.

On the seventh of August, the expedition broke camp and, striking a course due north, headed for Fort Abraham Lincoln.

CHAPTER

➤ 15

When Julian had first seen the river at Brown's Landing—boiling and furious, a demon of a river—he knew
he would never forget it. He knew that the river would
run through the deepest part of his memory, become
part of that subterranean stream of remembrance that
would forever prompt the rawest of sensations.

They had ridden alongside it on their way to the
fossil beds, and twice they had had to cross it. Where
it ran slow and high, the river spread indiscriminately,
spilling over banks, eating up trees. Where it ran fast,
it broke loose—leaping, tearing, gouging out the banks.
In the middle, the current erupted into foamy crests

like the spiked back of an armored dinosaur. This was the Missouri, and in the face of its wild power, he could not think of the order and divine destinies that were the focus of his father's work.

Their destination was a region called Medicine Buttes. There they camped on a flat-topped hill that overlooked the Judith River Badlands. The flat basin from which the buttes rose was mostly prairie, with ample grass for their horses. The Cretaceous sea had deposited the sandstone sediments from which the buttes had risen. When the sea had drained and the swamp evaporated, the river began its work, carving out its mad course and slicing the countryside into a maze of gorges, canyons, and ravines. It was into these deep cuts that they went in search of fossils, and it was from the crumbling dark shale—the mudstone, and the sandstone, and the siltstone—that the story of the terrible lizards began to emerge.

No longer were they finding mere fragments of the story of life. It was as if entire sentences and then paragraphs could begin to be read and understood. There were dinosaurs at the bottom of the strata and small mammals in the higher levels. It seemed as if all the smaller players of the Mesozoic era were there. They found traces of an ancient sea urchin, the prints of crinoids, or sea lilies, the ammonite, a sturdy fellow with coiled shell that was honeycombed for strength, allowing it to sink to great depths in the sea. There were scales of garfish and skulls of ancient terrapins, the turtles. And then, of course, there were the reptilian monarchs of the Mesozoic era—the dinosaurs.

Comparisons could be made, new species defined, new concepts concerning categories and classification of types could be built. And this was exactly what DeMott was doing. Cores of horns, frills, and pelvic girdles had melted out of the sediments in lovely entirety.

It was late afternoon when Julian saw the odd fellow entering camp. They were beginning to take tea in the lab tent when the man walked into the tent. "Ah, Mr. Henshaw!" DeMott exclaimed. He apparently knew the man, although Julian had never met him. "Bobber Henshaw, my team."

Henshaw was a grizzled man with a clouded eye. Built low to the ground, he appeared in his general shape to be bowed—his legs, his back, even his arms hung curved like semicircles at his side. He stood bent but powerful, built to withstand heavy loads. Like so many living things found in the wildest and harshest environments, his very contours seemed to possess the natural geometry that would let him endure despite the stresses nature served up.

DeMott had begun a hurried introduction of the team, dispensing with titles and often first names. The men seemed as mystified by the man's presence as Julian. "Mr. Wilbur, here, and next to him, Ormsby, Hamilton-Phipps, Albert Blanchford, and my son, Julian DeMott." Bobber fixed Julian with his one clear eye and seemed to incline his head toward him in a kind of nod. But it was the clouded eye that disturbed Julian. It had a strangely disorienting effect on him.

The temperature was 110 degrees. Algernon DeMott stroked a thighbone supported on two sawhorses while looking at a small row of horn-shaped pieces set in front of him on the ground. It was too hot for lively chatter. What little conversation had been taking place evaporated with the arrival of Bobber Henshaw. The gentlemen gradually began to make excuses to leave the tent. Julian, however, was in the midst of sorting some very small bone fragments for his father. He was supposed to have completed it the day before and was worried that if he got up to leave now, his father would be displeased. So he felt compelled to stay, although he would have preferred to broil in the sun than remain in the presence of this strange man.

"Guess who's finally here?" Henshaw asked as the last man left the tent.

"Cunningham," DeMott replied. His voice was level, without a hint of inflection. "We must have Cunningham and the entire Yale team for tea. It is only proper. I'll send Hamilton-Phipps with the invitation."

"And guess who's coming in a matter of days?"

"Babcock, no doubt."

"No doubt," Bobber said, looking at DeMott. He turned to Julian. "If it wasn't for me following Babcock out here, your father would never know 'bout this place," he said proudly.

"Nor would Cunningham," DeMott said crisply. It

had been one of Cunningham's colleagues from Yale on a visit to England who had told DeMott about the remarkable sediments of the Judith River Badlands.

"What's taken him so long?" DeMott asked.

"He got hung up on that fool expedition into the Black Hills."

"Oh," DeMott said. There was almost a yawn in his voice. "The one under the command of the ever-so-dashing young general—what's his name?"

"Custer."

"Was it a success?"

"Guess so. Never thought the Sioux would let them in there."

"Why not?" Julian asked suddenly.

"Them's their sacred grounds," Bobber said. "The *Paha Sapa* they call them. They're real tetchy about that country."

"But this Custer," DeMott continued, "went in with government permission?"

"Yes, sir," Bobber replied.

"I don't understand," Julian said.

"Nothing to understand. There's gold in the hills. There's land. Lots of white folks interested in that land. Naturally, the government would stick up for them."

"But I thought you said it was sacred to the Sioux?"

"Son . . ."

Julian bristled at Henshaw's familiarity. "I beg your pardon," he said sharply.

Bobber looked up as if he did not understand his offense. He coughed a bit and then began to speak. As he spoke, he looked down at his feet and shuffled them rather nimbly in an odd little dance. "What an Indian thinks is sacred and what a white man thinks are two different things."

"But . . ."

"They're just savages, son. You goin' to go round asking every groundhog, rattlesnake, and toad his idea of religion, and then come up with one that fits all?" Bobber then turned to DeMott. "Pardon me, sir, maybe I'm out of place speaking to yer son this way."

Julian felt the man was totally out of place speaking to *anyone* this way.

"No! No! Not at all." Algernon DeMott spoke heartily. "You put it very well, Mr. Henshaw. Although you might not be familiar with my theory of Divine Intelligence, your notions are quite compatible."

"Are they, Father?" Julian asked, mystified. Until now, he had pretty much thought of his father's theory in the abstract. There was this gigantic framework with niches for everything, from trilobites and slugs to reptiles, birds, and mammals. Once the crowning achievement of the reptilian age had been accomplished—the dinosaurs—and the Lord had moved on to creating man, Julian for one failed to see the gradations. He knew that there were people in service, like Mrs. Oliver and McGuff, and then there were masters, like his father and Lord Bartholomew. He could understand that McGuff would never learn Latin or Mrs. Oliver, square roots. Maybe they weren't smart enough, or maybe they simply didn't need to know. He did not know whether he was clever enough to make a lemon tart or pull colors from the earth as McGuff did.

Julian was feeling overwhelmed by the conversation and the company. He had no notion of where his father had picked up such an odious man as Bobber Henshaw, but he was not going to stick around to sort bones.

Later that evening after supper, as the the last embers of the campfire burned, Julian listened while Sammy Wilbur and Ian Hamilton-Phipps discussed a recent find.

"Would you call this a horn, Bertie?" Hamilton-Phipps asked.

"A horn? Good heavens, no! More of a cratered plate, I'd say." Wilbur twisted his neck as he spoke, as if trying to escape some phantom of the clerical collar that he had almost immediately ceased to wear in the extreme heat.

"Hard to tell, though, without more of the facial structure," Julian offered. He had been sitting on a keg a little bit off to the side of the conversation, and just then he became aware of someone behind him. Bobber Henshaw, crouching low. He nudged Julian lightly in the ribs in what he supposed was intended to be a friendly gesture.

"I know where you kin git the rest of that fella's face," he said softly. Julian felt his skin prickle. He turned his head as if he had not heard but was still focused on the conversation of Hamilton-Phipps and Wilbur.

"Sundowner's Ridge—was just telling your pappy about it. The place is jam-packed with them fossils."

"Oh," Julian said coolly. "Well, I'm sure Father will organize a survey and do some preliminary digging there in the near future. I think I shall turn in now." He got up to leave.

As he lay in his sleeping bag, he tried hard not to think about Bobber Henshaw, but it was impossible not to. How had his father met him? And why was Henshaw so proud of having trailed this Professor Babcock out here? It was not a particularly reputable pastime to go about spying on people. He had seemed to be trying to impress Julian when he had told him this, as well as when he had sidled up to him that very evening and dropped the information about the place called Sundowner's Ridge.

It was two days later, and elaborate preparations were under way for tea. Bertie Blanchford had tried to no avail to describe to the camp cook, a man named Rooster, a crumpet, in hopes that Rooster could achieve some semblance of one in his tin oven.

"This whatcha had in mind?" Rooster said, walking over with a lumpy thing on the long-handled spatula that resembled a buffalo chip more than anything else.

"Hmmm," said Bertie. "Somewhat larger, but may I try one and we'll see."

"Help yerself."

Bertie drew a fresh handkerchief from his pocket and scooped up the aspiring crumpet.

"Tad heavy," he muttered. He took it over to a table.

"A crumpet, Bertie?" Ian Hamilton-Phipps had walked up.

"More like pre-Cambrian rock—Lewisian formation." He sliced it in half and took a bite.

"Whatcha think?" Rooster asked.

Bertie's teeth ground on the gravelly texture. "Well, Rooster . . ." he said, swallowing and thinking of the impressive set of choppers he had just plucked from some strata the day before. "Quite good, actually. Not perhaps the subtlety of texture of an English one, but quite respectable. I think that instead of clotted cream as a spread—which we don't have, anyway—some antelope meat would be more suitable. We still have some from last night's supper, don't we?"

"Yes, sir. I'll slice it up."

"And if we do have any jam left, that would be a nice touch, too."

The would-be crumpet, the antelope meat, and the nice touch of jam were all part of an effort to extend a most civilized welcome—in the form of the venerable English institution of high tea—to Nathaniel Cunningham and the newly arrived team from Yale.

As Ian Hamilton-Phipps had so carefully explained earlier to Bobber Henshaw, Rooster, and the two Crow Indian guides, "We're very good at this—we English. We love friendly competition. Look, here's Bertie, Christ Church College, Oxford, and Sammy, Trinity College, Cambridge, both working side by side. We can do the same with the Yale gents. Let bygones be bygones. The Revolutionary War was over one hundred years ago. So why not have the chappies for tea?"

Bobber Henshaw, Julian observed, was noticeably absent that afternoon. This did not surprise Julian. He figured that if Bobber had trailed Babcock out to the Badlands as he'd claimed and then reported back to Cunningham about the rich fossil deposits Babcock had found, it was only common sense to assume that Cunningham would not be thrilled to find him in the DeMott camp. Tea or not, the Americans would look askance at seeing their informer working for the British. It would be awkward at the very least.

The Yale team arrived and were cordially greeted. Any competitive fervor was kept neatly under wraps, and the spirit of the occasion was maintained in the best English tradition as described by Ian Hamilton-Phipps. As the Cunningham group was munching away on their antelope crumpets, Julian was surprised when he heard his father's response to an inquiry about a nearby ridge.

"The ridge just to the west of here?"

"Yes, that's the one," Cunningham responded. "Two miles beyond the draw."

Cunningham was a tall man of easy elegance. Tanned, with sparkling blue eyes and dark-brown hair streaked with gray, he cut a handsome figure. They were taking tea outside under a canvas shade, as the lab tent was too small to accommodate the group. Also, they were not particularly keen on having the Yale team see all of their bones on display. Cunningham got up to point in the direction of the ridge.

"Yes, do you see that very rounded-looking one, about a mile and a half off? Almost directly beyond it, there's a steep ridge that runs between two buttes."

He looks at home in this setting, Julian thought, natural, much more so than my own father. When he arrived he had even spoken some words to the Crow in their own language. It was evident that he had very good relations with the Indians. He must be wondering how we got here, Julian reflected, how in the world we heard about the Medicine Buttes all the way over in England. Yet Cunningham was too gracious to inquire. He would only wonder in silence.

"Oh well," DeMott continued, "I'm afraid that ridge is a bit of a disappointment."

Julian opened his eyes in wide dismay as his father spoke.

"Really?" Cunningham said, and took his chair again.

Julian stared at his father. That very morning DeMott had returned from the ridge terribly excited about the prospects for excavation. Bobber had accompanied him. The camp had been empty except for Julian, who was still sorting bones in the lab tent. His father had gone in to share the good news, and to praise Bobber Henshaw's uncanny abilities for finding rich fossil beds. They would commence new excavations as soon as they had finished up in the areas they were currently digging.

How could his father now be saying that he found this ridge a disappointment? Julian wondered whether Cunningham believed him. The man might be gracious, but he was no fool. He had a hard edge to him and would not, Julian imagined, give up on a notion so easily. Apparently Algernon DeMott sensed this, too. He therefore elaborated a bit, but casually, as if what he was saying could hold little interest for a man of Cunningham's intelligence.

"My guide and I surveyed it quite thoroughly. Not much there. Indians seem to visit it quite a bit. Several of their, uh, religious or sacred drawings about the place; a small cave filled with what I suppose are their amulets and charms."

"Don't touch them!" Cunningham leaped to his feet. "I have always prided myself on maintaining the best of relations with the Sioux. You cannot trespass on their sacred grounds." He sat down abruptly but continued to speak with vehemence. "This ridiculous expedition of Custer's is going to take its toll. I would have nothing to do with it. And, I might add, it only confirms in my mind what a genuine idiot George Babcock is that he would drag Harvard into such folly."

If Julian was shocked by his father's deliberately misleading Cunningham, he was horrified when he followed his father and Bobber Henshaw later that night. They were making their way toward Sundowner's Ridge.

They're just savages. You goin' to go round asking every ground-hog, rattlesnake, and toad his idea of religion . . . ?

Bobber's words echoed in Julian's ear as he watched the two men in the moon-streaked night. They dipped their brushes in a mixture of water and rich red clays and began to paint symbols on the rock walls, symbols that had been created by those beings that they scorned.

Julian had given them a wide berth because he was fairly sure where they were heading, and he knew that there would be no place to hide on the bare flanks of the ridge that slid down into a kind of miniature valley. On the other side of the valley, not more than two hundred feet away, the valley floor began to sweep up again into a cliff. It faced west and had been scoured out by the wind, leaving a large overhang. Hidden from the moon and pressed between shale and shadow in the broad margins of ancient time, Julian watched as the hand that had written volumes on theories of God and law and the history of the earth and all matters of living things now raised the brush to counterfeit a faith it had so recently mocked.

CHAPTER

16

Professor Babcock's intention was to get to the Judith River Badlands before winter closed in. They had barely ridden a day north toward Fort Lincoln when it was decided that Thad would break from the expedition and ride south to Nebraska and the Red Cloud agency, which served as a liaison between the federal government and the Sioux. Once at the agency, he would act as a representative for Babcock and the Harvard team in requesting permission from the great chief Red Cloud to pass through Sioux territory on their way into that part of Montana. The Badlands were not considered to be sacred grounds by the Sioux, but Babcock felt it was judicious to obtain permission to pass through their country. He intended to be every bit as cautious and diplomatic in his relations with the Sioux as Cunningham.

Thad had succeeded in getting an audience with the chief. Red Cloud had seemed old and tired, not nearly so fearsome or powerful as Thad had imagined. Thad stated his business and then politely listened to the old chief's complaints, which ranged from his back troubles to his troubles with crooked agents, to his grief over the cantankerous young upstart Sioux like Crazy Horse. Thad was shocked by Red Cloud's garrulousness and relieved when he finally said that Babcock and his team could pass through the Sioux country and look for bones in the Badlands. The day before Thad left the agency, he had received a telegram from the professor confirming that he would be going to Montana almost immediately:

> *Arriving by September 5, Fort Benton. Field season will be short, but we'll get a start and establish base camp so we may recommence promptly in the spring. Have wired three hundred dollars and a credit letter for the bank. Please purchase four pack mules when you arrive, camp outfit, team ponies, wagon, hire cook and driver. Best of luck with Red Cloud. Sincerely, George Babcock*

Thad had been anxious to get away. The agency was a depressing place. Its purpose—the purpose of all the federal agencies—was to distribute food, medical supplies, and clothing to the Indians. Often the supplies were spoiled. And Thad found that the agency Indians were either old and defeated like Red Cloud or angry and sullen like the young men Thad had seen about the agency buildings. He could feel their bristling anger whenever he passed a group of them, and dared not breathe a word about how he had ridden with the Custer expedition.

The country seemed to open up in the Montana territory. He took a diagonal route north and west across prairies thick with grass. There were herds of elk and deer. When he came to a soddy stretch of uprooted grass, he learned that this was the sign that a grizzly bear had passed that way searching for the delicious wild artichokes that grew in the prairie grass and that the bears savored. Thad always camped near a tree, slinging his food high up in the branches in case a grizzly came in search of his crumbs of hardtack or bacon rind left from supper.

He skirted around the Judith River Mountains through a stretch of badlands with high broken hills, some rounded off into the domed sandstone mountains called buttes. Rising lower than the buttes were some gentler hills called bluffs. But there was hardly a tree in sight and water was hard to come by. Then he emerged into a great open plain. To the west, the Rockies rose, their snowy peaks burnished by the morning sun.

Thad slept where the day ended, without a tent but

encircled by a crown of mountain ranges—to the south, the Judith River Mountains; the Sweet Grass Mountains to the west; the Rockies to the north; and to the east, the Little Rockies, and the Medicine Bow and the Bear Paw ranges. Thad leaned back against his pack in wonderment. Had these mountains really risen from the sea as Babcock said? Was this what the Lord was talking about when He commanded, "Let the waters under the heavens be gathered together unto one place, and let dry land appear"? Mr. Jim used to read aloud from Genesis at least once a week on the trail. It would take eight or nine verses to describe the Lord's work. Seven days for the whole shebang. This seemed pretty short to Thad—maybe the Lord counted time differently than people did.

Thad gazed up at the night, tatted with stars. He might have touched one, they hung so huge and still. And if they were really millions of miles away, what difference did that make? He felt that he could touch them. Distance seemed meaningless to Thad that night; the time it would take to cross to the stars, useless to measure. And if one forgot about measuring time, then somehow those dim tracts of the past became brighter, and one could imagine further back than the mountains, when there was a sea, and before the sea . . . Thad fell asleep under the light of ancient stars and dreamed of that time before time.

CHAPTER 17

"Goldarn it," Thad muttered, "I'm going to have to start making a list of all the queer stuff that hits me. First a chicken and now this!"

"This" was a drunken man who had been sent flying headfirst out the swinging doors of the Hang It Up saloon. He looked unsteadily at Thad and tried to raise himself up. He succeeded only as far as to hoist himself onto all fours.

"Yer callin' me a queer chicken, boy?" He swung his head back and forth, his jaw hanging loose.

Thad was about to step neatly over the fellow when suddenly the man vomited.

"Shoot!" Thad leaped backward. His buckskins were plenty dirty, but he didn't relish having this fellow puke on them.

"Ah ha!" A deep voice rumbled from the doors of the saloon. "The Northwest Mop-Up Police!" The voice was that of a man with two holstered six-shooters and a fan of cards in his right hand. He wore a fancy vest under his sharply cut jacket and leaned against the frame of the saloon doorway. He was watching a young man in a uniform who rode up and dismounted.

"What's this all about?" He seemed full of self-importance, although he did not look that much older than Thad. To his dying day, Thad would regret his next words, spoken in goodwill because the young officer had not looked when he had dismounted.

"You're standing in puke, sir."

Five stupid little words and Thaddeus Longsworth found himself in jail in Fort Benton, Montana. He was charged with disturbing the peace, insubordination to an officer of the law, and finally, possession of stolen money.

"Boy, you just don't come by three hundred dollars by rightful means. Not your kind," the pompous young officer was saying—Sergeant Peterson of the Northwest Mounted Police.

"I told you. You got the letter right there from Professor George Babcock, Harvard University."

An older man had been listening to Sergeant Peterson's charges. He glanced down at the letter.

"He stole it, sir," said Sergeant Peterson. "It is quite

clear that a young hooligan like this would not be in the employ of a professor of Harvard University."

"Put him in number three, Sergeant."

The young sergeant yanked Thad up savagely by the arm and led him away.

"Restrain yourself, Sergeant Peterson," the older man called as Thad was led down the hallway.

Thad was flung on the floor of the cell.

"Stay there! Right there!" he barked. Thad wasn't sure what he meant. There wasn't much choice as to where to go in the tiny cell, but there was soon no doubt as to where he was supposed to stay. Sergeant Peterson's boot was right by his head.

"I recall that you mentioned something about where I was standing before. My boots must be soiled. Do you mind if I clean them off?"

Thad saw a dark flash and felt the cold muzzle of the Colt .45 pressed against his temple. Then a boot heel ground into his face for what seemed to be an endless time. There was a short laugh and then the sound of the lock turning. But Thad could still feel the boot heel and hear the laugh as the sergeant walked away from the cell.

He felt rage fill his entire being, and then he let it settle into a tight little ball somewhere deep within him while he thought. The order of business was simple: Get out of the cell, kill the sergeant, get Babcock's money, and find Jasper. His brain was working as it had never before worked. His eyes were drinking in every detail. The walls of the jail were made of granite, the windows barred. He wouldn't make much headway there. They had taken his belt, but they had forgotten his spurs. They were his best bet. He would have himself a pair of sharp, tiny little knives in no time, with which he could possibly pick a lock or certainly pierce an eyeball. All that would be left to plan was the strategy for getting to Sergeant Peterson.

When he heard the fall of footsteps, Thad quickly hid one spur under his shirt and slid the other one into the palm of his hand. It was the sergeant. He barely looked at Thad as he unlocked the cell door. This might be easy, Thad thought. The door swung wide open.

"You're a free man, scum." The sergeant turned and walked away without even looking back. Thad sat, stunned, on the narrow cot.

"He coming?" Thad heard a vaguely familiar voice question from down the hall. He jumped up and ran out of the cell. In the office where he had been interrogated was the man with the pair of six-shooters.

"You ready to go, son?"

"Need my money and my belt."

The older officer handed over a box. Thad counted the money. It was all there.

"Believe you owe Mr. Stevens some for your bail." The older officer nodded toward the man.

"That wasn't bail. It was a bribe," said the man called Stevens. "Don't kid yourself, there's not going to be any trial. You boys think being bullies means keeping the law, but this time it's not going to work. The Northwest Mounted Police is going to look about as serious as the rear end of a jackass after I get through talking with Hop Sprague, editor of the *Helena Reporter*."

The words slipped like silk through the air, and cut like razors. Thad felt his rage dissolve into rapture. The man was astonishing—a gentleman and a varmint at the same time.

"Oh, and boy," he said, casually looking over at Sergeant Peterson. "This here's for you." He flipped the sergeant a five-dollar gold piece. "Miss Lulu said she didn't have the heart to take money from such a green 'un. Give it another try when you're a bit more mature."

Sergeant Peterson turned bright red while the older man slapped his knee and guffawed. Thad was speechless.

Mr. Stevens winked at the older officer. "Thank you, gentlemen, for your time. If either of you ever would care to join me for a little poker, you know where I can be found. Good day, sirs."

Thad followed him out into the white noon light of the day.

"Mr. Stevens, I can't—"

"Call me Rap, son. What's your name, by the way?"

"Thad—Thaddeus Longsworth."

"Well, pleased to meet you." He stopped in the middle of the street and shook hands. "Everybody calls me Rap, except people who are scared of me."

"Good day, Mr. Stevens." A man was hurrying by with a parcel under his arm. "Fine day, isn't it, Mr. Stevens, for this time of year?" said another.

In the short time it took them to walk from the jail to the Hang It Up saloon, no less than six people had addressed Rap Stevens as Mr. Stevens.

Thad tried his best to thank him for his generosity at the doors of the saloon.

"Well, sir, I mean Rap, I don't know what to say except I sure wish you'd let me pay you back the money it took to spring me from jail. I know Professor Babcock would want me to. It's, after all, part of the expenses, and I might even have enough from my own salary from last summer."

"You keep that money, Thaddeus, my boy."

"But why, Rap? I don't understand."

Rap Stevens got an odd look in his eye.

"Well, son, maybe we can cut a deal. I don't know who said it, Shakespeare, Thucydides, or John Milton, perhaps"—he had rattled off a bunch of names Thad had never heard—"but as I recall the saying goes, 'money earned is fine, but money won is sweeter.' Draw poker, stud poker—name your game."

"I don't play cards real good."

"Well, then, that wouldn't be very much fun."

"I'll buy you a drink," Thad said suddenly. "I don't drink but I'll be pleased to buy you one."

Rap looked at him and smiled curiously. Then he looked across to the levee, or pier, where the steamboats and river packets, two or three abreast, were tied up. Men with mules and teams of oxen were beginning to line up, waiting to load their wagons with the goods that had been carried up the Missouri River.

"In another hour," Rap said, "you won't be able to see the river through the freight stacked up on that levee. This street will be chockablock full with mule skinners, bull whackers, roustabouts, clerks, and merchants. Dogs will start yelpin' and pigs'll break loose. It will be crazy. But right now, do you see those hawsers wrapped around the bollards?" He pointed toward the ropes leading from the boats and tied to posts on the banks. It seemed as if there were almost ten just in the stretch across from them.

"Yes, sir, I see them," Thad said, mystified.

"Well, I bet you, Thaddeus Longsworth, a sweet twenty dollars that you cannot clear every rope on that stretch in one minute."

Thad looked directly at him. "Well, I'm pretty sure I can, but why the heck do you want to wager a fool thing like that?"

"We got a bet, then?"

"I guess so." Thad paused. "But why?"

"Haven't you ever met a gamblin' man, boy?"

"Not like you, I haven't."

"Well, now you have," Rap said. "Let me call Cap'n Haskell over here to timekeep so everything's on the up-and-up. Cap'n!" he shouted across the street at a man who was standing on the deck of a packet named the *Nellie Beck.*

"Yes, Rap. What can I do for you?"

He went down the gangplank and crossed the street to where Rap and Thad were standing. "This here is Thaddeus Longsworth. He and I just wagered."

Captain Haskell closed his eyes and nodded silently.

"What did you wager this time, Rap?"

"I bet this fine specimen of young manhood that for twenty dollars he could not within sixty seconds clear every hawser from the bow of the *Nellie Beck* to the stern of the *Flo Belle* without falling."

"Well," Haskell said, "as long as you don't bet my cargo. You know what I brought up from Bismarck in this three-hundred-ton load?"

"What'd that be?"

"A grand pianer."

"You don't say! We must be getting a classier group out here."

"I s'pose you want me to be timekeeper."

"I s'pose so."

It would be about a three-hundred-foot run. First, Thad walked the stretch so that he could gauge the intervals between the ropes. Sometimes they were as much as twenty feet apart, sometimes just five or ten. It was going to be more difficult than he imagined, because there would be no way to get a rhythm going. He returned to the starting point.

"Okay. I'm ready."

"Got a bet goin' here, Rap?"

"Sorry, Chester, it's a closed game for now."

Thad wondered what Rap meant by "for now." If he had notions about him doing this a second time, he could forget them.

Captain Haskell raised his arm. "All right now. I'll give you a twenty-five-second countdown."

Thad crouched down and dug the toe of his boot into the dirt.

"Twenty-five . . . twenty-four . . . twenty-three . . . twenty-two . . ."

On twenty, Thad curled his knuckles under and braced his fists hard against the ground.

"Twelve . . . eleven . . . ten . . ."

Why the heck had he agreed to do this?

"Eight . . . seven . . ."

Because Fort Benton was a crazy place and everything had been queer since he had arrived.

"Five . . . four . . ."

With the way his luck was running, he'd probably not only lose, but fall into a mud puddle and be stepped on by a mule who would then drop a few muffins on him for good measure.

"Three . . . two . . . one . . . go!"

He cleared the first rope. Then the second. Holy Moses, here was the third already. He felt his britches graze it but that was okay. It still counted as long as he didn't fall. He was ready for the fourth and fifth. But Lordy, hadn't he noticed before—the sixth one was high, really high! He didn't know whether he could do it. Okay, calm down. You got space here to build up steam, he told himself. But he was running breath-short, and there was a stitch coming up in his side. He thought he might have heard some cheers. Some words, "Go! Go! Go!" "Go, Thad!" Someone had called his name. The *go*'s dropped out of the air like hailstones in a summer storm. They stung. They goaded. He forgot the stitch in his side. He forgot his breath. He felt only the sting of the *go*'s and then as he felt his feet leave the ground, the *go*'s seemed to turn into a billow of air and he sailed across that hawser like a hawk soaring on a warm current over the prairie. He landed on both feet, then dropped onto the bank, spent.

He heard the cheers, and then there was Rap waving the twenty-dollar bill over his head, as if the mere scent of the "sweet" money would revive him. But for Thad, it was still just plain money. He knew Rap would have bet him again if he had had the breath. The man was the gamblingest creature Thad had ever met.

It was over dinner in the Bullwhacker saloon that Thad found out more about Rap Stevens. For one thing, he owned the *Nellie Beck* and the *Flo Belle,* as well as another steamer called the *Ethel K.*

"They're all named after fine lady friends. I call all my packets after them, and all these ladies"—he spoke slowly, as if to make a point—"always call me Rap."

Thad found out all about the Fort Benton river trade. The discovery of gold to the north and west in the early sixties caused a boom for the region. Fort Benton was the natural place of entry for reaching the gold territory, and the town nearly burst with the activity as tiny stern-wheel steamers carrying wagonloads of gold dust, miners, and their equipment plied their way to the port. These boats turned over fantastic profits until the gold trade began to fizzle. Business was improving again, as more and more settlers streamed in from the east.

"Four hundred tons of freight," Rap explained, "and I collect a hundred thousand dollars for moving goods and folks in from St. Louis. You know what kind of profit that is?"

"No, sir," Thad said, cutting his steak.

"Sixty-five thousand dollars."

"Whew!" Thad put down his knife and fork. He'd never heard of such money.

"Yep, the late *Celina Grace* cleared sixty-five thousand dollars one trip."

"The late *Celina Grace?* You don't have her now?"

"No. Lost her in a game of stud poker."

"What? You lost a whole boat in a game of stud poker?" Thad was stunned.

"Close your mouth, son. You got a big hunk of half-chewed beef in it."

Thad quickly shut his mouth and began to chew.

"It wasn't so bad, really. I lost the *Celina Grace* just about the time the gold trade went bust—'69 to '70. But I see better times coming. See, I bought the *Flo Belle* and the *Ethel K* real cheap. Buy low, sell high is my motto."

"So sometimes you do buy things and not gamble for them?"

"Only if I can't help it." Rap rocked back on the hind

legs of his chair and hooked his thumbs into his vest pockets. Thad hadn't noticed until now what a fancy dresser Rap was. He wore a silk vest in a dull-pink color embroidered with tiny roses. A gold watch chain stretched across his vest, and when he took out the watch, it was in a black enamel case with a gold eagle's head on the cover. His shirt was a creamy ivory color and he wore not a string tie like most gentlemen Thad had seen but a big fancy wide one with a tangled design of lines and leaves in soft browns and purples, and there was a big pearl-headed stickpin that tacked the whole thing down. "I got the *Nellie Beck* in a game," Rap continued. "I'm just now thinking of starting my own overland freight company, buying up wagons and hiring drivers. Then we'll have the transportation sewn up—land and river."

The next day Rap Stevens bought twenty-five wagons and fifteen more pack mules. He sold one wagon and four of the mules to Thad at no profit to himself. He also recommended a cook, and by suppertime that evening, Thad had found himself a pair of ponies for the wagon, a driver, and a string of horses for a very reasonable price. In another day, he had gathered the rest of his supplies. By September 20, just as the telegram had promised, Professor Babcock had arrived with Jonathan Cabot, Oliver Perkins, and other members of the Harvard team. There were three newcomers—Isaac ("Ike") Van Camp, Frank Trowbridge, and

Alban Mallory. Trowbridge was in his last year at Harvard and Van Camp had already graduated and would be starting medical studies soon. Alban Mallory, a graduate student of Professor Babcock's, was introduced to Thad as an expert in "small-scale surface survey."

They set off in an easterly direction, moving quickly, for Babcock knew exactly where he was going—a region called Medicine Buttes. He did not waste any time along the way, even though the terrain provided some tempting sediments in terms of possible fossil treasures. They crossed the Way Creek, the Arrow Creek, and finally the Judith River. Then they angled north and when they reached the Cow Island Landing on the Missouri River, Babcock said, "We're at the heart of it."

They loaded part of their equipment and livestock on the ferry. The poleman pushed off and then announced calmly—for after all, what did it mean to him?—that he had poled two other groups across recently.

"Two!" Babcock exploded. "Two!"

"Yes, sir," the man said placidly, pushing on his pole as the ferry slid through the water.

"Who else besides Cunningham?"

The poleman reflected. "Cunningham—now he's your Yank, right, sir?"

"Yank as opposed to what?" Babcock asked. "A southerner, would you say?"

"No," replied the poleman. "I was meaning the English folk."

"The British! The British are *here?* How can they be?" Babcock was stunned by this news.

"Same way you is, I guess," the poleman said.

Babcock scowled darkly at the man, who poled harder while looking down into the muddy swirls. It took them two trips to get everything across.

They made camp, which was to be the base camp for all the future excavations, at the head of a short, steep ravine that opened into a valley between two long ridges. The butt ends of the ridges made a sheer drop of twelve hundred feet to a floodplain. The high end of the valley swooped up into a grassland where they pitched their tents.

After the expedition into the Black Hills, it felt good to Thad being in an encampment of only ten men and eighteen animals. It had turned chilly after supper when Jonathan Cabot suggested a walk. Thad readily agreed, happy to stretch his legs after a long day in the saddle. The others, however, were more inclined to stay close to the warmth of the campfire.

They walked on a slant up the eastern slope of the valley until they gained the top of the ridge. Far off, in the dwindling purple light, they could see the river winding through the dome-shaped buttes that punched out of the plains. The tops of these buttes often appeared like dark blisters and at their bases some were wrapped around with pale gray and almost white bands of limestone. The limestone marked the time when the inland sea had retreated, leaving behind its deposits of sand and mud.

"That must be one of the other camps," Thad said, pointing to tiny dark marks on the flat top of what appeared to be a shaved-off butte. "Why would they camp so high?"

"Keep an eye on things," Cabot offered.

"Professor seems mighty upset."

"He is. I hope . . ." Jonathan hesitated.

"You hope what?"

"I hope it doesn't get too intense." Jonathan kicked a rock with his foot, scuttling it ahead of him. "Science shouldn't be that way." Then he laughed a short bitter laugh. "But it is. Imagine, a war about bones!"

It was unimaginable to Thad that the competition between the paleontologists would get as bad as all that. "It does seem kind of stupid, don't it?"

Jonathan looked at Thad intently. "Yes, because in the end that's all there is—bones, ours and the ones we search for." He bent over and picked up a very small piece of fossilized animal bone. "Ours and theirs. That's all there is."

Jonathan stooped to pick up something else.

"Think about this." He tossed a piece of quartz crystal to Thad.

"What is it—quartz?"

"Yes, from deep within the earth. Millions, or dare I say, billions of years ago, the immense pressures began to squeeze this vein of pink quartz up through the granite that housed it. Finally, the quartz hit the rock lid of the overlying formation. The lid wore down through erosion, gradually exposing the quartz until one day the lid popped, so to speak, and the crystal weathered free."

"So what should I think about?"

"When the lid will pop," Jonathan said softly. "When the crystal will weather free."

CHAPTER
18

It was an enormous creature, its frill flaring back like an armored collar. The single horn, sweeping forward from what must have been a massive head, had been capable of delivering a lethal thrust that could rip open an opponent's belly. The legs were as thick as large tree trunks. And even in death, its monstrous bulk still cast a long shadow across the canyon of time. It was a shadow in which the team now stood, wondering what even fiercer creature had brought this one down, for it had not died a natural death. They had discovered scarring on several of the bones, scarring from a beast that possessed a deadly set of teeth and an agility to bring down any opponent, even one of this size. Because of its single horn Babcock had called it monoclonius.

"What did you say that measurement is, Oliver, from the tip of the beak to the beginning of the frill?" Ike Van Camp was standing with his feet tangled in a latticework of shadows cast by the ribs of the fallen beast. Only one part of the rib cage had been excavated.

"One and a half meters," Oliver replied.

"One and a half!" Babcock exclaimed. "Mother in heaven, this creature is going to be enormous. We might be dealing with a two- or three-ton beast. What a formidable character." He walked over to where a jaw fragment was just beginning to be exposed. Thad was working with a thin chisel and wedge. "Look at those teeth," said Babcock. "Blunt, packed tight as cobbles—millstones, really, for grinding, not tearing. This was a plant eater. Used his horn for a plunging-style defense. Quite effective."

"Scarring, Professor, more bone scarring over here," Alban Mallory reported. He had been sifting the debris around the site through a fine-mesh screen, and was now examining a bone fragment through an enormous magnifying lens.

"Ah ha! You see, Mallory." Babcock picked his way over to Mallory and peered through the lens. "You and your looking glass are invaluable."

Then Jonathan Cabot called, "Big scarring over here, too."

Babcock, despite his portly build, practically jumped three feet into the air. "Ah, the plot thickens." He

scrambled up the shaley incline to where Jonathan
Cabot had chiseled out a good portion of hipbone.

Babcock's *ah ha*s seemed to tumble down the face of
the butte like pieces of loose rock. "This scarring definitely brought down the beast. Mallory, you must
check this with your microscope against other samples
you have been collecting. I'll wager that despite his
vegetarian ways, this monoclonius could lower his
head and swing into a devil of a charge with that saberlike horn. The question at hand now for the forensic
experts in the group is what terrifying creature made
these marks. He was a killer, this thug of the Mesozoic
world, who dared take on a creature of the size we are
now excavating. I shall include notes on the attacker in
my 'separate' for the journal of paleontology. And I
seriously doubt if Professors Cunningham and DeMott
have found the equal to this!"

That evening in camp, excitement ran high as the rest
of the excavation of the enormous creature was plotted
out.

"So finally, Mallory, your obsession with the small
scale is paying off," Ike Van Camp said as they finished
supper around the campfire.

"I don't know what you mean by 'obsession.' "
Alban Mallory indignantly slapped down his tin plate.
"My conviction is a screening box and microscope are
legitimate tools for scientific inquiry. Those instruments are amply capable of identifying a variety of
tooth marks that could help in the identification of this
great predator."

"Here! Here!" Frank Trowbridge held up a morsel he had just taken from his antelope soup. "You don't suppose you could run this soup through your screening box before it's served, do you? There seem to be occasional bits of foreign matter floating about."

There was a swell of hearty laughter.

"I'm not the cook," Alban replied dryly. "But I do think it might be helpful to run a few more buckets of dirt through the sifting screen from that spot I was telling you about, Professor."

Babcock sighed. "We shall! We shall next season. I swear, Mallory, you are fixed on this. Every expedition has its priorities. Here is this gorgeous creature melting out of the sandstone, a new species, and I can hardly stop midway to nitpick through every bucketful of soil you bring in."

"Yes. Yes, sir," Alban replied quietly. "Suppose you're right."

The excavation took several days to complete, and while the pieces were coming out of the sandstone, Babcock had started to write his "separate" on this strange new creature that he had dubbed *Monoclonius crassus*. "Separates" were articles in the form of letters from the field. They were speedily published and read by the scientific community in the east. Their main function was to establish a scientist's claim on the first discovery of a species.

Two days after the excavation was completed, Babcock's separate was ready and Thad was to ride with all dispatch to the Cow Island Landing to catch the next steamer. Just as he was saddling up to leave, Jonathan Cabot went up to him.

"So you are off to the Cow Island Landing. Thaddeus, I don't mean to pry, but may I ask how many copies of the letter Professor Babcock gave you?"

"Just one. This one here to the . . ." Thaddeus began to read the words slowly, sounding out the long names. *"Scientific Journal of Vertebrate Paleontology."*

"Darn!" Jonathan exploded.

It was the first time Thad had ever seen Jonathan show even the slightest trace of anger.

"What's the matter?" Thad asked.

"The professor has just directly violated his agreement made with Nathaniel Cunningham two years ago."

"What agreement?"

"They had promised to send each other copies of any papers to be published, dated in order to avoid arguments about dates of publication, concerning new species and their descriptions."

"Why didn't he do it?"

"He's just being stubborn. He's mad at Cunningham for invading what he considers to be his territory. But this kind of thing is going to do no one any good at all. Cunningham has at least always been most scrupulous about adhering to these ground rules. Now we are moving into a no-holds-barred situation. It's going to be absolute chaos. Cunningham will be furious when he finds out."

Thad wondered whether Jonathan meant that the lid was about to pop.

"Well," Jonathan then said, summoning up a wry smile, "thank heavens it takes them a while to publish these separates, and we'll be out of the field by then."

Thad rode hard. From a high bluff, he had seen the steamer coming round the bend in the river, and he and Jasper arrived at the landing at the same time as the boat. Thad had barely noticed the man who had followed him on board. But the man had closely watched Thad or, more precisely, the path of the large envelope that Thad had handed to the mail clerk. The mailbags were put below. From the bluff where he had first caught sight of the steamer, Thad now watched it as it pulled away. He watched the crew working with lines but he didn't see one figure slide stealthily down into the hold where the mailbags had gone.

Babcock was distracted from further work on monoclonius by the promise of another significant find. It was early in December, just as the cold was moving in. Alban Mallory, out on one of his field surface surveys, had discovered a concentration of very interesting small fragments west of the camp. He managed to convince Babcock to dig a few test trenches at the site, which indeed proved rich with a most interesting assortment of bones. They gave every indication of yielding an entire new species of dinosaur. Once again, Thad made the ride down to the Cow Island Landing to deliver another separate to the east that described this most recently excavated creature.

The first field season ended a week before Christmas. The snow was late that year, but when it did come, it fell heavily. The larger fossils were wrapped, marked, and cached in caves. Those that could be moved were packed into the wagon and driven to the river landing to make the long trip back to Cambridge, Massachusetts.

CHAPTER

19

The new field season would begin in April. Thad had had little desire to spend the winter in Fort Benton. Instead, he headed south and east toward the Wyoming territory. Jonathan Cabot had told him that Cheyenne was a growing town with a railroad station and a market for just about anything. Jonathan had met a man named Wild Horse Charlie who had made a business capturing mustangs to sell. He caught them in the winter when they were slower and hungry. Cabot thought that Thad might get a job helping him. But when Thad arrived in Cheyenne, he found that Wild Horse Charlie had gone out of business. The enterprise had proved unsuccessful because the mustangs were small and only suitable as saddle animals and for light-load drivers. Indian ponies and saddle horses came cheaper out of Texas. Thad realized that he should have figured that one out, but chasing after wild horses had seemed a fun and tempting way to make money.

Instead, he found himself chasing and killing antelope. It had all started at the Union Pacific Hotel, where Thad had been hired to work in the kitchen. He heard the cook and the chief steward discussing the problem of getting a steady supply of antelope meat since their regular supplier had gone on to Denver. The hotel was competing with other eating houses in Cheyenne, and there was scarcely enough meat to go around. Thad did not particularly cotton to the idea of working in the kitchen for four dollars a week, so he figured he would try hunting for a spell. He shot antelope all winter.

It was cold, bloody work. He had to butcher on the plains in order to efficiently transport the meat and the hides back to Cheyenne. Although he could cut the joints with his gloves on, he could not seem to manage the skinning except bare-handed. His fingers would grow stiff and, when the job was finished, the snow would be stained red with blood all around him and piles of entrails would be steaming in the chill air. Thad took great care to clean and dress the meat properly, and to preserve the hide. He knew that if he was careful in the cutting, and later the stretching and drying of the hides, he could sell them at a good price to the buyer who came from the hide and fur house of Oberne and Hosick out of Chicago.

Soon Thad had customers beyond the hotel and it was all he could do to keep up with the work. He hired another boy from the kitchen to help him dress the hides. But he always went out alone to hunt. He got elk, as well as antelope, and once, early in the winter, a bear. A year before, under a Colorado sky, he had thought of this as big-game hunting. Now it was butchering, pure and simple, and lest he forget, all he had to do when he left the site with his joints of meat and bundled hides all neatly tied up was to turn around and see the bloody prints—his own, Jasper's, and the pack mules'. When he rode into Cheyenne, crusted with frozen blood, he dreamed, however, of another kind of hunt—the thrill of bringing those extinct animals closer to life.

Every week he deposited money in the bank and he could have made even more. The hotel steward said he should take on a real partner, and set up a camp on the prairie with a smokehouse and salting and pickling equipment. But as far as Thad was concerned, this was temporary employment. By the first of March, he had earned himself enough to buy a Sharps .40–90 target rifle and some new clothes. He had long ago outgrown Mrs. Cody's buckskin britches, but he saved them carefully just the same. By the middle of March, he was ready to head back north into the Montana territory and set up camp for Professor Babcock. He packed up

his few possessions into two saddlebags and included
a letter from Jonathan Cabot that had taken nearly a
month to reach Cheyenne:

February 21, 1875

Dear Thaddeus,

*Well, we returned home safely for belated Christmas celebra-
tions. All the bones arrived safely, too. This semester we have
been doing some serious study of the fossils with the help of
the staff and the good equipment at the Museum of Comparative Zoology. Although we can all count our excursion into
the Medicine Buttes region a success, we have recently received
some alarming news in regard to that last site we dug. It
appears that we spent our final weeks excavating a totally
mythical creature. There is no doubt in anyone's mind now
that this was the result of the Yale team seeding the site with
a phony assemblage of bones.*

*I'm sure that this started as a prank, a get-even gesture
aimed at Professor Babcock for his violation of the agreement
concerning the publication of separates. It's a puzzle how the
opposition discovered this so soon but they retaliated all too
well. The professor's separate on this latest find was published, and now a letter comes in to the journal from someone
with "the utmost esteem for the Harvard professor," saying
the animal as described in the separate possesses "an unlikely
and erroneous mixture of anatomical parts which suggest that
this creature simply does not exist." You might imagine how
Babcock reacted to this. You might as well tell him that he
does not exist. . . . Well, in any case, we all look forward*

to seeing you in the not-too-distant future. Plans as they now stand are for us to arrive in the Judith River Badlands in early April. I imagine that if you have not heard from Professor Babcock yet concerning preparations, you shall be receiving a letter soon.

Hope this finds you well.
Sincerely,

Jonathan Cabot
Quincy House
Harvard College
CAMBRIDGE, MASSACHUSETTS.

Julian DeMott had spent the winter in Chicago. His father had managed to find him a tutor, and Julian was soon amazed how the country that he had once thought so vast and wild had suddenly shrunk and acquired the sameness and dreariness of his old life in England. Chicago, of course, was much different from London. It seemed to be growing in a wild, sprawling, higgledy-piggledy manner. Some streets were still unpaved but the railroads, bringing in cattle cars of Texas longhorns by the hundreds, were making it a crossroads for slaughter and commerce. New steel rails, laid by the tycoon Cornelius Vanderbilt, and a network of nearly completed bridges promised to cut the running time between New York and Chicago from fifty hours to twenty-four. In anticipation of this shrinking distance, there had been a flood of new businesses and commercial adventurers into Chicago. The ornate Grand Pacific Hotel, built at the staggering cost of 1.5 million dollars, was constantly filled to capacity. There was an incredible pulsating energy to the city. It resembled nothing Julian had ever known and yet his father kept him away from it. He insisted on the kind of orderly life Julian had led in Eaton Square.

Julian closed his eyes and forgot the Cicero translation before him. He forgot how estranged he had become from his father over much more than just Latin, and he tried instead to remember that other land—the hot blue sky that poured down on the flat prairies with their endless grass seas, the broken terrain of the Badlands with the wire and scrub grass, sere but still blooming with the sego lilies, the pungent smell of the sagebrush, and always the massive buttes thrusting out of the land. Striped with their layers of sandstone, limestone, shale, and river silt, these were the graves of the terrible lizards.

He often remembered the boy on the pinto viewed from the train window when they had first traveled west. He remembered the gray-green eyes, the eyes the color of prairie grass. Now, as he sat in the room that had been designated for his studies under the direction of Mr. Moncrieff, his new tutor, the memory of those eyes was a welcome intrusion as the winter shadows crept across the floor. He wondered where that boy was now. Mr. Moncrieff slept in an easy chair in the corner. In a few minutes, he would jolt into wakefulness, ask "How goes it?", look at Julian's partial translation, declare it enough for today, and then mumble something about starting logarithms tomorrow. Julian's father would return from whatever lecture he had been giving, and then go on to one of the clubs in which he had been given a provisional membership as a visiting person of high rank. He might go dine with General Sheridan, who owned a grand house in Chicago. Julian thought the general was downright scary. So he found himself eating alone most of the time and counting the days until they would be back at Medicine Buttes.

Mr. Moncrieff finally tottered off and Julian went into his father's study to get some paper for his Latin translations. He noticed on his father's desk a letter in the hand of his cousin Lord Haversham. Julian hesitated. Lord Haversham had talked of Julian spending some time with him in New York, which Julian would have welcomed. He was strongly tempted to scan the letter to see whether there might be any mention of this trip. Just beside the letter were some yellow sheets with the legend of a Chicago bank printed on the top. They were copies, but they bore the signature of his cousin and were obviously bank drafts made out for large sums of money to Algernon DeMott.

This surprised Julian, but not greatly. He knew that his father's wealth did not compare to that of Lord Haversham, from his mother's side of the family. Julian had suspected that his cousin had arranged for a bank loan for his father's expedition, but these drafts indicated that Lord Haversham had lent the money directly.

Julian stood in the darkening room, considering his aristocratic cousin's reasons for funding this expedition. He was fond of Julian, as the only son of his favorite cousin, Lady Pamela. And the notion of having his name linked in some manner to an intellect of the stature of Algernon DeMott must have pleased him. There was also the promise of some ancient species bearing his name, Julian supposed. The Havershams had a relative buried in Westminster Abbey, and a chair of literature in their honor at Cambridge University. Why not a species to round things out? At family gatherings Lord Haversham, no great intellectual himself, could now make references to paleontological finds and sprinkle his conversation with allusions to various species.

Julian finally read the note, which referred to the honor and pride of being associated with DeMott's noble undertaking. He smiled to himself, imagining his cousin's delight. Too bad there did not seem to be any indication of a trip east for Julian. Well, he decided, his father would be out late tonight, so why not take a turn around the nearby Grand Pacific Hotel? The ornateness both inside and out of that building never ceased to amaze him.

Julian entered the lobby of the Grand Pacific Hotel, which was abuzz with people. There were decidedly more men than women, but the few ladies who were there were ornately dressed, with feathered decorations perched on their heads like exotic birds and low-cut gowns exposing generous amounts of white skin ablaze with jewels. He had just turned a corner when, through the fronds of a potted palm, he caught sight of a familiar figure. It was a man in a severely cut suit who was talking animatedly, punctuating the air with an unlit cigar. Was that the same man that he had met in New York months ago—Mr. Louis Woodfin, with his grand notions about the New World Museum? Yes, it was— the man his father had so disdained. Julian wondered whether Mr. Woodfin would remember him. He stood watching for several minutes until Mr. Woodfin broke away from the group he was talking to and headed at a quickstep to the dining room. He went right by Julian.

"Mr. Woodfin!"

He turned abruptly. His eyes bore into Julian. "Oh," he said suddenly. "Young Mr. . . . Mr. . . ."

"DeMott, sir. Julian DeMott."

"Why, of course. So you are still here?"

"Yes, sir, yes indeed."

"And how does the bone business go?"

"Quite well, sir, quite well. We shall be commencing our second season in a matter of weeks."

"Tell me all about it. I'm most eager to know. Won't you join me for dinner?"

"Well, certainly, sir. That's very kind of you."

It was a wonderful dinner. Julian felt he had never had a better listener than Louis Woodfin. At the end of the meal, Woodfin leaned back in his chair.

"Do you mind if I smoke?"

"No, sir, not at all."

"They seem to be more relaxed about smoking out

here. Not so many ladies, you know. Frankly, I would prefer the company of the ladies." He lit his cigar and settled back. Julian felt himself being studied. Finally Woodfin spoke.

"Mr. DeMott . . ."

"Please, sir, just call me Julian."

"All right, Julian. I have an odd proposal to make to you. I realize that you are now working with your father, but in a few years you will be independent. You already are intellectually independent, as I have ascertained through our conversation this evening. I am quite impressed with your knowledge of fossils, in particular, dinosaurs. If there ever comes a day when you would be inclined to collect for something other than private interests, namely a museum that promises to open its doors to the world, we at the New World Museum would be most happy to facilitate you in any way we can."

Julian felt the color rise in his face.

"I did not mean to suggest any kind of act of disloyalty, Julian, to your father. I think we can be very frank with one another. It is no secret to you or anybody else that I do not approve of private collection."

"Of course, sir. I understand that you meant no such thing."

"There will come a day when you will have to decide how you are going to share your knowledge with the world. If that decision leads you to work independently of your father, call on me." Woodfin peered at Julian through the smoke from his cigar and nodded as if satisfied. "Now tell me more about these Badlands of yours."

Woodfin and Julian would meet one more time in Chicago so that Julian could hear more of the man's plans for the New World Museum. Woodfin's notions and the assistance he offered excited Julian beyond anything he could imagine. But it also frightened him. With his sense of growing estrangement from his father and the intense competition already occurring among the three teams in the Medicine Buttes area, his life had suddenly become very complicated. Woodfin was right. Sooner or later he was going to have to decide where he stood.

CHAPTER

20

Thad's trip back to Montana would have been un-
eventful and quickly accomplished if Jasper had not
gone lame three days short of Fort Benton. It was severe, and as Thad dismounted, he realized how hard it
would be for the poor animal to cover the rough terrain.
By the next day, Jasper's leg was swollen beyond the
hock and the horse was in agony. Thad knew what had
to be done. He had seen this happen more than once on
the drive up from Texas. He led Jasper into a grove of
cottonwoods and shot him through the head. That was
it. Jasper had been his last link with Mr. Jim and with
Texas. Although his mother had been dead for over

nine years, he guessed that another link in the long chain that still connected him to that fragile memory was gone. He was grateful that Jasper had died instantly. His eyes stinging with tears, his vision blurred from the wind sweeping straight down into his face, Thaddeus Longsworth set off walking for Fort Benton.

Waiting for Thad in Fort Benton was a bank draft from George Babcock for four hundred dollars— enough to buy supplies for a prolonged stay in the Badlands. The professor and his team would be arriving within three weeks. Thad had to hire a cook, buy himself a new horse, a string of pack mules, and two wagons, and then get all the provisions onto the steamboat for Cow Island. He planned to spend as little time as possible in Fort Benton. Just long enough to do what he had to do. There was no sign of Rap Stevens, and blessedly, none of Sergeant Peterson. He found a cook, a Chinese man named Wu Chow. He also found a horse without a name. He quickly assembled all the provisions and arranged for the cook to take most of them by steamer to the Cow Island landing. Thad would take the mules by land. As short as his time was in Fort Benton, he could not miss the flurry of excitement over the news that gold had been found in the Black Hills. Miners were streaming into the hills by the thousands. One morning he was in the back storeroom of a local dry-goods store, helping the clerk pack up some crates for the steamer. From the front of the store, he could hear the talk drift back.

"They sent someone over to Sitting Bull with a letter

about giving up the land. Know what Sitting Bull said?"

"What's he talking about?" Thad asked the clerk.

"The Black Hills business. The government wants to buy them from the Sioux."

"What for?"

"The gold."

"There's not that much gold," Thad said. "I was there."

"You were?" The clerk looked up over his spectacles. "With Custer?"

"Yes, sir. And there's not enough to go round for all the people they say are flocking in there."

"They sure are flocking in, all right."

"Yesterday, I thought I heard someone say the army was out there trying to stop miners," Thad said.

"Guess they found it easier to buy the place than guard it. There's an article right here." He waved a folded newspaper that he was using for insulation in the top of the crate he was packing.

"What's it say?" Thad asked.

"Here, read it."

Thad had practiced reading all winter, and now he quickly caught the headline: CRAZY HORSE SAYS NO SELL. The article beneath it reported that Crazy Horse had steadfastly refused to meet with government officials in Washington and, instead, had sent them a message. The message was brief: "One does not sell the earth upon which people walk."

"Hmm." Thad folded the newspaper and handed it back to the clerk.

"In any case," the clerk continued, "the Indians are all getting mighty nervous round here. Where you heading? Toward Claggett?"

"Yeah, then on to catch the ferry at the Cow Island landing. I'm meeting our cook there, who'll be going on the steamer with the rest of my supplies."

"Best steer clear of the far side of the river—mess of Sioux and Crow down there."

"Didn't think they got on all that well," Thad observed while hammering a nail in the lid of a barrel of flour.

"They don't. But 'bout this time every year, they bury the hatchet for the spring buffalo hunt. This year, they've really buried it and something tells me they're after more than just buffalo."

Thad set out on his new horse, a dappled gray, toward Claggett, a trading post on the Judith River, where an Indian trader had set up shop. Thad had heard that he sold bolts of extra-lightweight duck cloth, which he felt might be useful in wrapping up the fossils. Across the river were the campfires and tipis of the Sioux and the Crow that the clerk had told him about. It did not take Thad long to pack up the mules with the additional supplies and get under way.

Soon he was seeing the familiar land again. In the brief shadow of a butte, he caught a glimpse of a mule deer grazing on some sagebrush. A jackrabbit sprang from behind a yucca. It was especially quiet now, for it was still too early for the rasping choruses of grasshoppers that strung the air with their song in full summer. Directly overhead, an eagle flew, and Thad paused on the dappled gray to watch its flight. The bird cruised higher and higher, barely needing to flap its wings as it rode the billowing updrafts from a warming earth.

He tethered the mules to a root jutting out from the face of an outcrop and rode up a ridge for a better view of the terrain. The country appeared to slope to the south and east. Rearing up through the earth, the buttes reminded Thad of a herd of powerful creatures lumbering across the country, their immense shapes printed now against the blue cloudless sky. Thad's gaze fastened on two buttes, almost twins that appeared to have been sliced in half. Their facing edges were so clean and sharp, one could imagine a giant cleaver chopping them in two.

Thad squinted at the banded layers of the buttes, clear and crisply marked in the noonday light: first, the brown muddy silts, then the dark-gray and tan of shale and sandstone, the black stripe of coal, and above that, a dull rosy streak. Finally, at the top, the color softened into a lighter buff. This was what Thad loved above all—the peeling back of present time, leaving only the past with its layers of history. It was the shadows of this time that had begun to fill the sky, the land, and be echoed by the wind, the wind that blew each day, scouring away more land, more rock, until the dead bones long buried rose again.

Thad kicked the dapple gray and moved on.

A few days later, he met Wu Chow at the Cow Island landing and they continued on into the Badlands until they reached the old base camp. Wu Chow proved himself to be a tireless worker and between the two of them, they had the camp set up quickly. There were the unmistakable signs that Cunningham was close by. And at the landing, Thad had seen several crates being unloaded with the name DeMott stamped on the slats. Thaddeus wondered how it would all work out this time. There were certainly plenty of bones for everyone. He was pondering this when Wu Chow went up and handed him a bowl of tea. Thad particularly enjoyed Wu Chow's tea, much preferring it to coffee.

"What's that horse's name, Mr. Thad?"

"What horse you talking about?" Thad asked.

"Your horse!" answered Wu Chow. "Your horse needs a name. How you call when he get lost? How you make mind? No fair."

Thad was startled. "How long you been thinkin' about this, Wu Chow?"

"Long time. Since I figured out that horse has no name."

"Then how 'bout Gray, seeing as it's gray and all?"

" 'Gray'?" Wu Chow made a funny face. His lip curled up. "What's *gray?*"

"That's what color he is."

"Why name him after color?"

"I don't know. It's the only thing I know about him."

"Naw! Naw," Wu Chow admonished, shaking his finger.

"Well, you name him then," Thad said.

"Not my horse. Your horse."

"Well . . ." Thad was getting exasperated. He knew he should try harder to see Wu Chow's point. "I don't know what to name him."

"Look at him! What you see?"

Thad looked over at the horse. "I don't know," he finally said. "He just looks like a big gray lump of a horse to me."

"Big gray lump—like dumpling?" Wu Chow asked, reflectively.

"Sort of." Then Thad hesitated. "Well, no, not exactly." He had no intention of riding a horse called Dumpling. "He's very strong and I guess, if you look at him real close, he's really more like the color of that spongy stuff."

"What stuff that?"

"That dirt with the rock in it that sort of swells up when it rains. They call it gumbo then. You know— everything gets stuck in it."

"You call him Gumbo?" Wu Chow picked up the cups with an air of having accomplished something.

"Yeah. That's not a bad name. Gumbo."

Babcock was in a decidedly ill humor when Thad met him and the rest of the team at the landing two days later. He seemed not the least impressed that they had accomplished the massive task of setting up the entire camp, just the two of them, and had done it all with thirty-five dollars left to spare, which Thad promptly handed over to the professor. "See any others about?" he said while putting the bills in his pockets.

"What others?" Thad asked.

"Cunningham and DeMott."

"Well, sir, I haven't really been looking that hard, but I believe Cunningham is here, and some fellow named DeMott has been unloading a lot of equipment," Thad said.

"Hrumph." Babcock walked back to where some of his bags were.

"Good to see you, Jonathan." Thad turned to Jonathan Cabot. "You too, Oliver."

"Nice to see your cheerful face, Thad," Jonathan replied, shaking hands.

"What's the problem with Babcock?" Thad asked as they mounted up.

"It's this business over the separate." Jonathan grimaced as they rode away from the landing.

"You mean that Cunningham really did salt the site with the crazy bones?" Thad asked.

"Yes."

"You sure?"

"Yes, indeed."

"God Almighty!" muttered Thad.

"And now we find that Alban Mallory has gone over to the DeMott team."

"What? I was wondering where he was this time," Thad said.

"Well, you need wonder no more."

Thad remembered Mallory standing for hours on end at his screen box, sifting through buckets of sand for fragments of fossils. It was his notion that these tiniest of pieces, which were often found in the first scraping of the trowel, were invaluable in helping to piece together the puzzle of ancient life, as well as indicating the presence of a rich fossil bed underneath. He would be valued by the British.

"How'd they get him?" Thad asked.

"His mother is English. They apparently have many connections in England. I believe that Alban at one time went to school there as a youngster. Babcock insists that DeMott 'solicited him' or actually 'suborned' him away. But I think it's very possible," Jonathan continued, "that he simply went of his own accord. He and Babcock were never really that keen on one another and with his family ties to England, it might have been attractive and easy."

"So now Babcock's mad?"

"Furious is more like it," Oliver said.

"Yes, I wish he'd get over it. Just forget it," Jonathan said. "He's a bit depressing to be around."

But the professor remained in his dark mood. That night as they sat around the campfire, he suddenly cleared his throat. "Thad, I have a, uh . . . suggestion."

"What's that, Professor?"

"Well, I would like to ask you to, er . . ." He coughed

again. "To begin to discreetly observe in and about the DeMott camp to be sure that, er . . . you know, that Mallory doesn't give away anything we might not want him to. For example, that site near where we excavated the monoclonius and where Mallory himself felt we might find something from the large killer who left those scars."

There was an uncomfortable silence and then Jonathan stood up. His face was pale in the firelight. His chin quivered and his eyes had an intensity Thad had never seen. "Discreetly observe, Professor? How does that differ from spying?" He had managed to keep his voice steady but then he inhaled sharply. "I can't countenance such activities."

"Jonathan, you are naive." Babcock spoke in dull, flat tones. "You think we are the first scholars to want to protect our research? Grow up, lad!"

But Jonathan was infuriated. "Thad is much too valuable to be wasted in this way. This is totally unproductive work. No one on our team should be involved with spying. If we don't, they won't. We should set an example—an example among gentlemen."

Oliver Perkins now spoke up. "I agree with Jonathan, sir. Harvard has always set the highest example. I believe we should continue to do so."

Babcock rose and left the campfire. He walked past his tent and on toward the clear starry horizon. He did not notice the figure standing in the overhang of a sandstone escarpment.

Bobber Henshaw had not planned on anyone walking by at this time of night. There was a quarter of a mile between where he was now standing and where he had tethered his horse. He prayed Babcock would not walk that far. He had overheard good information; information that DeMott could use to great advantage, not the least of which was Babcock's deep suspicion of Alban Mallory and a site of which Mallory apparently thought highly.

CHAPTER
21

It was very easy getting Mallory to open up about the site. DeMott invited him for an after-dinner brandy, and casually mentioned that from his studies of the geology and general lay of the land, he imagined that one mile north and east of their camp there might be something worth looking at—a surface survey might be in order. Mallory visibly paled.

"More brandy, Alban?" DeMott had asked.

"Sure. Thank you, sir."

"I must tell you that in the short time you have been with our team, I am most impressed with your abilities. If it wouldn't be too much of a burden, I would like to send Julian with you. He needs to have an opportunity to do some work with the screens and get some training in the problems and procedures of small-scale identification. I can't think of a better tutor than yourself."

Warmed by the praise, Mallory had regained his color.

"Sir, I know a place in just the area you are talking about that looks quite promising."

The next day, Julian found himself standing over a screen shaking dirt through into the catch box below.

"Here you go, Julian," Alban said, holding up something between the pincers of his tweezers.

"What is it?" Julian asked.

"Ossified tendon—possibly of a hadrosaurus, one of the duckbills. What have you got there?" he said suddenly.

"Where?" Julian asked.

"Freeze!" Julian immediately stopped shaking the screen. Alban leaned forward and picked out a small, flat, leathery piece that was less than a half-inch across.

"Fossilized wood?" Julian asked.

"No, Julian! I do believe we have here not fossilized wood at all but, rather, our first example of skin— fossilized dinosaur skin!"

"You don't say!"

This was indeed most exciting, but three hours later, the thrill had worn off for Julian. He had sifted through perhaps another twenty to thirty pounds of dirt, finding small bone and teeth fragments but not another piece of hide. Screening was the most monotonous work imaginable. But he dared not suggest they begin digging. Alban was immovable about procedure: First, screen all surface materials within a fifty-meter square; then, plot on a graph the position of all the small-fragment finds into still smaller squares. Only when it could be established that a "concentration of saurian debris" had been found within one of these squares did large-scale excavations begin.

They worked on this site for two days. At the end of the second day, when they were taking a different route back to scout other possible sites, Julian spotted the butte. What immediately caught his attention was its shape—steep sides rising into a high dome that gave it the semblance of a pudding, very much like ones that Mrs. Oliver used to make.

"Look at that butte," Julian exclaimed. "Precisely the shape of our old cook's Michaelmas pudding."

"Well," said Alban. "Perhaps we should go over there tomorrow and have a bite, so to speak. I've had it in my mind to head in that direction anyway. The shale changes a bit in color and texture over there. We could see what it all might yield."

The next day, they headed for "Pudding Butte." Alban immediately began his surface survey at the base of the butte while Julian looked longingly upward. These past few days had been tedious in the extreme. Small-scale survey largely consisted of sifting the screen, plugging anthill holes (so that industrious ants wouldn't disturb the site), or plotting the position of their finds on the chart of the measured squares. Julian was bored but trapped because Alban, basically a kind man, seemed so keen on having him as a student. He did not want to hurt his feelings. Alban had already alluded to how the Harvard team was somewhat scornful of his methods. He had obviously felt rankled by their treatment of him.

"Big bones, big bones . . ." Alban muttered while looking over the screen. "That's all anyone ever talks of, but half the time those big bones don't come out whole and you wind up with a bunch of slivers. So you better know what the slivers have to say."

Julian had to refrain from suggesting that perhaps it would be better if the technology of excavating the big bones was improved so that there was not so much damaged. Instead, however, he stopped shaking the screen and turned to Alban. "I think I'll just go over and plug a few anthills in square fourteen. My arms are getting tired sifting."

Julian was down on his knees, watching an ant carrying a grain of something nearly three-quarters its own size, when he noticed the scattering of garfish scales. This was not so remarkable in itself, as such scales were found all over the countryside from the time the fish swam in the old Cretaceous sea. The scales appeared like thin dark slivers approximately the size of a small fingernail. What was interesting was the concentration of the scales at this particular point, as if they had been sluiced down the side of the butte that was several meters away. There was something unique about the topography of the land. It seemed to tilt to the south and the east, toward where they were working. It struck Julian right then that he and Alban had been sifting through the washout from the butte as if they'd been standing in a drain and picking over the garbage. Julian immediately began walking up the butte.

It was a devilish face to climb. The height was deceiving, but he had not made his way upward more than fifty feet when he was able to turn and understand even better the topography. It was clear that the land sloped down as much as one hundred feet for every mile. With every step up the face of the butte, Julian knew that he must be covering tens of thousands of years. He began to perceive the whole picture. He could imagine how this ancient sea had fallen away and the mountains had risen through the old ocean floor. He could imagine the course of the glacier rivers tearing down from the melting ice cap in the north and west and leaving in their icy wake only the buttes.

Alban was going in the wrong direction! He could dig forever and find only those earliest of marine fossils—the jellyfish, the sponges, the mollusks, the still, slow, boneless creatures that oozed through the primordial slime. Julian raced down the butte to tell Alban his discovery.

"But I am finding signs of vertebrate life—look, here is a small spinal sliver right here, and only yesterday I found that fragment of a vertebrate column, not to mention all the teeth," Alban persisted.

"I know," Julian said patiently. "But it's all coming from there." He pointed to the butte. "It's washing down."

"That might be true to a point but, Julian, there is no way that you can categorically say there is nothing beneath here." He tapped at the ground lightly with the toe of his boot.

"There is something. But it's not dinosaurs. It's earlier marine life."

"How can you be so sure that where we now stand is some sort of drain?" Alban raised an eyebrow and looked over his thin arched nose at Julian. Julian regretted his choice of word. He knew quite well that one man's drain might be another's treasure chest. Julian's father's friend, Professor Wachter at Heidelberg University, loved marine fossils and had one of the largest collections of Cambrian mollusks in the world. He would be reveling in this "drain."

Julian was dying to say, "Hang the sifting screen, the microscope, and the magnifying glass. Get out the shovels, pickaxes, and plaster!" But he refrained and instead said, "No, I don't really think of it as a drain, but I do think that by staying down here, we choose to be on the wrong side of the sieve. We should be looking up there." He pointed at the butte.

"Well, Julian, I'm afraid it is impossible for you to be so sure about all this. I do not believe that this land tilts as you seem to imagine."

"I don't imagine that it tilts. It *does* tilt. Go up and see it."

"It is an apparent tilt—like the apparent wind one experiences when riding in an open buggy. Stop the movement and there is no wind. The earth is not so unstable as all that. I believe that Charles Lyell, your own great British geologist, said that change is steady, slow, and evenly distributed throughout space and time. Our planet has always looked and conducted itself as it appears now, more or less. So these violent convulsions that you dream of, these glacial rivers and vast expanses of land tilting at alarming angles, are entirely erroneous."

Julian did not know what else to say. It was as if Alban had stared too long and too hard through the fine mesh of his sifting screen. Granules had become mountains to him, bone slivers became whole creatures unto themselves. He had lost all sense of scale, not to mention sequences of time and even orientation in space. He looked down through his screen and thought it was up. He could not see the forest for the trees nor trust his own eyes to observe a distant vista or a scale larger than that of the microscopic.

Julian, however, did not relish returning to the site where his father was supervising an excavation. He knew that Bobber Henshaw would be there and he didn't want to witness his father's reliance on that man. In general, Julian did not like the tone of the excavation. Bertie Blanchford and Ian Hamilton-Phipps were both absent from the company, having decided to continue their studies at Oxford rather than with DeMott in the field. Julian sorely missed them, and suspected that their reasons for remaining in England lay in the unpleasantness and tension that was now growing worse. So he stayed where he was and went on plugging up anthills, sifting buckets of dirt, and plotting positions on the grid map. But even as he did so, the butte seemed to beckon Julian, and gradually the idea grew in his mind that someday he would return to it to dig on his own.

CHAPTER

22

There was no question about it. They were definitely in the land of the horned dinosaurs. The fossilized cores of hundreds of horns had been found. Fragments from the frills and crests associated with these dinosaurs had cropped up, as well as jawbones and teeth. But for the most part, they were coming up badly broken. It was very frustrating, for the team was anxious to find an entire skull from one of those horned creatures. With this in mind, Thad had set off, heading south and east from the camp. On a recent scouting trip, he had noticed that there was a stretch of reddish shale beds that looked somewhat different from where they had been working. He had brought back a handful of teeth and Jonathan Cabot had identified them as belonging to early mammals. Now as Thad rode, occasionally stopping to examine an outcrop, he had one of what Jonathan Cabot called his "famous hunches," that he was traversing some invisible border between the age of the dinosaurs and that of the mammals.

It was late in the afternoon when Thad spotted the bones sticking out of the high escarpment a few feet off his trail. It would be an easy place to dig, as the ground lay flat with no sudden pitches and the bones were weathering out from the horizontal plane rather than the vertical one of the escarpment. However, because they were close to the surface, the bones were made more fragile from the exposure. Thad never traveled without a small pickax and shovel, and he also had carried his bedroll and a few provisions in case he should decide to stay a night away from camp. After he had been digging for three hours, darkness settled in, and he knew there was no way he could stand to return to camp until he uncovered more of the floor where the bones lay. He had sensed the totality of the animal very early in the dig. The next day, he raced back to the camp to get help. He could hardly express his excitement, but he brought something none of them had ever seen—a slab of sandstone the size of a serving platter inscribed with the beautiful pattern of the dinosaur's skin.

"I don't believe it," Nat Forbes said in a stunned

voice. "The scales, look at the geometry of the scales." He ran his finger over the surface. "I never expected the hides to be so precisely patterned."

"Extraordinary!"

"Superlative!"

"Hah! I doubt the Brits or Yale have anything to compare," Babcock gloated.

All other work was stopped and the entire crew took off to complete the excavation. Even Wu Chow went with the chuck wagon so that the crew would not have to return to the base camp for meals.

Three days and over several tons of dirt later, a quarry had been excavated measuring ten feet wide by twelve feet deep and fourteen feet long. And within that quarry, lying on its back with its forelimbs outstretched as if futilely trying to claw its way out of eternity's sarcophagus, was a duckbilled dinosaur. There had been very little shuffling of the bones, which was unusual. The animal seemed to lie in the position in which it had died. Its neck was arched and contorted as if seeking a last breath and the head at the end of the neck lay behind its shoulder as if in a last convulsive toss. Had it choked? Had it drowned? Broken its neck in a fall? The men were all silent, for after days of painstaking digging, they had suddenly intruded upon the moment of death. The year 1875 seemed to simply melt away as they became witnesses on the edge of an ancient world. The gigantic rib cage seemed expanded with a final convulsive breath.

"It was not being attacked," Babcock said quietly. "You can see that the skin, so beautifully fossilized, has not been torn. I believe that it became mired somehow in the swamp and broke its neck in the struggle."

"Yes," Oliver said. "It appears to be drowning."

"If it had not broken its neck, it could probably have made it to safety," Ike Van Camp said.

"Yes," said Jonathan Cabot. "I agree. Look at that tail. Flat like a crocodile. Must have made it a good swimmer."

"Lucky for us, then, it did break its neck." Babcock chuckled.

The remark caught Thad off guard. Until that moment, it seemed as if time had vanished and together they had been watching a living thing die, helpless to intervene. But Babcock spoke as if the animal had died only for him—and there was fortune and fame to be gathered from its dying. Thad shifted uncomfortably and moved slightly away from the others. Had the magnificent reptiles been made only for the glory of men like Babcock? And just at that moment, as if to answer Thad's silent thoughts, Babcock's voice rang out. "A crowning achievement." And though he might later speak of the great university he represented and the enlightenment of the world, it was very clear to Thad that Babcock envisioned the crown firmly placed on his own head.

Thad kept his thoughts to himself. He felt as if he were in the minority here.

Even Jonathan Cabot seemed carried away by the stupendous find of a dinosaur complete with mummified skin. He proposed a special exhibit at the Harvard Museum of Comparative Zoology in honor of the fossil and a conference to explore the process by which it had become mummified.

"I believe that this region was a boggy part of the Cretaceous sea—a peat bog, really—and due to the peculiar antiseptic qualities of a bog, the skin was preserved, until through decay . . ." Jonathan relived nightly around the campfire the days following the death of the creature, trying better to understand the miraculous recovery of it in such entirety, and then each time he would finish by saying, "Well, I can't be sure, but by gum, we've got it!"

It was this notion of ownership of the past that Thad found so incomprehensible. He knew that Indians did not believe that land could be owned. He remembered the newspaper article that he had read back in Fort Benton and Crazy Horse's words—"One does not sell the earth. . . ." At the time, Thad could not really understand his words. But now he had come to think of time in the same way Crazy Horse thought of the earth. He had never thought of himself as owning the fossils he had taken out of the earth.

"I don't understand, Jonathan," Thad said one evening. "What do you mean, you've 'got it'? What exactly are you folks going to do with that Track over there?" The duckbilled dinosaur was a trachodon, a species discovered by Joseph Leidy some years before. The team had taken to calling their find "Track" for short.

"Well, he'll go into the museum and then we'll catalogue him and—"

"Hold it!" Thad raised his hands. "You mean you're going to chop him up and put him away in drawers or something?"

"No, no. Of course we won't do that. We'll take him as he comes out of the ground, largely in the matrix rock. We'll try to get rid of as much rock as possible when we get back to Harvard so we can have a better look. In some cases, yes . . ." Jonathan hesitated. ". . . parts will be separated. But never a bone that comes out whole."

"Well, are you going to put him back together whole?"

"Whole?" the rest of the team chorused.

"What do you mean by whole?" Jonathan asked.

"I mean whole. Set him up like he was standing in a bog or gettin' ready to go for a swim—like life."

"Like life?" Oliver repeated thoughtfully.

"Well, sure, why not? I mean, everybody's been bellyaching about getting a whole one. Now that you got one, why go putting it in little boxes where no one can see it?"

"He's talking about reassembling," Ike Van Camp said in a low voice.

One would have thought from Van Camp's tone that Thad had just suggested something terribly improper.

But Thad persisted. "Yeah, reassembling. Is that what they call it? Then everyone can go and see this old critter from times they never even dreamed about."

There was a snicker that rippled through the group. "But, Thad," Frank Trowbridge said, "people don't go into the Museum of Comparative Zoology. We do not have displays like an art museum."

"See, Thad," Jonathan said warmly, "we're set up for study. That is why I particularly want to have a seminar that addresses the issue of the hide. To do that, it is not necessary to reassemble the trachodon in the way you're thinking about."

Thad thought about this for a minute. "Well, how many people come to this seminar thing?"

"Perhaps thirty or forty. If we're lucky, who knows—seventy-five."

"Oh," said Thad. Seventy-five measly souls looking at parts of a dinosaur. Thad had envisioned thousands of people streaming through a hall with the creature all propped up, looking bigger than any life one could imagine, and a little sign with his name TRACK written somewhere, probably on a plaque near its toes, where everybody could step right up and see it. He could see that his ideas were very different from theirs and even from Jonathan's.

Thad had gone off to take a walk before turning in. Jonathan caught up with him and dropped his hand on Thad's shoulder.

"I know you wanted to see Track set up for the world

to admire. Don't think for a minute you won't get credit for finding him. Track is Harvard's property now, but in a sense, you are as much his owner as anyone."

Thad stopped. The night air was cold and crisp, the stars hanging sharp in the Montana sky. The buttes rose pale against the blackness of the night. "I'm not his owner, Jonathan."

"But—"

Thad interrupted. "No, I can't own Track or anything like him."

Thad read the confusion in Jonathan's eyes.

"But you should get credit for discovering it."

"Fine. Give me all the credit you want. But I never can own any of this stuff, and you can't either, and the same goes for Harvard."

"Wait! Thad." Jonathan touched his shoulder lightly. "Surely you know that you are no mere excavator. If you keep this work up, your reputation will grow. People will seek you out to lead expeditions. You will find your own fossils and they will become yours to keep or sell."

Thad shook his head emphatically.

"But what do you think you're doing, Thad," Jonathan continued, "when you excavate?"

"I'm tracking," Thad said simply. "I'm just tracking."

It was quite cold now, and Thad said he wanted to check on the horses before turning in. Jonathan watched him walk away. The moon had broken through some scudding clouds. The butte, the one called Camelback, was illuminated and the moonlight poured down through the two humps like a wash of silver rain. Thaddeus Longsworth was not a very big person and he walked with his shoulders hunched. His collar was turned up and his cowboy hat was smashed way down on his head. He was walking on a heading that aimed him dead center between the camel's humps. It was as if the moonlight made a path just for him. Was Thad saying it was folly to think of any of these fossils as possessions? Jonathan Cabot wondered.

Jonathan was an extremely intelligent young man, but this notion was hard to comprehend. Since colonial times, his family had been steeped in ownership—first ships, then real estate, now banks. And here was this penniless boy, Thaddeus Longsworth, declaring that fossils could not be possessions. It was a profoundly shocking idea to Jonathan Cabot, but it challenged his imagination. And there was something so very compelling about this figure moving away from him in a ribbon of silver light. Thaddeus Longsworth had been hired as a scout for sixty-five dollars a month but, for a fee Jonathan did not understand, he had become a tracker in the dimmest reaches of time.

CHAPTER

➤23

Samuel Wilbur had been on the track of a carnivorous dinosaur of unequaled proportions. The saberlike teeth alone measured six inches long by one inch across. They were sharply pointed, with serrated edges. One could imagine that teeth of these dimensions came from an enormous jaw, perhaps three feet long. The remains had been scattered over a wide area, and came out of the rock badly broken except for the teeth. A recent medial bone fragment had suggested that the lower leg of this creature might have been five feet in length. Samuel Wilbur had found three incredibly thick metatarsals, or lower foot bones. At first, because they were found in three widely separated places, he had not associated them as belonging to a single animal. But they had fit together like a puzzle to make an ankle designed for speed and enormous weight.

Together Wilbur and DeMott had calculated the size of the beast that had been supported by bones of this thickness. And they had concluded that when standing upright the creature would measure a minimum of 18 feet, or 5.25 meters, and might weigh upward of 5 tons. The rest of the creature was elusive. Try as he might, Wilbur hadn't found a concentration of bones. The evidence was fragmentary, and yet the terror of such a creature seemed real and pervasive. This terrible beast had raked his saber teeth on most of the horned dinosaur fossils they had excavated. The serrated edges had left distinct marks. DeMott knew for a fact, through Bobber Henshaw's surveillance, that both American teams were finding an equally high percentage of scarring. So although they were in the land of the horned dinosaurs, their real quarry was this killer—this carnivore with teeth like daggers that had felled its fearsome quarry.

And now DeMott, having discovered further evidence of this creature, was ready to declare that the bones were in his court, as it were, and the game was his.

"But, Father!" Julian was saying. "You can't do that. It's simply not fair. Sammy feels that the fossils you have found are part of the same creature that he is excavating."

DeMott snorted. "Feel! That is just the problem, Julian. Samuel Wilbur is an amateur, a hobby naturalist. He proceeds entirely by feeling and with no method."

Julian swallowed. His father was not yet angry. He was treating Julian as if he were simply too dense to grasp certain realities. But if Julian pushed on . . . Julian could not even bear to think of his father's rage. He could not, however, stand by and see his father behave this way toward Sammy Wilbur.

"I just don't understand."

"Of course you don't understand. You are a child still."

"What does it have to do with being a child?" The words just slipped out, quickly, boldly. Julian braced himself.

His father's eyes bulged in dismay. His face drained of color.

"It has everything in the world to do with being a callow, unreflecting child. I have devoted a lifetime to constructing a theory of great significance to our understanding of life on earth—God's creation—and I'll be damned, yes, damned, if my divine theory of creation will be undermined and sullied by the sloppy interpretations of the likes of Sammy Wilbur. As a child, you cannot yet appreciate the dedication of a lifetime's work, work devoted to the pursuit of an ultimate truth."

His father was right about that. But even a child could appreciate that a wrong was being done.

"Father," Julian said softly. His lips were trembling, and the voice did not sound like his own. But the words came out. "Maybe I am a child, but it is also true that Sammy has found over three hundred small bones, not to mention several teeth. You have found one tooth and a shard of something else and you are . . ." His voice dwindled off.

Algernon DeMott jumped to his feet. "I shall not tolerate such insolence." His eyes bulged out even farther.

Julian focused on a thin red blood vessel in one of his father's eyes, as thin as the filament of a spider web. But this time he was not simply concentrating in order to escape the rage and sink into some kind of self-hypnosis. He was focusing on those eyes because he knew that Mr. Woodfin was right. Someday he would have to make a decision.

"This is not fair, Father," he persisted in a trembling voice.

Algernon DeMott blinked and then moved forward rapidly. Julian expected a blow but it never came. Instead, there was another low voice behind him.

"No need, Professor. I kin do that."

They both turned around slowly. Bobber Henshaw stood in the shadows of the tent flap.

"I've given a lickin' to many a lad. Set them straight right off, you know," he drawled.

"Well, thank you, Bobber. A fine idea."

"Father!"

* * *

Julian had never been beaten in his life. Had he protested? He did not remember. Certain words did come back—not his but a muffled conversation between his father and Bobber. Something about taking him away from camp to do it and "blows only to the backside, Mr. Henshaw. . . ." "Nothin' that'll show, sir. You can bet. Just knock a little sense into him. . . ." "Precisely . . ."

But this was nonsense. Painfully, Julian reached around behind him. His fingers touched a wet gelatinous ridge on his skin. When he looked at his fingers, they were covered with blood. He had been left on his stomach, naked. He wondered if he would ever be able to sit down properly again. Bobber had taken him in the direction of Pudding Butte. He remembered that there was a creek nearby. He did not know what Bobber had used to beat him, but it had left his backside feeling like raw meat. And the pain of it pushed out any other feelings—anger, humiliation, the abject loneliness—these were nothing compared to this searing pain. His only thought was to get to the creek.

He groped for the clothes that Bobber had stripped off him and staggered to his feet. He found the creek a short distance away. It took him a full five minutes to ease himself into the water, for at first it stung. But once he had settled down into the soft, silty mud, every muscle seemed to relax. He watched traces of blood swirl away in the slow current of the stream. The sight was strangely fortifying. He knew that his was not the first blood that had soaked into these sediments. When he had first seen this land, he knew it would change his life forever. He remembered watching it unfold from the train, and knowing that his father could not maintain any real power over him. Now the prophecy had been fulfilled. Julian rested his head against a clump of scrub grass that grew down the creek's bank. He looked up into the vast dome of the western sky and smiled slightly. A red-tailed hawk soared on the warm thermal currents.

Yes, the prophecy had been fulfilled. The beating was not a demonstration of power but a sign of weakness, of abject failure. He, Julian, held all the cards now and he would play them cleverly. He followed the tracery of the hawk's flight until finally the bird melted into a distant cloud bank. Not twenty yards from the creek's bank was a tipi ring. Julian had seen many such circles of stones throughout the countryside in and around Medicine Buttes. They reminded him now of the Indians that he had seen on the train platform—vacant-eyed, blank-faced, the women selling glimpses of their babies. Lifeless caricatures they had become on that dusty train platform as General Sheridan, fat and swaggering, had expounded on his scheme for reservations. Then he remembered the baby, its dark-red moon face shining. He thought of that face as possessing a kind of innocent defiance.

These tipi rings belonged to those still-defiant Indians, the ones who refused to go into the reservations. As Julian soaked in the cool waters of the stream, he could imagine them all—the Sioux, Crow, and Cheyenne, and who knew how many others. He imagined that baby playing now in the grass sprinkled with the tiny white blossoms of the sego lilies. He imagined the warriors painted and befeathered, on their ponies, and the women, plain by comparison, wrapped in their blankets. Still and silent, the women were full of mystery. A powerful feeling swept over Julian at that moment. As he stared at the circle of stones, he remembered the tendrils of his own blood curling down the creek's waters, and he knew then that he would never return to England.

Algernon DeMott had not planned to see Julian so soon and would never have guessed, this being the case, that he would encounter his son alone and be compelled to look up from the work he was doing into those bright blue eyes. But he was compelled to do just that.

"Good afternoon, Father, am I in time for tea?"

Julian had whirled into the tent like a crisp wind. His color was high. There was an unusual brightness in his eyes. And although he seemed to be moving somewhat gingerly, he appeared calm and full of good cheer. Well, it just proved it. Nothing like a good thrashing to knock some sense into a lad. It was as if Julian had read his thoughts.

"You're right," he said. "It did knock some sense into me."

Suddenly Julian's face was just inches from that of DeMott's as the boy leaned over the table. Only he did not appear like such a boy now. His shoulders seemed to have thickened and broadened under his shirt, and close up, his eyes were bright with a lambent fury.

"Listen to me carefully, Father. Never, do you understand, never set that thug upon me again. If you do, I shall see that Lord Haversham, whom I know has poured funds into this operation, shall be apprised of certain ungentlemanly procedures that do not befit men of Christ Church College, Cambridge. This will be substantiated by Bertie Blanchford and Ian Hamilton-Phipps, who were most restrained at the time for giving their reasons for not returning with this expedition. I shall also be tempted to go to both American camps and inform them that certain sacred Indian markings on the north face of Sundowner's Ridge were counterfeited by you and Bobber Henshaw."

"How did you know that?" DeMott said in a stunned whisper.

"I know too much about you and Bobber."

"And what do you mean by that?" DeMott flared.

Julian was not exactly sure, but he had sensed some sickening bond developing between the two. He could not identify it precisely, but he felt that it had served to insulate them against any kind of reason or moral judgment. His only purpose now was to put his father, and hence Bobber Henshaw, on alert that he would in no way become an incidental victim of the rotten show they were running.

"I am sure," Julian answered, "that you know well enough for yourself." He turned and walked out.

His one desire was to help Wilbur track down the identity of the elusive killer. They must work steadily and amass enough evidence so his father would not have much cause to claim the creature as his own. There would be no arguments about his returning with Mallory for field survey, Julian felt certain of that. If he worked quietly and kept out of the way, he felt sure his father would be secretly relieved.

Julian knew that his discovery of Lord Haversham's involvement in the finances of the expedition made him safer still. For although his Lordship enjoyed his wine too much, as well as his cards and his games, he was a gentleman from start to finish and would never tolerate anything less than fair play. He would withdraw his support from any game where rules had been fudged and honor compromised. One hint of this and the game would be called. Julian knew this, and he also knew that his father was aware of it.

Life, therefore, became very simple for Julian. Bobber Henshaw never bothered him. The tedious field surface surveys with Mallory were ended. His time became his own and he spent it, as planned, with Sammy Wilbur. The rest of the team was occupied in the thrilling effort of excavating a beautifully preserved monoclonius, so Sammy was most pleased to have Julian's assistance. However, the search for the killer had become almost mystifying. They were still finding fragments, nothing connected, nothing articulated.

At last, they had some luck. "You're joking, Julian," Sammy Wilbur was saying. "You truly think that this is a vertebra?"

"Not one but two—a pair." Julian traced the outlines of the bones on the huge chunk of matrix rock.

"I see what you mean," Sammy said slowly. "Yes, indeed. They seem welded together—not a normal condition. This is certainly too heavy for us to get back to camp tonight. Perhaps we should get your father to come out and have a look-see."

"Yes. I suppose so," Julian reluctantly agreed.

DeMott was in a cantankerous mood. The excavation of the monoclonius was proving technically difficult. Bobber Henshaw had kept muttering about some fellow on the Harvard team who had a wondrous ability to remove bone from rock in one piece. "Well then, go and get the blasted fellow. Hire him! We'll pay him more," DeMott said. But the fellow—a young kid named Longsworth—would not come even when Bobber had offered him twice as much as he was making.

Bobber had then decided to snoop around with the team's strongest binoculars and learn how the fellow did it. He stole some samples of Longsworth's paper and lightweight duck cloth and went all the way to Fort Benton and then back to Claggett to get them. But still it was not working. Bobber and Ormsby and Chad Frawley, a student from the University of Chicago, had spent a day preparing the monoclonius skull, just as they had seen Longsworth do it, but it was wedged at a difficult angle in the rock. Bobber and Ormsby had succeeded in removing the "overburden," or the rock lying above the head, to within four or five inches above the level of the fossil. Delicately, they had tooled out the sandstone and shale to expose the outer surface of the skull, which included an eye socket and jaw complete with teeth. Bobber had then plastered, using Longsworth's technique. They would wait until the plaster had dried completely and then cut out the underlying supporting rock and invert the fossil head so they could tool out and plaster the underneath side. DeMott stood there livid as he saw the first good head of a horned dinosaur come out not merely in pieces but with most of it left behind.

"I guess we didn't cut deep enough," Ormsby said weakly.

"We should have gone for more of the rock," Bobber said.

"A little late for that now," snapped DeMott, and he turned away. Just at that moment, Samuel Wilbur and Julian arrived.

"What is it, Julian?" He scowled.

"Something of interest, Father. The killer."

It was a welcome diversion. DeMott followed them to where they had been working.

"Ah yes," DeMott said. He had taken out his magnifying glass. "I think you're right. A pair of vertebrae welded together. Astounding—but not really if we consider the probable weight of this beast. No, you are correct, Wilbur. Definitely a pathological condition— an indication of severe arthritis. Originally, these were flexible joints." DeMott was speaking rapidly. His eyes were bright. He was the hunter envisioning his quarry. This, Julian knew, was when his father was at his best—when he was reconstructing the creature in his mind, imagining and dreaming—before it belonged to him to be broken and tamed, analyzed and explained, owned and coveted. "You see," he continued, "the joints were under such an immense weight, a weight so enormous that it is hard to conceive. The bones began to rub together and then finally fused."

DeMott got his calipers from the case he always carried with him. He opened them as wide as he could to measure the wide blocklike vertebrae lodged in the rock. The calipers could barely embrace the full width of the vertebrae. "You see!" whispered DeMott in awe. "Each of these vertebrae, even alone and not welded to one another, was like a massive girder, designed to withstand great compression loads because of the creature's immense weight." DeMott paused and closed the calipers. He gazed across the land, now speckled with the white lilies. "We might imagine, lads, a beast of six to seven, even eight, tons."

"Eight tons!" whispered Julian.

"Good work, lads. Keep hunting."

Had his father changed so? Even though he knew that he could never really love his father, he wanted desperately to believe that his father could change. The very next day Sammy and Julian sat in DeMott's tent in rapt attention awaiting his response to yet another piece of the puzzle. Julian could not wait a second longer.

"Well, is it or isn't it, Father?"

"This is most bizarre," DeMott said, turning over the small pointed bone. He picked up another. "Wrist bones, but so tiny. . . . This . . ." He picked up the pointed bone again. "Obviously a digit . . . and this a second digit." He was now holding a blunted columnar-shaped bone. "But amazingly delicate, absolutely small by comparison. And did you say you found them near the spot of the vertebrae?"

"Yes, Father."

"I can't believe they would be associated. The scale is so different. I mean, this is an absurdly small limb. We must assume that it looks rather like it belongs to an enormous chicken."

"You mean, then, Professor, that you don't believe it could belong to the same creature that possesses the giant vertebrae?" Wilbur asked.

"Hardly. There is no correspondence in terms of scaling. We were thinking, Wilbur, if you'll recall, of a beast of up to eight tons. Now what is a monster of that size going to be doing with these little claws? This is too ridiculously small to be of service to such a beast. No. No. I'm afraid not."

But Julian was not convinced his father was correct.

He dared not counter him, for his father had been more than accommodating of late. DeMott was clearly piqued at Bobber Henshaw and his botched attempts at excavating the monoclonius, and whether it was because Bobber had sunk in his father's favor that Julian had risen, he was not sure. In any case, he did not want to upset the delicate balance of rapport they had been able to maintain.

But after his father had left, Julian picked up several pieces that seemed to assemble themselves readily into a kind of clawed forelimb. His father was right, it did look as if it could be the claw of a giant chicken. It was absurdly small. He raked at the dried dirt of the tent floor with the curved, pointed digit—small for what, however? Julian wondered. Small for attacking? Small for a true offense, for a weapon. But perhaps not so small for the finer work of a monster. Now what would that be? Could the monster possibly have used this claw for a grappling hook of some sort? Or as a support when raising itself up from resting? For these tasks, there was nothing miniature about the structure. It would be a form absolutely in scale with its function.

Julian spent the rest of the evening measuring and drawing. He had become much more skillful of late in his renderings, and was especially good in the shading and stippling that showed the contour and volume of these bones. The more time he spent drawing it, the larger this claw seemed to grow in his mind. There was nothing ridiculous about it at all. It was the efficient tool of a most immense creature—the killer whose long shadow was cast across this land. Julian decided to go back the next day to the base of the butte where these claw bones had been found. They had avalanched from higher up, and Julian planned to climb the butte to find more.

CHAPTER
24

Julian left at dawn the next morning. He had packed some cold venison, biscuits, and a skin of water. He watched the morning star, a dazzling point in the thin dawn light, begin to fade as if it were receding behind layers of gauze. A cold pink began to steal over the horizon. The rising sun burnished it to a warmer red. He walked on toward the butte where he and Sammy had been working, stalking the killer. Why, he wondered, had the creature come to them so fragmented? Was it so terrible in its strength, so elusive and cunning, that it even defied the processes of fossilization?

He reached the butte, which appeared in the distance

to have the shape of a loaf of bread and which they had taken to calling Bread Loaf Butte. He ascended three-quarters of the way and was following a ledge just below the summit, moving very slowly to examine every foot of the shale slope for signs of fossils. Julian had been thoroughly absorbed in this task for almost two hours when he had inched his way to the edge of a gap that had been made by a large chunk of ledge falling away—perhaps the very chunk, he was just thinking, that had contained the fused vertebrae. He had turned slightly to reach for his pick, which was slung in the holster over his shoulder, wanting to check the gap to make sure it was firm before crossing over. He remembered thinking that from this height, the few trees he could see in this barren land looked like the seedlings McGuff might set out in the garden in late March for hardening off.

Then suddenly he felt himself plunging into the gap. He tried to grab hold with his fingers but tore instead at the sandstone, hands flaying the shale as if it were soft flesh over the underlying hard bone of the rock. McGuff was not his last thought at all but merely the first as his life seemed to unravel before him in a bizarre chain of images. Some part of his subconscious mind must have fought through the spinning images and ordered his body to extend and span itself in the narrow gap before shattering on the bottom. For he stopped—wedged, his hands and feet braced against the side of what he realized was a deep shaft.

Beneath was a fathomless pit. Above—good Lord,

had he really fallen that far? Above, there hung a square of blue sky. Julian had no choice. There was only one way out—up. He was cross-braced in the narrow shaft, but he could not claw his way out, for the sandstone was too crumbly and any sudden movement not only rained a shower of dirt on him but threatened an entire avalanche.

A chill swept through Julian as he realized that this shaft might very possibly become his coffin. He braced himself harder against the shuddering thought when something flashed deep within his brain. Like an imageless memory, it came back to him, the feeling on his shoulder—a pressure, warm, quick, firm. Yes, he could feel it just as it had been. The truth exploded, filling his skull with its harsh light—he had not fallen. He had been pushed. Just at that moment, a shadow passed over and eclipsed the square patch of blue sky. Only a sliver of blue remained. What was it? Had his only exit been closed, the lid put on the casket? Then, from the shadow, there came a disembodied voice.

"Someone down there?"

"You're bloody right," shouted Julian. "There's someone down here. You ought to know."

"What do you mean, I ought to know?"

"You're the bloody fool who shoved me down here into this hellhole."

"What the heck are you talking about?"

"I felt it. I felt your hand, and I would very much like to know if there is any reason why I should exert the effort to climb out of this bloody hole, because if you're

going to push me down again, it seems rather pointless,
doesn't it?"

"I didn't push you down any darn hole. Not that you
don't deserve it after all the spying you British been
doing."

"Spying! What the bloody devil are you talking
about?"

"Look, do you want me to help you out of that hole
or not?"

"No, no, of course not. I thought I'd take tea down
here." The shadow slid away and the square of blue sky
suddenly floated blank above him. "No! No! Come
back," Julian shouted. "Just joking. Good heavens, no
sense of humor at all. Come back. Please." Julian cursed
himself. He hooked his fingers, trying to gain a purchase, but the wall became dust in his hands. So
he quickly flattened his palms and spread his fingers,
then pressed with all his might against the sides. At
this moment, he was nothing more than a human
wedge within the cleft of a mountain, a mountain that
threatened to grind and crush him into its stone
heart.

He tried to concentrate on the physics of his situation, then thought of the god Atlas holding the vault
of the sky on his back. Atlas had it easy compared to
himself. A bunch of air and some clouds, that was all
the sky amounted to—nothing like holding apart two
halves of a mountain. Julian feared he was losing control. He stared directly ahead now. Despite the dim
light, he could see every grain of dirt in the wall. He

had a dreadful feeling that he would become more familiar with this little piece of sandstone wall than any other thing on earth. This was his destiny.

"Hey!" The shadow slid over the square of blue. Julian looked up. Some grits of sand fell from high up.

"I do want to be rescued, you know. Just joking about the tea."

"Hold on. I'm letting down a rope."

Just at that moment, he saw the loop of a rope slap against the wall. "I see it!" Julian called.

"Can you grab it?"

"I don't . . . don't know." There was a problem. If he unbraced himself, what would happen? He was afraid to let go. If he fell again, how far would it be before he stopped? "Lower it a bit more," he called. When it was just at his shoulder level, Julian inhaled sharply and grabbed with his right hand. He had it. Then he grabbed with his other hand.

"You got it?" the voice called down.

"Yes."

"Start climbing."

Julian had never climbed a rope before but he learned fast, keeping his feet away from the walls. There was no way he wanted to disturb the innards of this butte any more than he already had. He pulled himself up with nerve-racking slowness, feeling like a feather in the throat of a huge beast.

He must have fallen almost thirty feet. When he had climbed up a good twenty, he began to feel a tug on the rope.

"Hold up a minute," the voice called. "Let me get another loop around this rock."

Julian paused. There was no doubt about it. This bloke wanted to help him. He could still swear that he had been pushed. It was as if the print of that hand was still pressed on his shoulder. He had begun to climb again. The square of blue was nearly obliterated now. He was moving through different shades of darkness. The walls were a murky brown, the air within the hole nearly black but swirling with gray dust, and straight up where the sky should be, it was solid black. There would be an occasional crack of blue as the person above shifted. For his helper now seemed to be crouched over the hole. Julian could hear him breathing, or was it his own breath? He began to discern a shape. First he saw the hair, a shock of it, very shiny, coming over the forehead, and then the eyes, and suddenly he was transfixed in this clear, dreamless light. He stopped climbing and caught his breath.

"It's you!" They were the same eyes he had seen just a year before from his train window. They were the gray-green eyes of the boy on the pinto horse by the railroad track.

"You weren't spying, then?" Thad asked.

"Of course not! Why would I do a thing like that?" They were sitting at the base of the butte under the shade of an overhang.

"I don't know, but someone wants to find out awful bad how we get the bones out whole. They sent some fellow to try and hire me."

"So you're the one!"

"Yeah, but I wouldn't go."

"Can't say as I blame you," Julian replied, and Thad raised an eyebrow in surprise.

"Why not?"

"Oh, nothing." Julian shrugged.

"I got this feeling after the fellow—what's his name?" Thad asked.

"Bobber—Bobber Henshaw."

"Yes, after he tried to hire me. I had this feeling that this Bobber fellow wasn't going to give up. It was almost as if I could feel his eyes following me around, felt as though they were stuck to my back. Wasn't long before I found his track. He's as easy as they come to track. His horse has got one wedged shoe. This Bobber fellow walks kind of strange himself. I think maybe his right leg's shorter than his left. So he gets a purchase with his left leg. Like over there." Thad pointed a few feet away and then casually tossed a pebble in that direction.

Julian jumped to his feet. "You mean that's his heel mark over there?"

"All over the place here," Thad said.

"Then he's the one!" Julian exclaimed.

"The one what?"

"The one who shoved me."

Once again, Julian could feel the hand hard on his shoulder.

"Are you sure?" Thad asked.

"Positive."

"But why would someone from your own team try to kill you?"

"I don't know," Julian said vacantly. He and his father were getting on better. Maybe that didn't sit too well with Bobber Henshaw. Bobber hated Julian, as he well knew. Or perhaps his father had simply fooled him into thinking he had softened. Maybe he was biding his time, waiting to claim Sammy Wilbur's discovery as his own.

Julian stared across the flat valley to the edge where a herd of buttes reared against the morning sun. A shadow crossed over the blue sky, and it was as if the same shadow somehow crossed over his mind. Could he no longer trust his own feelings? Was it possible that his father had sent Bobber?

CHAPTER

➤25

That night in camp, Thad thought about Julian De-Mott. If you took a person like Julian straight on, Thad reflected, he seemed a mite strange, what with all that curly orange hair and more freckles than prickles on a cactus. Lord, he had never seen so many freckles in one place. Seemed like his face was just one big freckle. Only the Lord, Thad thought, would take the time to divide up all that tawny gold into little specks. And he had the strangest accent that Thad had ever heard. He sounded older than his years and a darned sight smarter than anyone. And it wasn't just that he sounded mouth-smart. He sounded thinking-smart. He did not,

Thad thought, sound as if he had all the answers but as if he was positively thinking about all the questions. And some of those questions were the same ones that Thad had been considering.

"I thought I climbed this butte to stalk a killer," Julian had said after telling Thad his notions about the bone scarring, the same kind of scarring that Thad had also seen on many bones. "But it appears as if the killer is stalking me." He had taken out a handkerchief and dabbed it at his mouth, which was bleeding from the fall.

"Do you think you'll find him?" Thad had asked.

"Dunno," Julian had replied and then said the strangest thing of all. "Don't know what I'll do if I do find him."

"What do you mean? You'll take him back to England, won't you?"

"To sit in the archives of some old university, or worse, my father's collection? I'd want the world to see it—not just a few old professors, but the whole world!"

Thad was stunned. He had thought himself to be entirely alone with such notions. Now he began to share his ideas with Julian.

"Precisely!" the English boy exclaimed. "Absolutely! Utter folly, I agree." And then finally, he said, "So what should we do about it?"

Again, Thad was caught off guard. He had never been asked what he should do about anything, except of course such practical matters as how to dig out a hunk of fossil, how to make a cantankerous horse be-

have, or how to find water. But what to do about bones,
old bones that belonged to the world, was a whole new
thing. They had agreed to meet the next day. Julian had
told Thad about the site he had worked with Alban
Mallory. It was convenient for both of them, being out
of the way from any of the three camps. There was no
chance of Alban returning to it for weeks, if at all.

It was shortly before sundown. The whole land was
bathed in a deep rusty pink. It was the time of day
when the light brought every object into sharp relief.
A pronghorn antelope stood still as stone, its spiraled
horns like twin scrolls against the sky. The prickly pear
in full bloom now seemed drained of its own color in
the vivid pink ending of the day. It looked to Julian as
if the sinking sun, in one last blast of furious brilliance,
wanted to take the rest of the earth's color with it. He
sat at the base of Pudding Butte, watching the sun's
dazzling display, and he considered the notion that
dinosaurs could be assembled whole to look just as
they had been millions of years ago, so people, not just
professors, could come and see and imagine this life on
earth.

"Tilts some, doesn't it?" Thad said. Julian was so lost
in thought that he hadn't even heard Thad approach.

"Goodness, you gave me a start. Where'd you come
from?"

"Camp."

"I know that." Julian laughed. "I just didn't hear you
come up."

"Came from downwind."

Julian's eyes widened. The fellow knew so much. He had already taught him some simple tricks for back-tracking and covering his own tracks to elude Bobber, should Bobber decide to follow him again. But that was no problem now, for Bobber and his father had ridden to Claggett for supplies.

"What were you saying now—something tilts."

"The land," Thad answered.

"Precisely," Julian exclaimed. "You see it quite clearly, don't you?"

"Oh yeah. I started to see it just east of Claggett on the other side of the river. Like the whole country starts to tip down."

"Now, how can you and I see it, and a bloke like Alban Mallory can't?"

"Oh, Mallory—you got him now," Thad remembered. "Professor Babcock got pretty rattled over that."

"He needn't be," Julian said dryly. "Unless he's very interested in doing a treatise on anthills. The poor blighter stood right down there." Julian pointed. "Right in the drain of this sink, if you will, sifting for the tiniest bits."

"Oh yeah, they must wash down that coulee over there." Thad pointed to a deep channel that plunged straight down from the top of the crest of the butte.

"Of course. But you tell me—where do the big bones lie?"

"Up here beneath the coal line." Thad pointed to a dark band that was several feet wide and twenty or thirty feet below the top of the butte's ridge. "Probably best on the other side."

"Why's that?"

"Weather side. Wind comes up from the west."

"Of course! More erosion."

"Yep. Let the wind do the work."

"Right-o." Julian chuckled, then paused. "Do you think the killer could be here?"

"Maybe."

"Thad." The jolly freckled face became sober. "What do you say we have a go at it?"

"A 'go at it'?" Thad appeared confused.

"Try to excavate. You know, I've had a feeling about this place since I first worked here with Mallory."

"But who do we dig it for—you British or Babcock and Harvard?"

"The world, dear boy! We'll dig for the world!" The words rang out jubilantly across the ancient terrains.

CHAPTER

26

If the creature was to be for the world, the two boys had not worked out precisely just how it was to be delivered. There was also the problem of how much time could be stolen to work on Pudding Butte. This was mostly of concern to Thad. The season was two-thirds over and in late summer it seemed as if Babcock's team were pulling fossils out of the ground faster than one could count them. But they remained baffled and frustrated because they had still failed to locate the complete skull from a horned dinosaur. In both camps, the fossil remains of the great predator had simply dried up.

The day after Thad returned from Pudding Butte, Ike Van Camp and Frank Trowbridge had finally uncovered a small fossil head, not of a horned dinosaur but of another real killer—a carnivore this time, outfitted with a deadly set of teeth. The head was quite small, no more than eight inches long. A fragment of its foot was found nearby. Its shape indicated the creature was quite swift.

"A vicious little package," Frank Trowbridge said, referring to its teeth and its possible swiftness. The excavation was painstaking, for the head was lodged at a peculiar angle. It took Thad several days to apply the first strips of paper and cloth. Midway through this delicate process, Babcock came rushing up in a fit of glee to announce a major hadrosaurus find. "It's going to be much bigger than the 1858 one Foulke excavated in New Jersey—much bigger—possibly a different species," he exclaimed. So between excavating the little killer and "Big Haddie," as the latest find was called, Thad barely had time to work on Pudding Butte.

Julian, on the other hand, had nothing but time. His father hardly paid any attention to him or to his work with Sammy. He was fully occupied with a promising excavation and the warm reception a paper of his had been given by the British Museum. The museum had sent an inquiring letter to him regarding the possibility of purchasing or buying some of the American specimens he was collecting. The few times they saw one another were at tea or other meals. On these occasions, DeMott was always perfectly correct with his son, but still, Julian could not forget the terrible doubts he had experienced after his fall into the chasm of the butte. He would catch himself observing his father, trying to imagine if he could have conspired with Bobber Henshaw. Finally, he concluded that if Henshaw had pushed him, he had done it on his own. For his father, Julian was certain that he constituted no more than a minor annoyance.

This became quite clear on one extremely hot day in the lab tent when they were having tea. Alban Mallory had never been able to accustom himself to this midafternoon ritual, and he had been set upon the night before by bedroll chiggers. This, in addition to the heat, had dissolved his usual equanimity.

That afternoon he sat in the tent looking quite prickly.

"Do try the tea, Mallory," Charles Ormsby suggested. "It helps."

"Indeed," agreed DeMott. "The heat and the bugs are merely the petty perturbations of this great land." Although he was not looking directly at Julian, Julian thought he felt swipes of a sidelong glance. "There is no use swatting the insects. You will only irritate your own skin. The best thing is to drink tea and ignore the disturbance. There is no need to even attempt to vanquish these perturbations." Then he added as an afterthought, "It is really a tactic the United States government should adopt in regard to the Indians. Better than going to all this fuss. As most aboriginal races, they are destined to recede and perish due to their inferiority. Why waste money trying to hurry up the process?"

Julian quietly left the tent. He had had enough of his father's lectures on racial inferiority and brain size. He had been forced the previous winter to accompany his father to Philadelphia in order that he might see what his father called a "craniological treasure trove" that had been assembled by one Samuel Morton. Morton had gathered over one thousand skulls, mostly Indian, and through study and measurement had arrived at a scheme for ranking the races.

Just as Julian was leaving the tent, DeMott had drawn out his precious Morton volume on American Indians—*Crania America.* One illustration showed white men's skulls on top, Indians in the middle, and blacks on the bottom. Within the white ranks, it showed Germans and Anglo-Saxons on top, Jews in the middle, and Hindus at the bottom.

It was all nonsense, Julian felt. He had seen his father do similar measurements with some of the skulls he had collected. Give Algernon DeMott a nice British skull or a German one and he would pack in mustard seeds—used for measurement—to overflowing by shaking the seed so they would settle and then pushing them down again with his thumb through the hole at the base of the skull so more seeds might be poured in. Of course, if he got a skull of any other race, there was no shaking or pushing down of the seeds. Naturally the volume of the seeds was always higher in the white man's skull.

Where would his father place an aberrant Anglo-Saxon son like himself, Julian wondered. He supposed somewhere between a Hindu and a Montana mosquito—not to be swatted, which would only cause further irritation. Rather, to be ignored, to let die due to its own inferiority. Neither he, a gnat, nor an entire race would be given the dignity of being anything more than a petty perturbation.

On this particular afternoon, Julian set off for Pudding Butte. He was quite careful to take indirect routes to the butte and never to appear too anxious to be getting anyplace in particular, especially when Bobber Henshaw was around. Julian and Thad had begun by meeting at night, in the hours just before and after midnight. However, too many midnight forays would arouse suspicion and so they often went in the early evening, each hoping to find the other.

This afternoon, within hearing distance of Henshaw, Julian had told Sammy that he was planning on going back to Bread Loaf Butte to retrieve something left behind. This was true. He headed that way but then did a kind of double loop that Thad had shown him across a very hard untrackable piece of terrain that led directly up to a stream. In this way, his trail was lost even before he crossed the stream, and he then headed off for Pudding Butte in the opposite direction.

With all the excavation going on in Babcock's camp, Thad's evenings began to be consumed. Still, the boys had found a rich vein of fossils. Several more parts of a small killer, similar to the one that Ike Van Camp and Frank Trowbridge had found, turned up and many fragments of crests and frills from horned dinosaurs. But still there were no entire skulls of these creatures or any bones of the great killer. Their best find so far had been the long flattened tail complete with skin of what they believed to have been a hadrosaurus. They also had found another mittenlike piece of fossilized skin that Julian had speculated was the webbing from between its toes or fingers. There was a large cave where they cached their finds and that Julian had begun to use as a lab. It was to this cave that Julian now went to seek refuge from the sun and his father, to wait for Thad, and to imagine how that mitten of skin might have served the animal in life millions and millions of years ago.

Thad arrived somewhat earlier than Julian had expected. His face was tight and the cool clear eyes had narrowed and hardened.

"What the devil is the matter?"

"I'm being sent off." Thad spat out the words.

"You mean you've been fired?" Julian asked. It was incomprehensible that they would fire their best excavator.

"No." Thad sank down against the cave wall.

"Well, what do you mean by 'sent off'?"

Thad sighed. "Cunningham is leaving soon with a cargo of fossils and I have to follow him and report every darn thing I see and hear."

"Cunningham from the Yale team? Why, it's still

early. There's almost three months until the winter snows."

"I know. Supposedly, he's just taking an early shipment to the railhead in Omaha. But Professor Babcock's got it in his head that the fossils are going to Omaha but Cunningham is getting off at Fort Robinson for the big meeting there with the commissioners and the Indians. All this fuss about buying the Black Hills."

Julian was confused. "Is Cunningham a commissioner?"

"No, no such thing. They hate him. He's a big pal of the Sioux, especially of Red Cloud's. He's the one who made the big fuss two years ago over the rotten food the agents were doling out to the Indians. Got written up in all the newspapers."

"So what's wrong with that? Sounds like a nice bloke to me. Fair and square."

"Course it does. But you got to understand Babcock. He has more fears than a dog has fleas. He called it 'grandstanding, shameless grandstanding'—Cunningham's helping the Indians. It got his name all over the papers, got him made president of some fancy scientific group and more money for his work."

"So he's scared he'll do it again?"

"Not just that. Babcock is 'fraid that Cunningham will strike some sort of deal with the Indians. He says things are going to be red hot out here by next field season and we're going to need the Indians more than the generals if work is going to go on. He sent me in to talk to Red Cloud to get permission to cross through his territory when we were coming out from Fort Lincoln."

"You talked to Red Cloud?" Julian's eyes opened wider. "What was he like?"

Thad thought back. The old chief had been somewhat of a disappointment to him. It was as if he had just grown too tired, too weary with age and with the troubles of his people, to show any of the fire that Thad had expected.

"Well," Thad began. "He's kind of grown old and a little bit ornery. He's got a bad back, full of ailment complaints—like a lot of old folks, I guess. Those other old folks don't have the whole government breathing down their necks, though." Thad paused. "Crazy Horse, now he is something!"

"Crazy Horse? You met him, too, I suppose?"

Thad nodded, but Julian was still trying to sort out his notions of Red Cloud. Everyone, even legends, Julian guessed, got worn down after a while.

"So you're going, Thad?"

"I don't have much of a choice. This is the only job I got right now. The professor's been good to me. I guess I got to put up with his funny parts."

"Funny parts?"

"His fears, you know. This thing he's got going with Cunningham. I feel kind of strange as it is, hunting fossils out here with you that aren't for Harvard."

"They're for everyone, Thad. I told you about Mr. Woodfin at the New World Museum."

"Yeah."

"So how long will you be gone?"

"I have to leave tomorrow. That's when the next steamer comes through. There was one yesterday but I missed it. The river's high, so the trip shouldn't take that long. I get off at Fort Pierre in the Dakota territory and ride on down to Fort Robinson in Nebraska. That's about a hundred and seventy-five miles. Got to plan at least two days for that. The meeting's called for late September. I don't figure I can make it back here much before the middle of October. Professor wants me to get some supplies to carry us through to the end of the season."

"By then, there won't be much left of it."

"Yeah. So I guess this is it for Pudding Butte," Thad replied, his voice full of resignation.

"Well, I'll keep picking around. I dare not excavate without you. But cheer up. There's always next season."

"If the whole darn show don't go and blow up on us," Thad added.

"Yes, yes. This Indian thing's bound to heat up, I suppose."

No farewells were actually spoken. They did not want anything to be finalized or finished. Thad gave Julian a friendly shove on his shoulder. "Don't fall down any holes," he said.

Julian craned his neck about in a rather nervous, self-conscious gesture and muttered something about the mitten of skin belonging to an ornithopod that they had found.

"Ornithopod?" Thad asked.

"Bird-hipped."

"Is that the name your father thought up?"

"Oh dear, he's thought up so many. I think that's one of his—ornithopod—you know, where the ischium bone lies directly against the . . ." Julian's voice trailed off. That was how they left each other.

CHAPTER

27

"He ate the tibia?"

"Yes," said Nat Forbes. "Wu Chow ate it."

"The whole bone?" Thad asked.

"Well, there was really only a shard," Jonathan Cabot said.

"That doesn't make it any better," Forbes replied. "It was enough of a shard for me to project what a decent foot might look like on the creature."

"And Wu Chow ate it?" Thad simply could not believe what he was hearing. "How?"

"He drank it, actually. Ground it up into a powder.

I believe he steeped it along with his Lapsang souchong tea leaves. Apparently"—Jonathan's face was beginning to redden—"it is believed by the Chinese to be an aphrodisiac."

"An aphro what?"

"Aphrodisiac—er, uh." Jonathan coughed. "It enhances the sexual powers, the lovemaking ability. Dragon bones. That's what he calls these fossils."

"Well, who is there for Wu Chow to love out here? For criminy sake, we're in the Badlands of the Montana territory," Thad exclaimed.

"Must be preparing for when he goes to Fort Benton," Nat Forbes offered dryly.

"Those girls at the Hang It Up don't have much truck with Chinamen."

"At the Silver Dollar, they do," Nat Forbes said.

"Really, Nat," said Jonathan, "I don't think you need to go into graphic detail."

"In any case," Nat continued, "Wu Chow's going to get to Fort Benton sooner than he anticipated. Babcock's fired him."

"Fired him!" Thad exclaimed. "That's terrible."

"Terrible. It's good riddance. God knows how many other fossils are rolling around in his gut."

"We all need Wu Chow," Thad said. "Who's going to cook? Who's going to help me pack up, end of the season? Wu Chow's as hard a worker as you can find. And he's the best trail cook I ever knew. You, Nat, you're going to miss him the most. You eat more of his sourdough biscuits, Fluff Duffs, and pies than anyone. Where is he? I got to talk to him and I got to talk to the professor."

"Wu Chow's packing up now."

Thad poked his head into the chuck wagon. It was as neat and orderly as the lab tent. Pots and pans hung scoured and black from their hooks. Bulk supplies such as flour and beans were stashed in bags or kegs under the bunks. The chuck box was closed. This was a bad sign, for the box was opened up when meals were to be prepared. The box had built-in shelves that were filled with most of the cooking utensils, plus working supplies of molasses, rice, beans, dried fruit, and lard, as well as simple remedies such as quinine pills, black draught, and horse liniment. The chuck box fitted onto the rear of the wagon. When its side was let down, it became the cook's workbench. It was not down tonight and it appeared that there would be no supper.

"Wu Chow? You in there?" There was no answer. In the dim light, he could see Wu Chow sitting erect, wearing his square black hat. From under it, his pigtail hung straight down his back. His face was as still as stone and his hands were folded calmly in his lap. He did not acknowledge Thad at all. Thad climbed into the wagon and sat down across from him on a keg of flour. Still, Wu Chow did not move.

Thad sighed. "Wu Chow, just how many bones did you eat?"

There was a long silence.

"Not many," he said finally. "Less than a pound."

"Less than a pound," Thad repeated.

"Much less. I only took little bones. Most, I find out on the buttes. Just two times I took bones from Mr. Forbes and lab tent—scraps, too tiny for Mr. Forbes to make good drawing."

There was no use trying to explain that size did not matter. Thad, indeed the entire team, had great respect for Wu Chow's medicinal know-how. He had patched up many a sprained limb and poulticed many an aching tooth. This, however, was going too far.

"Wu Chow," Thad said. "You just can't do it."

Then Wu Chow, suddenly animated, blurted out, "Dragon bones are good, Thad. Give plenty strong seed—lots of children."

"That's all well and good, Wu Chow. But you can't eat the dragon bones anymore—children or no children. If you promise not to, I think I can get the professor to take you back."

He slid his eyes toward Thad. It was impossible to see what Wu Chow was thinking but Thad guessed he must be trying to decide which was worth more, the job or strengthening his seed.

"You good man, Thad. I stay. I no eat dragon bones. Promise."

It was not hard for Thad to convince Babcock to take Wu Chow back. Babcock was not ignorant of the value of a good cook in the field.

That night, the team sat down to a late but delicious supper served up by Wu Chow: antelope steaks and a favorite dish called camp potatoes, where the potatoes were diced up and cooked in bacon grease, then sprinkled with the tiny fragrant leaves of the sagebrush plant. There were two desserts—Lumpy Dick, a spicy milkless pudding that Wu Chow boiled over an open fire, and a cake made of raisins, dried apples, and suet that was steamed in a bag over boiling water. It was a troublesome and tasty dish to make. The team members called it Fluff Duff, but it was the same dessert that Thad had eaten on the drive north from Texas, and the cowboys had called it Son-of-a-Gun-in-a-Bag.

At the end of the meal, Babcock rose and spoke. "Well, thank you, Wu Chow, for the delicious supper, and I think now that we understand each other, we can look forward to finishing up the season tastily if not too hastily. I feel we are far ahead of both other teams in terms of the quality of our finds. There is no question that we are getting our bones out in better shape." He nodded to Thad as he said this. "In the meantime, if Wu Chow should be seized by an irresistible urge for the taste of dragon bones, I would ask that you direct him to Nathaniel Cunningham's camp." There was hearty laughter at this, even from Thad. Jonathan Cabot remained silent.

Thad had planned to leave by midmorning to catch the steamboat at the Cow Island Landing. Shortly before Wu Chow beat the big pot to call for breakfast, Thad heard a commotion outside his tent.

"How dare you come into this camp and accuse us of

such a thing! Absolute nonsense." It was Babcock's voice.

"I repeat, sir. An entire metatarsal from our mono-clonius is missing. Until two days ago, the Yale team had a complete foot construction. We do not now."

"What makes you think we would have it? We have our own monoclonius materials. We don't need yours."

Thad came out of his tent buttoning his trousers. Cunningham was not with the group, and it was obvious these men were not college students. Thad recognized two as being from Fort Benton. They were rough-looking men but wore bland expressions. It was a stout fair-haired young fellow who was doing all the talking. "It has been reported . . ." he continued.

"By whom?" Babcock's eyes were dancing with rage. The rest of the Harvard team had gathered behind him.

"I cannot say."

"Where's Cunningham?"

"He's left on business. It was while he was loading at Cow Island that the piece was stolen."

"Stolen!"

This was a very serious accusation, and Thad felt the group tighten up like a wet knot.

"See here!" Jonathan Cabot stepped forward. "You have no evidence to support such a charge."

A burly fellow, one of the pair Thad had recognized, stepped forward. He shoved Jonathan back roughly with one hand. "We plan to get it." He scowled.

"I beg your pardon, sir!"

The very air seemed shrill with the accusations.

"Easy, Starkey," another of the men muttered.

"What kind of thugs does Cunningham employ?"

Thad saw a fist shaking in his own face. Then he felt his jaw explode. He came to within seconds. He was dimly aware of a terrible ache, but his jaw did not even feel as if it was part of his face. The dust swirled around him. Nat Forbes had one fellow in a headlock. Blood poured out of Jonathan Cabot's nose, and Ike Van Camp had wrestled to the ground the stout fellow who had delivered the accusations. He had him pinned, but just at that moment, the fellow began pointing and shouting.

"See! See! I told you so!."

One of the young men from the Yale team had emerged from the lab cave waving the bone. "Still has our code on it!" he said, referring to the catalogue number.

The fighting stopped.

"This is preposterous!" Babcock gasped. "Let me see that bone."

The fellow who carried it approached gingerly. He tightly held the bone, which was over a foot long.

"Sloppy work, Professor. Didn't even remove our catalogue code."

"Hard to do, seeing as I didn't know it was here."

"A likely excuse," sneered the young man.

The thugs from the Yale team departed quickly, carrying the bone, and they left in their wake a stunned camp, pondering how it could have possibly gotten into their lab tent.

"Who could have done it? Why would anyone do it? What possibly could be gained by it?" The questions swirled in the air.

"Our own discredit could be gained." Babcock spat out the words.

"You can't possibly think," Jonathan Cabot said, "that Cunningham would have planted the bone himself to discredit us."

"Precisely. He's tried to make me look a fool before. This is just a new strategy."

"You still want me to follow him to Fort Robinson?" Thad asked, rubbing his jaw. The words came out thick and he could feel some blood inside his mouth.

"Absolutely. I certainly don't want him making me look like a fool to Red Cloud and the rest of the chiefs. Having the Yale team burst in here is one thing, but having the entire Sioux nation come down on us is another."

CHAPTER
28

Thad's jaw ached. He had never thought that he would be glad to leave the Badlands, but now all he felt was relief. He tried not to think about the fracas in camp that morning but couldn't help it. It seemed unlikely that Cunningham had tried to frame Babcock. For one thing, he never would have left the catalogue number on the bone, because he'd know that Babcock would change it right away. Cunningham would have found a more clever way to incriminate the Harvard team. The British, on the other hand, might be unfamiliar with the American system of cataloging. Thad pondered this while urging Gumbo into a fast trot. The

British had tried to hire him away, then spied on them and even snitched some of his best plastering materials. But what motive could they have to create dissension between the two American camps?

Thad's head whirled. Babcock was so angry that he had given Thad a just-completed separate to send on to Boston. Its title was *"Ornithominus grandis* of the Judith River Formation," or as Thad translated it, "Bird Hips of the Badlands." Babcock had promised Jonathan that in accordance with the ground rules, he would wait until Cunningham's return and inform him of his plans to publish it. But it was obvious that all the ground rules had been thrown right out the window.

The Missouri River poured from the west, carrying the steamboat downstream past herds of buffalo, elk, and deer and bands of fleet white antelope. The river unfurled like a wide banner of water across the high sweep of the plains. Thad had heard that this river raced eastward through the terrain of the Ree and the Sioux Indians, then into that of the Omaha and the Pawnee and all the way to the Mississippi River. It did seem like an endless river, as endless as the throbbing pain in his jaw. At the junction of the Yellowstone River on the border between the Montana and Dakota territories, the boat swept by Fort Union and Fort Buford, then it continued southeast.

There were other river travelers, too, who were poling, hauling, or steaming their way up or down the Big Muddy. After the Yellowstone River, the Missouri

truly began to earn its name. There it became tawny-
colored and unruly, cutting into banks and tearing out
cottonwoods and other trees that dared grow near the
edge. But Thad was so preoccupied with the troubled
camp he had left behind that he barely noticed the
teeming river life. The hot wind was like a blade against
his sore jaw, but the evenings were cooler. Thad would
go below deck to the stalls where the animals were kept
to feed and water Gumbo, who seemed to be adjusting
well to river travel. Then he'd sit in the bow of the boat,
where he was able to feel better the life of the river.
Through the throbbing turbines of the steam engines,
he could sense the streaming, powerful current, the
heart of the river. It seemed to send a wild free feeling
through his entire body that was stronger at these times
than any pain he had felt.

He lost track of time. One day flowed seamlessly into
the next, and it was as difficult to separate the days as
it was to separate the watery strands of the river's
current. Time and water combined in an odd way. They
both flowed, interwoven, and were spliced into this big
river. When he had first set out, Thad had been very
concerned with the problems at Medicine Buttes, but
now they seemed to dissolve and simply flow away
with the river. The mission that Babcock had sent him
on was foolish, the foolish preoccupation of a frightened man. But it no longer bothered him. The river in
a strange way lessened such feelings, blunting pain,
taking the edge off fear, and making tolerable even the
most foolish enterprise. As they made their way down-

stream, he could imagine that flowing through the very heart of this river was a kind of spirit. He thought of it as a kind of weaver, a river weaver, who wove together not only time and water but all parts of life into one whole piece. The petty things, the silliness, the small fears and the old pains, were but the thinnest threads in a glorious design. Thad had never felt such freedom. It filled his heart and mind as they hurled down the watery course slanting across the Dakota territory.

A day past Bismarck, the steamer docked at Fort Pierre. Thad led Gumbo down the gangplank. Gumbo hoofed the ground, as if he were happy to see it again. Two days later, Thad rode into Fort Robinson.

CHAPTER

29

The meetings were to be held near Fort Robinson, on the White River between the Red Cloud and the Spotted Tail agencies. Thousands of Indians were streaming to the meeting place, and Thad wondered how in the mass of people he would ever pick out Cunningham. Babcock had said that Cunningham would be sticking close to Red Cloud. However, Thad learned that Red Cloud had refused to come. By September 20, when the meeting was to begin, Thad had still not seen any sign of Cunningham as the commission appointed by Edward P. Smith, Commissioner of Indian Affairs, assembled under a tarpaulin outside the fort.

The commissioners sat on chairs facing several thousands of Indians. They were charged with reaching an agreement on the fate of the Black Hills. Thad climbed a cottonwood tree and crawled out onto a branch that hung directly over the tarpaulin to gain a better view. Coming from the fort, he saw a long line of white horses ridden by cavalrymen. Why all white? Thad wondered. It must have been a bother to scare up that many. There was not a light dapple gray or a palomino among them. They made an impressive showing as the soldiers drew up in a formation behind the tarpaulin.

Thad soon noticed a stir among the throngs of Indians and realized that their chiefs were arriving. There was one large broad-faced man who seemed to cause a great deal of commotion. Thad saw the mass of people part as he made his way through with his wagon. His hair was not braided but flowed down over his shoulders from a center part. From each ear hung a large gold hoop earring. He wore a snug double-breasted broadcloth coat. Over the collar, a bright yellow neckerchief was knotted, and draped over his shoulder was a red blanket. His face appeared calm but firm. He was a man of about fifty. This chief was going to be tough to deal with, Thad realized.

Thad heard the soft, almost muffled sound coming from the Indians, and as it grew clearer, he could make out the words *Sinte-Galeshka.* "Spotted Tail." One of the commissioners, who was almost directly below him, said, "Spotted Tail." Of course—Spotted Tail, the Brulé Sioux. Just at that moment, he caught sight of

Cunningham. He was riding a few feet behind Spotted Tail's wagon. Some other chiefs were following, but there was no sign of Crazy Horse or Sitting Bull. Thad climbed to a higher branch. Over the crest of a distant hill, he saw a dusty smear rising against the horizon. It seemed to be moving closer, rolling like a dust storm full of turbulence and speed. Within minutes, a hard-galloping band of Indians was bearing down upon the assembly. Dressed for war and firing their rifles toward the sky, they slashed wildly on their ponies back and forth and in front of the white mounted cavalry before slowing down to form a line. No sooner had they quieted their ponies than another band followed, their war paint flashing through the boiling cloud of dust. Band by band, the Sioux warriors arrived, until over a thousand Indians encircled the gathering. Thad could see the commissioners grow pale and fidgety as they looked out and saw their world rimmed with Indians.

The meetings went on for several days. Thad was able to listen from his perch in the cottonwood tree. On the second or third day, Senator William Allison, chairman of the commission, realized that there was no use in trying to buy the Black Hills. He opened his remarks that day with a direct proposition for Spotted Tail.

"We have now to ask you," the senator began, "if you are willing for a fair and just sum to give our people the right to mine the Black Hills as long as gold or other minerals are found. If you are so willing, we will make a bargain with you for this right. When the gold or other minerals are taken away, the country will be yours again to dispose of in any manner you may wish."

Thad watched Spotted Tail carefully as he was read this proposal. He watched the chief's long eyes grow longer as he narrowed them, not in anger but in scrutiny. Then he saw a trace of a smile play across the solid mouth. He thinks, Thad thought to himself, that this is the biggest joke he's ever heard.

"Senator," Spotted Tail began. "Eight years ago, the Great White Father thought our Holy Hills of the *Paha Sapa* worthless and gave them to our people forever by treaty. Now you ask to break that treaty, to borrow our hills." He paused. "Senator, would you lend me a mule in such a way?"

The senator swallowed but looked straight ahead, this time addressing not just Spotted Tail but all of the Indians. "It will be hard for our government to keep the whites out of the hills. To try to do so will give you and our government great trouble, because the whites that may wish to go there are very numerous. But there is another country north of the Platte, lying toward the setting sun, over which you roam and hunt, and which territory is yet unceded, extending to the summit of the Bighorn Mountains."

"Not the Powder River country!" Thad muttered in disbelief. This rich hunting ground spread west from the Black Hills and extended to the Bighorn Mountains in the Montana and Wyoming territories—lush grasslands dotted with rivers and streams. Not only the

Sioux but the Cheyenne hunted there, and without these hunting grounds, the Indians would surely starve to death.

"It does not seem of great value or use to you," the senator continued.

Thad gripped harder onto the tree limb to steady himself. This was unbelievable. "And our people," the senator went on, "would like to have the portion of it described." The terminology was unfamiliar to Thad but he understood the senator's intent. The miners flooding into the Black Hills were to be used as a wedge toward obtaining an even greater prize.

Something had turned within Thad as he witnessed this profound violation taking place. His own part in it was clear, for he had ridden with Custer into the *Paha Sapa*. And now the government, after invading the Indians' sacred grounds, was trying to take away their hunting grounds in the Powder River country and, by doing so, threatening their very existence.

The chant then began to roll down from the distant bluff to the west. It was an old Sioux chant.

> *The Black Hills is my land and I love it*
> *And whoever interferes*
> *Will hear this gun.*

It was September 23. Three hundred chanting Oglala Sioux from the Powder River country trotted toward the commissioners. A striking-looking man with deep coppery-red skin stretched tautly over his chiseled features rode his gray pony up to within inches of where they sat. Thad recognized him as Little Big Man, the warrior who had stood just behind Crazy Horse in the tipi in the *Paha Sapa*. He had come now as Crazy Horse's envoy. Stripped to the waist with a slash of paint across his chest and two revolvers in his belt, he began to speak.

"I will kill," he shouted, "the first chief who speaks for selling the Black Hills." His voice split the air. He wheeled about and danced his horse in an odd, nervous step along the open space between the assembled chiefs and the commissioners. It was not simply a performance or display. Little Big Man was the live coal, the embers of the Indian anger. The commissioners had felt the heat. They could now imagine the raging fire.

The next day, Thad heard that the meetings would be continued in the headquarters building of the Red Cloud agency, which was just a few miles away. Thad went along. Just outside the headquarters building, he came face to face with Nathaniel Cunningham. Cunningham squinted for a brief instant, as if he were trying to place Thad's face, and then proceeded through the doors. Thad followed.

Talk went on for three more days. Thad noticed that Cunningham became an intermediary between the chiefs and the commissioners. He also became the link between the meetings and the newspaper reporters who would feature his picture and his words in newspapers from Chicago to Washington, D.C., to New

York and Philadelphia, where accounts of the meetings would be laced with quotes from the distinguished professor from Yale.

On the last day of the talks, Thad saw Cunningham walking toward him with a kind of purpose in his gait, which tipped him off that the man had recognized him.

Cunningham got straight to the point."So what kind of work are you doing for Babcock here?"

"Same kind of work you are, I guess—seeing what's going to happen between the government and the Indians."

Cunningham scowled. "It'll be bad any way they cut it." He paused, took out his pipe, and put it unlit into his mouth. "I want to talk to you for a few minutes. Come along."

Cunningham was obviously a man who used few words and was accustomed to being obeyed without question. Thad followed, knowing full well what Cunningham was going to ask him.

"So how much would it cost me?"

Cunningham was looking directly at Thad. He clenched a pipe in his teeth and when he spoke, his mouth hardly moved. They were sitting in a small annex of the headquarters building. The meeting had adjourned a quarter of an hour before.

"You mean me?" Thad replied. He did not especially like being called *it*.

"Your services? How much?"

"You mean digging?"

"Yes, yes." There was a trace of impatience in his

voice. He took the pipe out and pressed his lips together. "I heard that you're good. Very good. You get
the stuff out in one piece."

"Most of the time," Thad said levelly.

"So what does he pay you?"

"Babcock?"

"You working for someone else?" Cunningham said
acidly.

The man was tough, hard as nails. He was more like
a bull whacker with brains than a fancy university
professor.

"No. Only Babcock."

"So how much does he pay you?"

"Sixty-five a month."

"I'll double it—one hundred and thirty."

It was a lot of money. A year ago, Thad would have
been staggered by the thought of it. But last winter, his
hunting had brought him in more than that. So he
appeared impassive.

Cunningham shifted in his seat. "All right, I'll go to
one fifty, but no more."

"No need."

"You mean you'll take it?"

"No—" He had started to say he was sorry when
Cunningham broke in.

"You mean you can't be bought?"

The eerie sound of the words seem to bore into Thad.
Now not only time and history were property to be
owned but himself, as well. "Naw, naw, 'fraid I can't
do it. I'm happy where I am."

Cunningham had turned his head so he was staring out the window. A knot of Brulé Sioux stood in the yard of the agency. He seemed to be focused on them. With his head in profile and his pipe clenched between his teeth, he continued to address Thad in an even voice.

"You won't be so happy by next field season."

"Yeah?"

"Yeah. The whole works are going to fall apart out here. Talk is cheap, you know." He nodded in the direction of the room where the meetings had been held. "Red Cloud is disgusted. Spotted Tail is a bit more than that. He's going to go in there this afternoon and ask the commissioners to put something in writing—a leasing proposal with definite dollars and time periods. The commission will come up with some harebrained, insulting offer and that will be the end of talking and the beginning of war."

It was almost precisely as Cunningham had predicted. The commissioner proposed $400,000 a year for the mineral rights to the Black Hills, or if the Sioux wished to sell outright, the offer was for $6 million in fifteen installments. Spotted Tail rejected the proposal firmly. The commission packed up and returned to Washington.

By the time Thad was back in Medicine Buttes, the first snow had fallen. He wondered as he rode Gumbo over a bluff just south of the camp whether there would be anyone still there. The layer of snow was thin, but it had transformed the landscape and pulled a gauzy white veil over everything—time, bones, and men. Sun dogs climbed high into the sky, shimmering on either side of the sun. For now, everything seemed still and frozen. The barbs on the cactus glared like icy needles. Thad's breath hung in a billowy cloud. He saw ice crystals on Gumbo's withers.

"Too cold to snow," Thad said as he dismounted. Wu Chow had come out to meet him from the chuck wagon.

"Yes, Mr. Thad. They all go. Too cold for them. Fear snow. Fear Indians. Fear Yale. Fear British. Want to get bones out fast. They leave with some."

"And we do the rest, right?"

"Right." Wu Chow laughed.

Within three days, they had broken camp. The rest of the bones were crated and packed and waiting for the steamer *Carolina* at Cow Island Landing to go to Omaha, where Babcock, according to his letter, would be waiting. Wu Chow would board the next steamer coming upstream and head back to Fort Benton. There he'd find work as a hotel cook. Thad would return to Cheyenne in the Wyoming territory.

Thad and Wu Chow got the fossils on the *Carolina.* Thad briefly wondered whether this boat was one of Rap Stevens's, named for an old ladyfriend. He didn't feel much like inquiring. There was a sadness that set stone-cold, quartz-cold, he thought, inside him. He missed Julian but he knew he would see him again next season. Inside his pocket, however, there was a small crystal chunk. He reached his hand in and felt the sharply faceted surface of the rock that had weathered free from the vein of quartz. The note from Jonathan was short and to the point.

The lid has popped. I have to get out. I know you will understand, Thaddeus. And I shall understand why you must stay, if you so choose. With fondest regards.
　　Jonathan Cabot
　　8 Louisburg Square
　　Boston
　　Commonwealth of Massachusetts

He felt an emptiness, and yet worse than this emptiness were those last words of the letter—"if you so choose." He wondered what Jonathan would think of his work with Julian. Were they fooling themselves? Could they really bring these creatures to the world—if they so chose?

Thad rode the nearly seven hundred miles to Cheyenne. The hunting business was still good, better than before, since a new hotel had opened its doors. In exchange for meat, Thad had a small room back at the Union Pacific Hotel.

Cheyenne had its own newspaper, and the hotel received several others for the guests, including an occasional month-old *New York Herald*. Thad found that reading newspapers was very easy after a year or more of sounding out the Linnaean taxonomic chart. The news was ominous. War with the Indians seemed unavoidable, as the government had set out on a course of destructive actions. "They might as well be using bullets now!" Thad muttered as he read a November 9th edition of the *Cheyenne Standard.* The article reported that a certain E. T. Watkins, special inspector to the Commissioner of Indian Affairs, had told Congress that those Plains Indians living off the reservation were "lofty, independent, and downright uppity." They were also well fed and armed, thus making them a "definite threat to the reservation system." Inspector Watkins's recommendation was reported in the last paragraph of the article: "Troops should be sent against these Indians in the winter, the sooner the better, and whip them into subjection."

Thad put down the paper. He could not help but think of his frail friend Black Elk. Black Elk was strong in spirit but weak in body. The reservation would kill both. For the next few weeks, the papers carried warnings from government officials that unless something was done to gain the Black Hills, they could not control the miners who were streaming in. But it was on Christmas Eve that there was a shocking turn in the news from the east. Thad had come in from a long hunt. The cook and the kitchen help were all poring over a three-week-old *New York Herald.* It was no longer threats and warnings. Thad looked at the headline over their shoulders. PLAINS INDIANS CALLED IN. The article went on to report that on December 3, 1875, Edward P. Smith, Commissioner of Indian Affairs, had notified

Sioux and Cheyenne agents to order all Indians living off the reservation to come in and report by January 31, 1876, or "a military force would be sent to compel them." After this date, all Indians still off the reservation would be considered "hostile."

"How do they expect those Sioux to come in?" Thad looked up from the paper at the hotel cook and the manager, Mr. Wiley. "Blizzards all over the place, cold. They'll never come in now."

Two weeks later, the Cheyenne paper reported that Sitting Bull had sent a messenger back to the agent saying that if he did move back at all, it would not be until the "Moon When the Green Grass Is Up."

"Crazy Horse, I hear, is up near Bear Butte, where the Thieves' Road goes into the Black Hills," said the cook. "You can bet he ain't going to budge. He's all set up perfect for raiding in the spring when the miners come into the *Paha.*"

In the *Cheyenne Standard* of February 7, Thad read that General Sheridan had been authorized by the Secretary of War to begin operations against "hostile Sioux," including those bands of Indians under Crazy Horse and Sitting Bull thought to be in the Powder River country. Then, on February 8, the news came over the telegraph and a busboy came running straight through the lobby of the hotel. "Crook and Terry are starting!" Generals Crook and Terry, serving under Sheridan, had been ordered to mobilize their troops. Thad and several others went out into the drifting snow and made their way to the telegraph station. Thad watched as the op-

erator, a young man with a blotchy complexion, took
down the code, his face growing tenser by the second.
No one said a word. The window of the telegraph
house was fogged with the breath of the anxious people. When the last signal came through, the young man
put down his pen. "So what does it say?" Mr. Wiley
asked.

The young man picked up the piece of paper. "Generals Crook and Terry are to begin preparations for
military operations in the direction of the headwaters
of the Powder, Tongue, Rosebud, and the Bighorn rivers, where Crazy Horse and his allies frequented." And
the operator added, picking up his hat and putting it
on, "I'm going home."

"I thought you lived here at the station, Corey," the
busboy said.

"Portland, Maine. And I intend to keep my scalp just
where it is."

It was shortly after that when Thad received a letter
from Julian. He opened it excitedly. Julian had promised to write, but this was the first letter he'd received.

January 12, 1876

Dear Thaddeus,

*I didn't want to write you until I had something to write
about, and unless you consider learning Latin from an old
tutor who constantly breaks wind, or yet another visit to
Philadelphia to examine the Morton collection of skulls of
inferior races (remember I told you about my father's obsession) intensely interesting, there hasn't been much to write*

about. But by Jove there is now! Last month, which will probably be three months ago by the time you get this letter, my father and I traveled to New York City. It was there that I was able to make contact once again with Mr. Louis Woodfin. Mr. Woodfin is terrifically enthusiastic about our work. Seems like Harvard and Yale are being very piggy about their fossils—won't lend any, won't let people see them, even professors from other institutions. The general feeling here is that both Babcock and Cunningham are behaving miserably. The scientific community, by and large, is fairly fed up with their bickering and ungentlemanly behavior. (They would be equally fed up with my father if they knew him as I do.)

In any case, Woodfin took me over to meet some of the New World Museum people, and what a dandy lot they are! Thad, it is so exciting. Their ideas are so much like ours—bones reassembled to give the most accurate representation possible. They are even talking about dioramas and painted scenes to recreate the Cretaceous swampland. We must keep an eye out, by the way, for some fossil plant materials. Their artist, an awfully nice chap named Maxwell Knight, would love a good palm frond. In any case, they are not just enthusiastic but supportive. Woodfin is going to foot all the costs and has already given me money for next season! He owns railroads. He, that is Woodfin, as well as the others, have promised me that they will be discreet. I explained to them my differences with my father. They are not so keen on Englishmen "robbing American fossil beds" to quote Dr. LeMoyne Frank, one of their curators.

Of course, they do wonder how the next field season will go with the heating up of this Indian situation. It's all rather appalling—ordering those poor devils into reservations in the middle of winter. This, however, is not slowing down our intrepid paleontologists. Did you not say that Babcock is preparing for another field season there? We hear that Cunningham is going, too. My father is already making preparations—writing that disgusting Henshaw fellow. Henshaw actually came to Chicago for a visit. I can't understand why my father would employ, let alone entertain, such a vile human being. Henshaw has him convinced of many things, one of which is that with the threat of war, our friend is indispensable in terms of protection from the Indians. He has my father believing that he is a great friend of the Sioux. I give the Sioux more credit and better taste than that.

Thankfully, I was not around when Henshaw was. My cousin, Lord Haversham, took me on a trip through the south. It was very much fun. The young ladies are extremely pretty, and for the first time ever, I think some of them really liked me. It is probably just that I'm different. You know my accent and all, but Cousin Edward says that I have lost my baby look and I guess some baby fat. My trousers are sure looser. Anyway, I danced with several of these "Southern Belles," as they call them. The dances they do here are much livelier, very bouncy, and the young ladies are given to wearing their hair in these masses of corkscrew curls that jiggle all over the place. Quite enchanting, really. How have you been? Don't write and tell me because if my father should get hold of any letter from you, it would be disaster. But know that I think of you often and cannot wait until the new field season begins.

Sincerely,

Julian

CHAPTER

> ### 30

It was the first week in March, and Thad had just finished strapping an antelope to his saddle. He was noticing how the animal's fur felt different. The pelt on all the animals was beginning to change just slightly as winter finished. As if to confirm this change of seasons, he suddenly felt a fresh wind blow softly against his face. "The chinook," he said aloud—the warm wind, signaling the end of winter. It seemed to curl across the country now in a low hush. Thad knew there could still be a spring blizzard, but he began to imagine the frozen creeks unlocking their water to flow like black ribbons through the still-snow-blanketed land, and the deer

lean and hungry, their coats winter-stiff and beginning
to shed, their antlers losing their husks and becoming
velvety in the spring. The grizzly, too, would awaken
finally from his long sleep, his winter fat diminished,
his coat dull. Sleepy and cantankerous they were.

*Beware of the grizzly in earliest spring, hungry and feeling light,
a shadow of his September self.* That was what Thad would
write down later that evening after his long day out. He
kept some paper to practice his penmanship. He had
always copied things from newspapers or books for
practice, but recently he had begun to write things
straight out of his head. It made him feel very peaceable
to do it after a long day of blood and ice and killing.

As he felt the wind on his cheek, he knew it was time
to start heading north into the Montana territory. He
would finish up his business in Cheyenne and head off
as soon as he could.

That evening when he returned to Cheyenne, there
was another letter from Julian.

Dear Thaddeus,

*Only time for a quick note. Met a most interesting gentle-
man at a dinner given by General Sheridan the other evening.
I was surprised to hear he is an acquaintance of yours—none
other than the incomparable William Cody—Buffalo Bill!
He remembers you well. Since my father was there, I could
not let on that I also knew you. Somehow your name came
up in connection with Babcock and the Harvard team. Buffalo
Bill allowed as how he had got you the job. He struts around
like a peacock with all that blond hair. Rather bombastic,*

*only mildly entertaining. I can't say I was really taken with
him. Especially his views on the Indians. He came roaring
into Chicago straight from his last stage appearance to enlist
as a scout for Sheridan in his old outfit, the Fifth Cavalry.
We should ourselves be arriving shortly behind the Fifth in
early April.*

    For now,
    Julian

Two days later, the Fifth Cavalry had indeed arrived,
detraining in Cheyenne. Their final destination was
Fort Laramie, northwest of Cheyenne. Within hours of
the cavalry's arrival, Buffalo Bill rode into town.

"A one-man parade if I ever saw one," Mr. Wiley
observed. He, Thad, and some of the other employees
watched from a second-story window as Buffalo Bill
galloped up to the hotel. "Good grief." Mr. Wiley
craned his head for a closer look. "I saw the show back
in Springfield a few years ago. He never wore anything
that fancy." Buffalo Bill was dazzling in a black velvet
and gold uniform of no army Thad had ever seen. The
uniform was decorated with silver lace, and on top of
his head he wore a white sombrero with one side
pinned up.

"He's going to fight Indians in that?" the cook asked.

"Lord only knows," someone else replied.

Thad had not really wanted to meet up with Will
Cody in person. He was grateful that Cody had given
him the letter of introduction to Babcock, but he could
not understand why the man was scouting for Sheridan

now. The first time he had seen Cody, over two years ago, he had been running around in a dirty undershirt and buckskin britches. Thad could not square that with what he was hearing about the man who had just ridden into Cheyenne. Avoiding Cody proved impossible. He was staying at the Union Pacific, and Buffalo Bill found out that a fellow named Thad Longsworth was winter hunting for the hotel. The busboy came pounding on Thad's door. "Mr. Buffalo Bill wants to see his old friend Thad!" he called out. There was no choice.

Cody made a big fuss over how Thad had "grown and filled out." This was terribly embarrassing for Thad, as they were standing in the bar at the time and everyone was naturally hanging on to Buffalo Bill's every word. Buffalo Bill was painting a picture of what a puny runt Thad had once been. He managed to convey that he, Bill Cody, was due the credit for this magical transformation.

"I sent this boy up to Custer a skinny little critter. Now he's almost as tall as me and filled out! My word!" he said, looking at his audience rather than Thad. "In all the right places and . . ." He paused, then winked. ". . . some of those other places." This drew a large guffaw from the people in the bar. Thad was scarlet. Of course, he had grown some. That was what kids were supposed to do. But he was still short for his age, and he didn't shave yet, either. If this was some sort of stage performance by Buffalo Bill, Thad sure didn't want any part of it. Finally they sat down at a table in the corner. Cody fixed him with his bright-blue eyes.

"I'm proud of you, son!"

Thad wanted to ask why he was making this unholy fuss. If Thad had not stepped between him and that chicken Louisa Cody was throwing, none of this might have happened at all. He sounded so tinny to Thad.

"Where's Mrs. Cody now?" Thad asked, trying to change the subject.

"Back east." Cody sighed and grew sober. "We've had a bad piece of luck, a real tragedy. Lost our son Kit."

"Kit? Kit died?" Thad had remembered the little boy, bright, sharp as anything, with curly hair in ringlets to his shoulders. He was about three or four when Thad had met him. He would have been six by now. "What happened?"

"Died of the fever, scarlet fever."

"That's . . . that's terrible, Mr. Cody."

"Hard . . . hard, hard, Thad. Hard to bury a child. You bury a lot with him." He sighed deeply. "But I said to Louisa, I said—'Mamma, I can't go back to that—that mockery. Up on a stage, hollering and speechifying and shooting off guns. What's the point of all that foolishness?' And she says to me, 'Will, it's spring. They're starting up the expeditions now, back home. It's your land out there. We've got enough money. We can live.' " Buffalo Bill's eyes grew misty, his voice soft. " 'I want you,' she said, 'to go back out west again.' " His voice grew intense. " 'To ride and fight—and I know you won't forget us.' 'No,' I said, 'I won't forget.' "

It was a stirring performance, but Thad for the life of

him could not imagine Louisa Cody saying those things. Furthermore, Thad did not understand how fighting Indians was going to help Will Cody get over his son's death. He had thought that Cody was better than that. Thad asked him point-blank.

"Why you doing this? That Powder River country was guaranteed them back in the Treaty of 1868. Why you going in there with the Fifth? What d'ya want to kill them for?" The question took Cody by surprise. His eyes grew dull as he stared at Thad. "That's treasonous talk, son. You got to be careful." His voice was low.

"Treasonous? Government breaking their own treaty?"

"Thad," Cody said slowly, "there's a higher law operating than treaty law. White man's coming, no matter what. It's our destiny to be here. Even Red Cloud said it."

"What?"

"Yes, son. The great chief said to me not more than a year ago, 'Our nation is melting away like the snow on the sides of the hills where the sun is warm. While your people are like blades of grass in the spring when the summer is coming.' He said that, Thad."

But Thad couldn't answer. It was true that Red Cloud might have said that. Red Cloud was old and had lost his will to fight. But Thad doubted that he meant for the government to help melt the snow from the hills. So all he said was "It's not right, Mr. Cody. The Indians aren't snow. The white men aren't grass, or whatever, and the Fifth Cavalry shouldn't go round pretending like it's the God Almighty sun."

The Fifth Cavalry pulled out of Cheyenne and proceeded to Fort Laramie, where Sheridan ordered scouts to patrol between there and the Black Hills. They were to stop any war parties of Indians that were heading to the Little Bighorn River in the Powder River country.

Thad, however, moved quicker than the Fifth. He left the day he met with Buffalo Bill and headed northward. The most direct route back to Medicine Buttes went right through the Powder River country in the southeast corner of the Montana territory.

CHAPTER

➤31

The chinook had stopped blowing and the wind had backed round to the north and east, blowing a bitter cold down across the land. It was the Moon of the Snowblind. Thad knew the Sioux names for each month from Black Elk, who had translated them into short word strings that were like pictures.

Thad had been riding north across the Wyoming territory for days, finally reaching what he was certain was the Little Powder River. For the last several hours, he had done little else but think of Black Elk. The snow was driving in hard now and making it difficult to see. He headed Gumbo down closer to the river. Even in the snow, he could detect signs of Indians all over—the tracks of a travois, and small patches where bark had been peeled from trees that the Indian ponies found tasty. He stopped Gumbo and slitted his eyes against the snow. In the failing light, the world blurred and seemed to appear as if it were behind a screen. At that moment two figures appeared. Thad knew immediately by their dress that they were from Black Elk's people. They fell in on either side of him. The three rode together along the river for the next quarter of an hour until they arrived at an encampment on the Little Powder. There were one hundred or more tipis along the river.

"There was a thaw," Black Elk said, "late in the Moon of the Dark Red Calves. So we began the journey to the Soldiers' Town, but then the cold came again. Now we stop here with Crazy Horse."

Thad was sitting in Black Elk's tipi. His mother and father were there. Black Elk was the same. Unlike Thad, he did not appear to have grown even an inch. Standing Eagle came in and greeted Thad warmly, but now he did not need to translate as much, for although Black Elk had not grown taller, his English was better and Thad had an easier time with the Sioux language.

"I do not want to go to the Soldiers' Town." The rest of the family had left the tipi, and Black Elk began to speak in a low voice, guardedly. "But the old ones are tired. They think only of blankets and food."

Looking at the bone-thin youngster, Thad wondered how he could not be tempted by the same.

"Two Moon was ready to go in," Black Elk continued, speaking of the great Cheyenne chief. "But now not so sure after talking with Crazy Horse."

"What does Crazy Horse say?" asked Thad.

"We fight the Bluecoats. My father not certain. He is old now." Black Elk cast his eyes down.

"Who else is here besides Two Moon?"

"Little Wolf, Old Bear, Maple Tree, White Bull, and Crazy Horse—up the river farther. Low Dog, too, he's here."

"We brought many ponies—seven hundred," offered Standing Eagle.

"Where?" asked Thad.

"Behind the bluffs."

The storm worsened. There was no use trying to go north against the blinding snow. Thad knew he still had plenty of time to reach the Medicine Buttes before Babcock. Then, on the third morning of his stay, he awakened, suddenly aware that Black Elk was sitting straight up beside him. He was trembling under his heavy buffalo blanket. It was as if Thad could feel Black Elk's tremors coming directly up through the skins on the tipi floor. Black Elk let the blanket fall and, as he sat naked on his pallet, his dark eyes were as large as black moons.

"They come!" he shouted in Sioux. But Thad had heard nothing. Black Elk pulled on his leggings and Thad his britches. Now the family was up. Thad, Black

Elk, and his father ran out of the tipi. The air was brittle with the cold. It seemed as if every branch, every rock, were ready to shatter. Their own breaths hung in thick clouds in front of them. Black Elk stopped and raised his hand. His eyes grew even larger.

"I feel the hoofbeats," he said. "Hundreds—they come! *They come!*"

Standing Eagle shot from his tipi. "Help! We must get the women and children safe. Up to the edge of the bluff."

Black Elk's mother, White Cow Sees, had come out of the tipi, a parfleche, a bag made of rawhide, on her back. She headed toward her sister's tipi. Then Thad saw a woman, the one called Red Leaf Woman, struggling with several bundles, a baby on her back and one in her arms. He ran over to her and scooped up the baby. A three- or four-year-old girl came wandering out of another tipi. Thad grabbed her hand. "Come on!" he said, but the child began crying. The mother came out with an infant at her breast and hurried the little girl along as they followed Thad to the bluff.

There were many running now to the bluff. He saw Black Elk, a baby on his thin narrow back, another in his arms, just ahead of him on the icy hillside. He slipped but held on to the baby. By some miracle, Thad got up the icy ledge and Black Elk was just behind him. The air was laced with gunfire, and as soon as Black Elk and Thad had led the children and their mothers to safety behind the ledge, they turned around and saw tipis on fire and the encampment overrun by Bluecoats.

An old man stood confused in the middle of the melee, holding the hands of two small children on either side of him. As a soldier rode straight down upon them, the children seemed to fly off to each side, clear of the horse, but Thad could hear the old one's skull crunch under the hooves of the Bluecoat's horse. The soldier wheeled around on his horse as if scanning for the children he had missed. In that instant, it was as if Thad's and Black Elk's minds had conjoined. Like twin furies, they hurled down the bluff's slope and scooped up the two children.

By now, the smoke was so thick it was hard to see. One old woman ran out of a tipi, her back on fire. Thad was leading the child through the billows of thick smoke when he felt something soft underneath his boot. His leg seemed to freeze, and he forced his free hand to reach down toward the soft thing. He felt the downy curve of a baby's head. He did not remember picking it up, or even the run up the side of the bluff, this time carrying the infant and leading the child. All he remembered was the look in the women's eyes. He had brought one live child and a dead infant, cradling it against his shoulder. It was the child of Starblanket Woman. Starblanket lay slain in her tipi, but her mother, Sweet Willow Woman, took the infant tenderly from Thad.

As soon as they had returned, Black Elk headed off in the direction of the ponies. But Thad remained, stunned. It was as if the tiny infant had left a print against his shoulder. He could still feel its limp little body, warm and curled against his breast, its downy head resting on his shoulder in death. From the bluffs he watched the destruction of the camp. He watched the Bluecoats, their swords slashing through the smoke, their huge cavalry horses trampling anything underfoot until there was nothing left to slash or burn and everything had been wasted.

Thad was not sure how much later it was when Standing Eagle found him. "It's Colonel Reynolds and Three Stars Crook. Our scouts know their faces," Standing Eagle reported. "Who would have thought they come now? They got the horses, too. But tonight, we get the horses back. Tonight we surprise them."

And they did just that. As the soldiers slept, confident in their victory, the warriors stole softly into their camp and recovered their horses.

Once more Thad found himself in the presence of Crazy Horse. The fugitives from the burned-out camp had moved swiftly up the river to where Crazy Horse was camped. Crazy Horse welcomed them with food and blankets. The air in the tipi was tense as Two Moon gave the account of what had happened. Thad could sense the anger of Little Big Man. He could visualize the warrior's anger coiling within him, tightening, ready to spring.

Two Moon finished his account with: "I am ready to fight now. I have fought already. My people have been killed. My horses were stolen. I am satisfied to fight."

"We will," Crazy Horse replied. "In the Geese Laying Moon, we break camp."

And then Crazy Horse turned to Thad. "Today you went into battle. Carrying no weapon, but you fight to bring back life, you and Black Elk. You run through the fire for the seed of the tribe, Thaddeus Longsworth."

That night, the warriors gathered in the medicine lodge. Almost two years before, on the banks of a creek, Thad had become a blood brother to the Sioux as he had drunk the handful of water from the bloody hand of Black Elk. Now the memory of his face and Black Elk's, reflected in the dark stream's waters, came back to Thad as the warriors encircled him in the lodge and Crazy Horse slipped the eagle's feather into the band tied around Thad's head. In the eyes of the Sioux and the Cheyenne, he was a warrior. For his act of bravery during the attack on the encampment, he had earned his first eagle's feather, and to the Indians, he would no longer be known as Thaddeus Longsworth but as Man-Who-Runs-Through-Fire.

CHAPTER
➤ 32

Thad would never forget the March attack on the Sioux and Cheyenne encampment, nor the ceremony in the Sioux medicine lodge. But he was surprised how easy it was for him to tuck that bloody day into some corner of his mind and become immersed in camp life and the work of excavation. It was amazing how far away the attack on the Little Powder seemed. For it was as if Babcock and his team from Harvard had brought an entire world of their own with them. Thad had never been to Cambridge, Massachusetts, where Harvard University was, but he felt as if he practically knew the place. Babcock's students talked about the awful dining-hall food and how glad they were to be back to Wu Chow's antelope steaks and Fluff Duff.

Thad learned that the bickering with Cunningham had continued over the winter. Babcock had been reprimanded by the Boston Society of Natural History for violating standard publishing courtesies. But the same society had chided Cunningham for his too public endorsement of the Indian cause, which caused Babcock great glee. No, it was the same tight little world, and if anybody had suggested that there was any cause for concern, let alone alarm, over the conflict between the government and the Indians, Babcock and the others would have hardly been ruffled at all.

If there was indeed anything ominous or threatening about the first few days of the field season, it was the dull, thudding sound of explosives rolling across the flats, in and around the buttes. The British and the Yale team had begun to use dynamite to blast open new exposures. Babcock was categorically against the use of dynamite, and Thad had to agree with him.

"They say that they are using it," Babcock began one night as they sat around around the campfire. "That they are using it in a very limited way, just an opening wedge or to clear away overburdens. But it's not that controllable. They cannot tell what fractures it's causing several meters down. They don't even know what they might be losing in the process. They're pigs, you know. That's it—pure and simple." Babcock got up and started pacing. He walked within the bright rim of the fire's light and cast a long slashing shadow. "They want it all and they want it now. I have a good mind to write to the Society about it and formally complain about these deplorable methods."

The work for the camp was going well, and Thad was able to find time to meet with Julian again at Pudding Butte. They were finding small but interesting pieces. The butte just above the coal line was loaded with very early mammal fossils.

"Hundreds and hundreds of these little teeth," said Julian, turning over the pieces in front of him as the boys sat in the lab cave, which they had been happy to find undisturbed.

"What's the meaning?" asked Thad.

"The meaning is, we're in too high a strata, too young a layer for the dinosaurs, especially the big killer. You can wager that none of the possessors of these little choppers"—Julian held a tooth between his thumb and forefinger—"could have made much of a show against the big fellows. No, the jaw that this came from belonged to a creature who was too big to hide in a nook or cranny from the big monsters, but certainly not big enough to meet them in a fight. But the fact is that we are finding so many of these teeth that we must assume that these creatures flourished."

"What about the dinosaurs?" Thad scooped up a handful of the teeth.

"Well, the game was over for them. Curtain down on the terrible lizards. The day of the mammal had begun." Julian paused and looked out of the cave at

Pudding Butte. "This butte has taken us right to the borderline between dinosaurs and what followed."

"Borderline?" Thad whispered, and looked out toward the butte. Something seemed to click in Thad's mind when Julian said "borderline." "These teeth were almost in the coal, weren't they, Julian?"

"You bet. Virtually on the edge—one or two right in it. Note the high cusps. Good for slashing little wiggly things."

But Thad was not thinking about the cusps of the teeth. "Julian," he said, still looking out toward the butte. "We got to go up there to the northeast end, just to the right of that hump there."

"You mean to where we got these teeth?"

"Yes. Just below the coal line—eight feet or so."

"You really pick the spots, Thad. The slope is at least fifty-five degrees."

"Well, think of it as downhill once we get up there."

"Yes, I suppose gravity always has its uses."

"And there's a rattlesnake nest, too, if I remember."

"Oh, great! How will we use that?"

"Kick it downhill along with the gravity, I suppose." Thad smiled.

"But Thad, why are you so set on that spot?"

It was hard to say. He couldn't really answer. He had just sensed something about that face of the butte. That despite its steepness, it was a good place for something big. It was just below the coal line, so they were still in the time of the dinosaurs, and it seemed a perfect place for something big to stay put, out of reach, protected for a long time.

The grade was too steep for a direct ascent, and as they crisscrossed the face in a series of switchback moves, Thad felt more and more confident about something within the structure of this butte—a ledge, perhaps, that would support something big. When they had gone up seventy-five feet, Thad stopped. He got out his trowel and scraped furiously.

"What is it?" Julian asked.

"I just have to know how this butte runs."

"What do you mean?"

"There's a harder tongue of something running through here," Thad said.

"You mean a cross-bedding?"

"I don't know what you call it, but it's not as crumbly as most of this shale. It hasn't weathered out much yet. It's earlier and harder, and I think it makes a kind of shelf. Look. See here."

Julian went over. Indeed, the dark mud-brown shale was becoming a lighter buff color. "Yes, yes. We've seen that a lot before, haven't we?" Julian said.

"Yep. But I don't think it beds back as far in other places as it does here."

"Beds back?" Julian asked.

"Yeah, runs back, right into the heart of the butte. Like a big tray sliding in there, nice and even."

It was getting very steep. "Where is the rattlesnake nest?" Julian whispered. "I really don't fancy battling those fellows with my one free hand—*mano a mano,* as the Spanish say!"

"The nest is over there. They're not going to bother you. Okay. Here," Thad finally said. "Here's where we stop."

"Right here?"

"Yes."

"This is definitely the steepest place on the whole bloody butte, Longsworth!"

"What did I tell you? It is going to work for us."

"For us . . . yes, I keep repeating that to myself—gravity is supposed to work for us." Julian tried not to look down.

Thad was unhitching two coils of rope while he talked. "What did you say gravity was again? Falling down? No, you said it a fancier way. What was it?'

"Really, Thaddeus, I am not prepared to give a physics lecture at the moment." Julian was on a very narrow foothold, clinging to a shale lip directly above.

"Just hang on," said Thad. "We're going to fight gravity here with these ropes. Now, what's it again that you said it was?"

Julian sighed. "Gravity is the universal ability of all material objects to attract one another. Us to the ground unless you get those ropes ready pretty quick. Rattlesnakes to us."

"No, no." Thad was tying a figure-eight knot in one rope. "That's not gravity. I know better than that. Rattlesnakes don't just fall down on you. Fear. That's what draws them."

"Then they should be flocking to me right now!" Julian muttered.

"Who'd you say thought up this gravity business?" Thad persisted. His equanimity amazed Julian.

"Sir Isaac Newton," Julian replied evenly. "Cambridge University."

"That in England?"

"Yes. Not Cambridge, Massachusetts. Although I understand that the town of Cambridge, Massachusetts, was named for the one in England."

"Pretty smart guy, this Newton, figuring out gravity, I guess."

"And calculus."

"Calculus?" said Thad. He was now eyeing a spire of sandstone some twelve feet above him. He paused in his conversation, swirled the rope in a wobbly O shape above his head, and let it fly. It plopped down on the spire. "What's calculus?"

"Mathematics, actually," Julian replied, stunned at what he had just seen. "It's really the study of slopes and curves," he said, looking up. "Accelerations, maxima and minima, by means of . . ." His voice dwindled off. Calculus was lower mathematics compared to what Thad had just done, which was to calculate the vertical height of the spire and its angle in relation to where he stood. The spin of his rope loop had then been gauged in terms of its potential velocity in relation to these variables, as well as the length. All this had been accomplished while standing on a sandstone ledge no more than nine inches wide with his free hand wedged in a tight crevice.

"So, would Harvard like to have this here Newton fellow? I mean, he sounds smart enough for them."

"Yes, I think Harvard would have been more than happy to have Isaac Newton on their faculty."

"I wonder why they don't."

"He's dead, for one thing."

"Oh."

"He figured all this out a long, long time ago."

Thad was now lassoing another spire. The loop floated down easily onto it.

"How long ago?" asked Thad.

"Oh, the sixteen or seventeen hundreds. Last century."

"Pretty smart for then. But it doesn't seem so long ago, does it, compared to all this?" Thad was looking straight up at the butte. "Now get ready to hang."

"Hang?" asked Julian.

"Yeah, like this." He slid the rope under his rear end and then slowly swung over to Julian and handed him his loop.

"Are you sure this will hold us?"

"Pretty much."

"Pretty much? That's not really reassuring, Thad."

"Look, I'm going to fix a safety backup." Within ten minutes, he had fashioned another harness for each of them by threading the rope through his spurs, which he had removed. He had then wedged the spurs into a crevice in the rock. "It'll do for now. Let's start working."

This rock face would become their home for the next six weeks. Their butts became sore from the ropes. They tried to cushion them with blankets and even by putting old rags into their pants. Neither seemed to help. But the very first night after they had begun their work, the first promise of an extraordinary find was revealed.

"I've got a point here," Julian cried.

"A point?"

"Yes."

"A tooth?"

"I . . ." He hesitated. "I'm not sure. It doesn't appear to be the right material for a tooth." He dug and scraped with his trowel for another quarter of an hour. Then, in a voice of studied calm: "Thaddeus, all the horns you have found belonging to the ceratopian dinosaurs—have you ever found an entire one?"

"No, just cores really—seven-inch chunks, twelve-inch chunks."

"Nothing with a tip, I suppose?"

"Naw." Then he said, "Tip? You mean point?"

"Yes, Thaddeus. I think I've got a whole one here, and I won't wager how far back it goes."

Thad swung over. The night had grown dark. Only a sliver of the moon could be seen riding behind a thick herd of woolly clouds.

"I'll be!" Thad whispered as Julian held up the kerosene lamp. "It's horn, all right. Not bone."

Three and one half inches of the horn tip protruded from the shale face. "If there's this much in this good shape, there could be . . ." Thad paused.

"A face?" Julian whispered. His breath hung in the air, the words on it.

"Yes, a face."

"It'll be the first," Thaddeus said.

"Let's not count on it yet."

The boys' voices had grown progressively lower, as if they feared the mere vibrations of their whispers were enough to dislodge and fracture what millions of years might have miraculously preserved. At last, they dared not speak or hope or even pray. Even silent prayer would seem to scream against the delicate balance of this proposition posed by time, earth, and death.

There were no stars before the dawn.

"We have to quit," Thad said.

Another four inches of the horn had emerged.

"Yes. I suppose we must get back to our camps."

"It's not just that." Thad paused and looked at the horn that jutted out from the face of the butte. "If any more of this sticks out, it might get knocked off by a rockfall. When I come back, I'm going to have to bring wood and stuff to splint it up. If it keeps going back . . ." He paused again. ". . . the way I think it is going to, we're going to have to build a whole darn cage around it."

CHAPTER

➤ 33

One week later, there was a cage around the horn—a very long cage, for the horn measured one meter, or forty inches, long. Within the cage, they had splinted the horn, then wrapped and plastered it. As the enormous horn emerged, the upper edge of a brow bone appeared directly underneath it. Finally, on the tenth day of the excavation, Julian swung back from the shale face of the butte. It was another starless night with a wedge of moon as pale as an old man's eye shining feebly through a thick cover of cloud. But another eye, darker and even stranger, holding the secrets of millions of years, peered out into the night. Thad stopped scraping and swung back, too, bracing himself against the butte. Both boys looked at the vast, gaping socket and then at each other. A shiver passed through them like a telegraphic current, and both of them felt the spark of some old and ancient fear.

"Well, chappy," Julian said with a rather desperate joviality. "I think indeed that we do have a face here."

"We might have a face," Thad said, "but I'm sure as heck losing my butt!" It was getting on toward dawn, and they started to lower themselves down. They had arranged the ropes so they could manipulate them like pulleys. They no longer bothered walking up from the base but now hauled themselves up on the ropes. On his last provisioning trip to Fort Benton, Thad had purchased two block and tackles and additional rope, which he stashed in the lab cave. The money came from the cash Woodfin had advanced Julian in New York. With the two block and tackles, they had gained a mechanical advantage of three to one, or that which roughly enabled them to haul three times the weight with the same effort. It beat walking. They had become adept at moving about on the vertical rock surface of the butte. Their hind ends, however, never quite got used to the cutting ropes that supported them.

On this particular night, as their feet touched the ground after they had lowered themselves, Julian stood rubbing his hind side vigorously. His head was flung back as he looked at the sky.

"Thad," he said suddenly. "Thad!"

"What is it?"

"Thad, we are too stupid for words!"

"What do you mean by that?"

Thad sat rubbing his backside and wondering how he was ever going to get himself in the saddle the next day to deliver Babcock's latest separate to the steamer.

"Thad, why in heaven's name have we never thought of stringing a plank for a seat? Please tell me."

"A plank," Thad said in soft wonderment, as if the very word conjured up the downiness of a goose-feather pillow. "Good Lord, Julian, we are stupid!"

They had a plank the next evening.

"If sore butts could sing hosannas, ours would!" Julian sighed as they hauled themselves up.

And the two boys laughed in the moonlit night.

Excavation work proceeded rapidly. After the eye socket was dug out, it was not difficult to speculate about the other half of the face.

"A bloke like this could not run along with just one horn over one eye, at least not one a meter long. He would tip over," Julian said at the finish of one long night's work. "It has been my experience to observe that God goes in for the practical—except for certain breeds of English lapdogs whose long, shedding fur and twitchy temperaments are not at all suited for life in a mistress's lap! In the case of this creature, however, common sense dictates that there should be another horn of equal length over the other eye—presuming, of course, that the other half of the creature's face has been preserved. Might you hazard a guess as to where this other horn might be, E. C.?"

"E. C." was Julian's occasional nickname for Thad, and stood for Esteemed Colleague. Thad took a guess as to where the other horn might be. Within one quarter of an hour, another point, pearly in the moonlight, shone out of the ancient shale sediments.

Thad silently considered this second horn, trying to imagine how much of the mid to lower section of the face they might be dealing with. Some rather fancy buttressing was going to have to be connived to keep this head intact, if indeed it was an entire head. They certainly did not want to have gravity help out too early in the game. They had not been working long on this section when Julian cried out, "Thad, another point!"

"Another!"

"Yes!"

"A third horn?" Thad leaned over to examine more closely the place where Julian was scraping. "It can't be as long as the other two," he added.

"Why not?" Julian asked, and then realized, of course, that if the Lord's common sense were to prevail and there were three horns, each forty inches long, it would be very hard for the creature to maneuver let alone eat, with the third horn in this position. "It appears to set," Julian continued, "right where one would expect a nose. Let's stay on another hour or so and get a start on it."

"Don't you think you better be getting back to camp before someone gets suspicious?"

"Don't worry, Thad. My father is fully occupied with a trachodon. He's so determined to get this one

out whole that he is personally supervising every shov-
elful of the excavation. Neither he nor Bobber notices
my absences or my fatigue, for that matter. Bobber
never leaves his side."

Indeed, within another two days, it was revealed that
the third horn, which was considerably shorter than
the other two, was fused to the nasal plate. Thad was
taking no chances. He cross-braced the three horns
using a system of struts and wires and devised a separate scaffolding to slide in under the lower part of the
face, for the jaws on the animal, which were just
emerging, promised to be immense. The face had had
to sling forward beyond the range of the upper horns
in order for the animal to eat.

There was a four-day interruption in their progress
when Thad had to shore up a cave where Babcock was
excavating a duckbilled dinosaur. He had worked long,
hard hours at the duckbill site, and then the boys had
a stroke of luck. Babcock observed that Thad was looking rather "peaked" and should perhaps take it easy for
a couple of days.

Thad, of course, took it easy by spending his time at
Pudding Butte. When he returned after his four-day
absence, he found that Julian had not only made progress but had strutted and braced the exposed surfaces
and had started to work backward toward the rear part
of the skull.

"Put your hand in there!" Julian pointed at the right
eye socket of the creature.

"What d'ya have in there—a rattlesnake?" Thad asked.

"No. Just reach around toward the right side."

"Yeah—feels like a knob or something."

"Right-o. I'll wager it's part of a ball-and-socket joint, Thad."

"What for? What did it join?"

"This massive head to the neck, therefore giving this creature incredible balance. You see, this has to be the natural balancing point for the head. With a ball-and-socket joint like that, the creature could sustain huge neck muscles and be able to toss his head in any direction with the greatest precision. Those horns could be lethal with a precision like that, and part of one of the most exquisite defense machines ever invented."

"Defense?"

"Yes," Julian said soberly. He pulled something from his pocket. "He's not our killer. I found this yesterday." A tooth glistened in his hand. The tooth, unlike the killer's, did not curve and end in a tearing point. Nor did it have the sawlike serration along the edges. "You see," said Julian, "despite its wear, this never was a tooth designed for tearing—not like the killer's, at least." He paused. "It's more of a slicing edge. Like scissors. Depending on whether it came from the upper or lower jaw, I'll bet that the tooth above or below this met it at a complementary angle. Met it in just the same way the blades of scissors meet—vertical slicing action—and they would continue to sharpen themselves against one another."

"But you don't think it's a carnivore tooth?"

"No. Not efficient for attack, for meat on the run. Good, however, for slicing thick fibrous plants—stalks, leaves, cycadeoids."

"Cy—whats?"

"Cycadeoids—palm fronds."

"Palm fronds," Thad said softly.

Julian looked at him. "Disappointed we don't have our killer?"

"I don't know."

"I actually think we've got something better here."

"How do you mean?"

"Well, I can only hunch now. Be patient. Let's get a little more of this head freed up and then I'll tell you."

A week later, the entire beaklike snout and lower jaw jutted out of the sandstone rock face. Five days after that, they had scraped and chiseled away in the area directly behind the two horns and rear portion of the skull to reveal the beginning of a frill.

"And not a skimpy old piece of frill," Julian whispered breathlessly. "But the whole bloody thing!" He sighed as he looked up at the bony cape flaring backward like a shield. "Marvelous! Marvelous! An engineering feat—a biological, anatomical engineering feat that adds up to extraordinary power . . . and . . . and elegance." Julian was ecstatic. "Do you see, E. C.? All this brute power combined with the flexibility—the creature could lunge and plunge with his entire set of horns. The frill is the perfect counterbalance!"

* * *

Between the ancient seafloor and the starry night, the two boys hung on their scaffolding, their legs swinging. A light breeze blew through their hair. For almost six weeks, they had been working, and now this primeval face surged from the heart of the butte.

"We do not have the killer himself," Julian said, turning to Thad. His stiff red curls shivered in the night wind. "We have his worthiest opponent. Between predator and prey, there has never been such a contest. The two most massive antagonists ever! What a creature!"

"We have to stop calling him creature," said Thad. "He's a new species of horned dinosaur and we get to name him—according to the rules."

"Well, he's a ceratopian, being horned. I guess you can consider that shorter horn a full-fledged one. Three horns . . . Yes, I suppose its name would be Triceratops."

"What about two and a half horns?" Thad said.

"Now that is difficult," Julian conceded. "What should we name him, then?"

"Do we have to give him a scientific name right off the bat?" Thad asked.

"Well, I suppose not," Julian replied brightly. "Suppose for now we just call him old Lunge and Plunge. I mean, that's what he obviously did so well."

"Lunge and Plunge," Thad repeated. "Yep. Fine with me."

The head was immense as it loomed from the western side of the butte. From the tip of the beaklike snout to the brow bone, the face measured seven feet. The frill extended back another three feet. The boys had estimated that the body must have stood a minimum height of nine feet, and from head to tail could have measured up to twenty-five. The body, however, was gone. Vanished. Only the head remained, hanging eerily now against the Montana sky. It could be seen a quarter of a mile away. So, carefully, they scrounged the nearly barren Badlands for brush with which to camouflage it. They dug up countless armloads of sagebrush and hung these from the scaffolding and from the creature's horns. Then they settled down to the very difficult business of planning its final dislodgment and transportation.

The objectives seemed simple as Julian scratched out a diagram on the floor of the cave. A horizontal arrow indicated dislodgment, or removal from the face of the butte. He made a vertical arrow to show the lowering of the head down the side of the butte. Another arrow, its tip pointing east, stood for its journey on the Missouri to the railroad head in Omaha, where it would travel by one of Mr. Woodfin's special cars to New York and the New World Museum.

"First things first," Julian said. "You think you can build a sliding scaffolding to get it down?" They had figured the weight of the head, including any matrix rock that they had to take with it, as close to seven hundred pounds.

Thad shook his head. "I've decided that a sliding scaffold would need too much lumber. Too much time putting it together. I've seen them moving huge dead-weight cargo off steamers in Fort Benton with these giant rope bags. The rope is almost three inches thick. That, with heavy block and tackles and lines at an angle of about like this"—he indicated a thirty-degree slope with his hand—"make that angle even lower—we'll gain distance. Any distance we can gain toward the river, even if it's just inches, counts."

"Okay," Julian said. "And now, about getting it to the river—reinforced wagon, you say? Double team of oxen?"

"Yep. You sure there's enough money for all this?"

"Yes," Julian replied. His voice was taut. He paused. "And what about the river?"

The river presented a particular problem. There was a shortage of space on steamboats, as well as a shortage of steamers, as so many had been commandeered for the Indian conflict that now seemed inevitable. The Geese Laying Moon had come and gone. Crazy Horse had broken camp on the Little Powder River and was moving into the country around the Tongue and the Rosebud rivers. Army troops, too, were on the move, and several of the steamboats that plied the Missouri between St. Louis and Fort Benton were now busy moving troops and supplies.

"I met a man once," Thad said slowly. "He helped me out of a jam. But I think I could call him a friend."

"What can he do for us?"

"Get us a boat. He owns a mess of them."

"There isn't that much time, Thad. And although my father is fairly occupied, if I start buying supplies in Fort Benton, that might arouse suspicion. So you'd better go yourself, on some pretext or other. And once we get the gear, our timing is going to have to be as good as clockwork."

"You're right. Look, everything is pretty much set here at the butte. To be really on the safe side, let's stay away for at least a couple of days. We can meet back here when I get back with the gear."

They knew they were so close to the end that they could not afford one mistake. From this point on, it felt to both of them as if they were walking on eggshells.

CHAPTER

34

He found Rap Stevens in the Hang It Up saloon, playing poker at a high-stakes table. One could tell by the way the players tended their cards and drank their whiskey, neat and slow, that it was a high-stakes game. There was no showing off and not much talk. One player looked as starched as a preacher. Another fellow, with a big bush of a salt-and-pepper beard, wore small wire-rimmed spectacles and a red bandanna tied around his neck; there was a carpetbag on the floor, stashed behind his legs. A third man had long silky sideburns. He was dressed nicely. Not as nicely as Rap Stevens, but he carried a yellow handkerchief that he

kept pulling out to wipe his sweaty face. Rap wore a
silk embroidered vest, and from where Thad stood, it
looked as if he had enough gold chain with watches
across the front to anchor one of his own steamships.
He wore pointy black shoes and they made his feet
look dainty and almost prissy. But there was nothing
prissy about the way he played cards.

"See and raise you five," the man with the spectacles
said after a player had tossed in two chips.

"Pass," said the next player.

"I see six," the preacher muttered.

"See and raise ten." Rap pushed in his chips.

"I pass."

"See sixteen."

"I retire."

"See and raise ten."

"I see."

"Pass."

"Pass."

"I retire," said the man with the yellow handkerchief, throwing down his cards without showing
them.

"Raise you sixteen." The man with the bushy beard
had frightened everyone out of the game except Rap
Stevens. Spectators ringed the table. Craning his neck,
Thad could see that the pot was high.

"See and raise ten." Rap pushed in more chips.

They both appeared as cool as could be.

"See and raise," said the whiskered man, squinting
through his spectacles.

Rap shifted in his chair. "I call." He laid down his hand. Rap Stevens had called on "threes," three eights. The other fellow had tried to bluff on a pair of sixes. Low cards in a high-stake game. Calling a bluff like that took guts, Thad thought. How had Rap known the fellow was bluffing?

Rap raked in the pot. The man with the whiskers and spectacles suffered his losses by taking a small sip of whiskey. It was his deal. He had just finished dealing the cards when Rap pulled out a pistol and laid it on the table. He spoke very quietly and in a funny sing-song voice that Thad had never heard him use.

"Loss is not boss. Cheats drink neat. Now, I'm not making any accusations or untoward suggestions here. I just want to say this. If I catch any man a-cheating, I'm going to shoot out all four of his eyes." He looked directly at the whiskered man with the spectacles and called for a new deck of cards. They played another hand and then Rap motioned Thad to a table.

"So," Rap said after listening to Thad's story. "You been rootin' round with the bone men all this time?"

"Yes."

"I like the idea . . . I do indeed." He rocked back on the two hind legs of his chair.

"Well, now, Rap, there's no gambling in it. It's just a question of moving this head."

"No gamblin' in it? Why, course there is! I could line up twenty people to bet on whether you get it down from the butte in one piece."

"Maybe you could, but don't. I told you this has got to be secret."

"Don't worry. Don't worry. I'll keep it a secret. I'll play all twenty bettors myself." Rap laughed. "It's the nature of the situation, you understand, that makes it a gamblin' man's dream. So you need a boat and a wagon with a team."

"Yeah. And we got the money. I can show you a letter of credit from Mr. Louis Woodfin of New York City, but we got the cash, too."

"No need," Rap said. "When do you need the wagon?"

"Ten days. Friday after this one. Just get it on the steamer that stops at Brown's Landing." Brown's Landing was far enough from either camp to avoid suspicion.

"And the boat for transporting this fossil of yours?"

"Two days after that, at the Cow Island Landing. It's got to be there on Sunday."

Thad's next stop was the Fort Benton bank. The clerk had to help him with his business, but it didn't take long. He then asked for an extra piece of paper and an envelope. Late that afternoon he caught the steamer out of Fort Benton for the trip downriver to Cow Island. That evening on the deck, in the flare of a kerosene pilot light, he began his letter to Babcock.

Dear Professor Babcock,

   This is a sad letter to write and I hope that you will understand. I am going to have to leave the expedition. I don't

*want to pull any punches. I'll tell you straight out. I found
a partner—Julian DeMott, the son of Algernon DeMott—
and we found the head of a great three-horned dinosaur. As
I have dug fossils over the past two years and learned to track
through time, I have come to feel that these bones belong to
the world and not just to places where rich and educated people
can study them all chopped up. I figure that in one sense people
can get educated just by seeing the bones, whether they can
afford to go to a university or not. Julian and I have decided
to give this head to the New World Museum in New York
City. I realize that I have dug this fossil on your time and
your money. I, therefore, have deposited in your account at the
Fort Benton bank all of my salary plus interest for the last
two years I have worked for the Harvard expedition.*

*I've learned so much in these past two years. But I guess
one of the troubles with learning is that you start getting ideas
of your own. Sharing the head of this dinosaur with the whole
world is one of mine. There's no real way I can thank you
for all you have done. I just got to say that I was kind of
unlucky with my parents. My father I never knew, and my
ma got killed when I was about five, but I consider myself the
luckiest person in the world because I've had two of the greatest
teachers—Mr. Jim Dundee and you.*

    So long and good luck,

    Thad

CHAPTER

➤ 35

Thad was back at the Medicine Buttes by noon the following day. Julian arrived shortly after he did.

"Got everything?" Julian asked.

"Yeah. Got the block and tackles. And Lord knows, it's good that old Gumbo is so broad in the beam and so strong. That net webbing weighs more than I do and was a devil to pack up."

"I see," Julian said, looking at the pile of thick rope that looked like a collapsed web of some monster spider.

"I had to travois it from the river up to here."

"Travois?"

"You know, how the Indians move their gear—on drags. Got some long branches from the cottonwoods near the river and lashed it to them and just dragged it on up here."

"So what's next? You got it fixed with the wagon?"

"Yep. I talked to Rap. It'll be here next Friday. Sunday, there'll be a steamer at the Cow Island Landing for us."

"So I suppose we just sit and wait for the next few days."

"Well, we can get the lines up on Friday. No sense sliding old Lunge and Plunge down till we have something to slide it into. I sure don't want to have to lift that skull straight up from the ground into the wagon."

"No, certainly not!" Julian said. He paused. "Have you thought about how you're going to break this news to Babcock, Thad?"

"Yeah," Thad said flatly, thinking of the letter in his pocket, then added, "I've written him a letter. Don't know how much good it will do. I'll leave it for him before we go."

"Yes, I suppose I shall have to do something similar for my father. This, of course, is the hard part of the operation," Julian said, trying to force a bit of a smile across his face. It came off as more of a grimace that might accompany a bad-tasting medicine. "I do feel that this is definitely the way it must be. The bones belong in a museum."

"Yes," Thad said.

"We both believe that. So that leaves only one course of action."

"Yep," Thad said. There was a long pause. "So what do you think your father's going to do when he finds out?"

"Well, I suppose he'll disown me."

"What does that mean?"

"Not much, in the usual sense. See, most of the money and property comes from my mother's side and passes directly on to me. The Eaton Square house, of course, is his."

"That the usual sense," Thad said, repeating Julian's words, "the money, the property, and the square thing?"

"Yes," said Julian slowly.

"But what about the other?"

"You mean, I trust, in the unusual sense."

"Well, apart from the money and all that."

"Yes. Apart from the money and all that, I suppose my father shall cease speaking to me, and we shall never see each other again."

"Never?"

"Never," Julian repeated. "He'll deny he has a son."

"You ready for that?" Thad asked.

Julian flushed and answered slowly. "It is not a question of being ready, Thad. This is difficult to explain. But in a sense, I have known that it has always been so—that my father has always denied me despite the fact that he is my father. One is never ready for that as long as one lives, but it does not change the truth."

"I never knew my father," Thad said quietly.

"Then perhaps we are the same."

That night when Thad returned to camp, he dreamed of the buffalo hunter for the first time in nearly three years. The beauty of a Montana sky with its moon riding low over the buttes became raked with blood, fingernails of blood. In the morning, Thad awakened to the soft, squashy sounds of dynamite exploding the face of a distant butte.

CHAPTER
36

They had dislodged the head but not removed it from its space. It had been cross-braced, strutted, and painted with one coat of varnish and another coat of a new resin that Thad had been using recently. The parts of the skull that were most vulnerable had been papered, wrapped, and plastered. There was no practical way to test the elaborate rope-and-pulley system they had rigged to lower the head down the side of the butte. Both Thad and Julian had tried it by climbing in the rope-mesh basket as the other operated the pulley system. Thad decided that he wanted to add one more block and tackle, thus increasing by one third again the mechanical advantage. He could get one in Claggett where he was to accompany Babcock the very next day. The Harvard team had discovered yet another fossil-rich site, and supplies were running low.

"But I think I won't come here for a day after that. Babcock really needs me to finish the plastering on the elasmosaurus. It's Tuesday now. I'll be back before our wagon gets to the landing on Friday night."

The elasmosaurus, a plated marine reptile, had been uncovered, and its exceedingly long neck was going to be difficult to excavate. Thad felt strongly about leaving things as tidy as possible with his old boss.

As Julian sat around the campfire the next evening, he caught himself watching his father, wondering if indeed these were their last few days together. As much as he disapproved of his father's values as a scientist, he now realized they were inseparable from the man. Yet Julian still felt that he had failed as a son in some way. If he had been better, more morally perfect, could he have persuaded his father to change? Julian sat silently as his father, animated even after a long day in the field, discussed the anatomy of a duckbilled dinosaur.

"One would imagine"—Algernon DeMott took a long draw on his pipe—"from the evidence of webbing we're finding in the feet that these creatures would be able to paddle about nicely in the Cretaceous sea."

Alban Mallory, Samuel Wilbur, and even Ormsby, who often was less than enthusiastic about DeMott's long-winded lectures, were rapt with attention. Bobber

Henshaw whittled in a corner. In a general way, it seemed to Julian that Henshaw was always attuned to DeMott. Nearly illiterate, hardly articulate, the man seemed to be able to understand DeMott in a way that none of these other men ever would. His comprehension had nothing to do with the intellectual theories of DeMott. It was something else, something that Julian could not put his finger on but that made the two men, Bobber and his father, soul mates in some strange and profoundly disturbing way.

They all turned in later that night. Julian's tent was near his father's. His father was a heavy sleeper, which was fortuitous for Julian, considering his recent nighttime activities. But Julian was not a sound sleeper, and tonight something wakened him. Had someone staggered against a tent pole? Shaken his bedding? In any case, he was awake and he could hear his father's voice, low but discernible, just outside his own tent.

"You don't say . . . Thaddeus Longsworth . . . the master excavator? Seems a shame."

That was all Julian needed to hear. He sat up quietly on his bedroll and listened.

"Someone on the Yale team is actually planning to kill Babcock? I can't believe it."

"Yes, sir. Heard it on good authority, and they're going to frame Longsworth."

"I never thought Cunningham would stoop so low."

Julian felt himself break out in a cold sweat. He had

to warn Thad immediately, but he ordered himself to stay calm and to listen.

"They're working over in those low bluffs, a few miles north on the way to that old ferry landing. Kind of a lonely spot. Only he and Longsworth working on the plastering now. They figure it's a perfect setup."

"Frame-up, I think, is a better word here." For once, Julian would have to agree with his father. "And you think it's too late to do anything to stop it? . . . Well, it is no business of ours anyway, I suppose." Their voices dwindled off into the night as they both moved toward their tents.

It could never be too late, Julian thought. If he got there only to witness the murder, at least he could attest to the fact that Thad had not done it. As soon as Julian could be sure his father and Bobber had retired for the night, he was on his pony and racing in the direction of the northern bluffs.

The night was just melting into that time before the dawn when the sky, too pale for stars and failing of light, appears thin and worn. It had started to drizzle lightly and the trail was becoming difficult, as there was much of the pulverized rock known as mineral soap along the way. The mineral soap had the peculiar ability to absorb many times its own volume in water. It was doing so now as the dust of the trail was becoming wet and thick and swelling into a sticky mess. Just as Julian was coming around an outcrop, two figures ap-

peared. His breath locked. Was he too late? One fellow
he recognized as the artist from the Harvard team, leading a pack mule with his kit of materials.

Julian trotted up to them. "You're from Babcock's
team, are you not?"

"Yes. I'm Nat Forbes and this is Oliver Perkins. And
you, I believe, are Algernon DeMott's son?"

"Is there something wrong?" Oliver asked, noticing
Julian's high color.

"Possibly. This might sound ridiculous, but I heard—
heard a rumor that someone on the Yale team was
planning on killing Professor Babcock at the elasmosaurus site."

"What?" Nat Forbes and Oliver Perkins both said at
once.

"Yes," Julian continued. "They were going to frame
Thaddeus Longsworth, your excavator."

"Well, Babcock is at the site right now eating a rather
hearty breakfast served up by Wu Chow," Forbes said.

"And is Thad there?" Julian asked.

"No, actually," Oliver continued. "A message came
for him late last night—why, it was from you!"

"What?" Julian was stunned. "From me?"

"Yes," Nat Forbes was saying. "We were all quite
excited—thought we were all being invited for tea by
the famous British scientist. Turned out it was just
Thad. He left about the same time we did this morning."

"He left!" Julian wheeled his pony around. He did

not need to ask where Thad had gone. It was unbelievable. The whole thing was a lie—a fantastic fabrication.
He had been decoyed away from Thad. And Thad!
Thad had been lured, through a forged letter, to Pudding Butte. Julian dug his heels into the pony's flanks
and rode, rode as hard as any man has ever ridden.

CHAPTER
37

Thad had thought it odd that Julian would be so bold as to send a letter directly to camp, but when he opened it, he understood the necessity. It seemed that a piece of the lower support struts, the ones that came up under the jaw, had somehow moved. Julian had attempted to reinforce the whole thing but was so nervous that he had actually spent most of the night on the plank, not willing to trust his own carpentry.

But when Thad reached Pudding Butte, he could find no sign of Julian. The plank was lying on the ground amid a tangle of ropes. Thad decided to go up himself and examine the struts. He was bending over to put the loops on the plank when he noticed the heel mark in the damp earth. The boot heel had ground in hard as a leg would, trying to gain a purchase. Then he felt something cold and the soft thud of something exploding right in his head. The world went dark.

When Julian arrived, breathless, the first thing he noticed was the line, the thin dark line, and along it, a spluttering tongue of flame. Three hundred yards away, at the opposite end of the butte from where they had been excavating, Thad was sprawled. Julian galloped directly up the butte and dismounted.

"Good God!" There was a stick of dynamite tied to Thad's head. Julian's fingers seemed to stiffen as they touched the knot.

"Julian! Julian! Get out!" It was his father, from across the flats. He had just stepped out of the cave they had used for a laboratory.

"Father!" Julian screamed. The flame was devouring the line just thirty feet from Thad's head. *Forget everything,* he told himself, *except this knot. Do not think of that tongue of flame hissing, like a snake's tongue. Do not look. Look means run. Knife. Thad's knife.* He reached under Thad and drew out the knife. Thad stirred and Julian cut the dynamite free. But he had cut it on the wrong side. It was still connected to the line, and the flame came, licking its way closer and closer. Julian's hand was wrapped around a live piece of dynamite and he could not move. He watched, paralyzed, as the flame crept closer. As if from a great distance, a distance of time as well as space, a voice called.

"Julian! Julian!"

Was that his father begging now for Julian's life, begging finally for his own son's life? He looked up. "Run! Drop it!" the voice called. The flame was so close, he could smell it now. Then, just across from where his father stood, he saw resting on the top of a boulder the two bores of a double-barreled shotgun.

Bobber Henshaw's drawn a bloody bead on me! The realization flooded Julian's brain. He hurled the stick of dynamite as far as he could. The boulder exploded. The air was splattered with shale and blood. A hat wafted down almost lazily.

And then the world became muddled for Julian. He could not remember Thad regaining consciousness. He only remembered him walking back from the site of the explosion. His face was pale and as tight as a knot, his eyes cold and old, very old.

"You don't want to see that over there. There's not much left of Bobber," Thad was saying. "Your father, a big boulder rolled on him. He's pinned. He's not got much breath left in him. You want to see him?"

Julian nodded. Thad took him by the elbow and steered him to where Algernon DeMott lay. By the time they got there, he had died. So Julian simply looked off into nowhere. "Why?" he asked softly. The rain had stopped and the larks wheeled in a flawless blue sky.

* * *

"I don't believe it." Oliver Perkins gasped as he looked up at the enormous head above, looming out of the butte. His face was caked with dust, his horse panting from the hard ride.

"What are you doing here?" Thad asked, stunned by Perkins's arrival.

"I followed Julian DeMott. He seemed absolutely terrified when he heard that you were not in camp. I thought something might have happened, that you might be in some kind of danger."

"I was," Thad said, and then began to explain.

"So you mean you and Julian have been working independently?" Oliver asked at the finish of Thad's story. "And this Henshaw chap and Julian's father were ready to do you in to get the head?"

"Yes," Thad said somberly. "I know my part in it doesn't look too good. But Oliver, you got to understand that we weren't working for ourselves. Julian met this man from the New World Museum in New York and . . ." Thad looked over at Julian, who seemed to still be in some kind of daze. There would be no help from him in telling this part of the story. "Look," Thad said, "I've got this letter here for Professor Babcock. I want you to deliver it to him, but read it now. It explains my feelings about all this bone stuff." Thad handed the letter to Oliver.

It was almost as if Oliver could not tear his eyes from the incredible fossil skull to read the piece of paper. "I just can't believe the size of this head." Finally he lowered his eyes from the butte to the letter. He read it once, and then Thad could tell he read it a second time. He swallowed, folded the letter up, and put it in his pocket. "All right," Oliver said quietly. "I think you might need my help if you really are going to pull this thing off. Your partner seems rather out of sorts. Let's get going."

"Do you mean it, Oliver?" Thad asked excitedly.

"I mean it."

"Won't you be missed at camp?"

"Not for the space of the day it takes us to get this creature off the butte. Most likely, the people at the elasmosaurus site will think I'm at the main camp, and those at the main camp will think I'm at the site. It shouldn't be a problem. You have a wagon somewhere, I take it?"

"I will by tomorrow. It's coming in on the steamer at Brown's Landing. I got to ride there now. I'll be back here by Friday night, Saturday morning at the latest. We load it as soon as I get here and then we go!"

The rest of that day and the next was like an eerie dream for Julian. He felt as if he were in a bubble, a strangely silent bubble. He thought he saw through the bubble another young man, with red hair that was paler than his own, ride up on a dusty, panting horse and jump down to stare in wonderment at the great head of Lunge and Plunge. Thad rode off on Gumbo and then after a time—was it long or short?—returned. Julian did exactly what Thad told him. But he could not remember hearing his voice and he felt as if he, himself, could not be heard. He would later have no recollection of putting the basket of rope over Lunge and Plunge's head. Nor would he remember operating the block and tackles, as he apparently had done, or any of the sound of the ropes straining and the small rocks falling. He would later see rope burns and blisters on his hands, but he would remember none of that. The great head floating down almost magically from the butte—that would be all he would ever recall.

Just after the head was loaded into the wagon, Thad took Gumbo's reins and walked over to Oliver. "Here, Oliver, take good care of Gumbo. When you get back to camp, say good-bye to the fellows for me and be sure to tell Wu Chow that I'll be thinking of him."

"I shall, Thad. I shall." Oliver held out his hand and Thad clasped it in a long handshake.

Finally they were on their way, the head secured in the wagon. Julian did not know how long the trip to the river took. It could have been an hour or a week.

CHAPTER

38

"What in tarnation do you mean?"

The silent bubble had burst. Every vibration of every syllable reverberated in Julian's ear. Thad was talking to a well-turned-out man in a fancy vest and boots with pointy toes.

"You what? You lost the boat in a poker game? I told you, Rap, this was not gamblin'! How can you do this to us?"

Thad was livid with rage. He looked at Julian for help in this impossible situation and then remembered that Julian was in some sort of daze. He had not said a word since Thursday. Thad slammed down his fists on the top of one of the crates stacked on the pier of the Cow Island Landing. He beat them furiously. After all their efforts, after nearly getting killed, it had come to this. He beat his fists even harder.

"Thad! Thad!" He felt someone touching his shoulder. He looked up. Julian's eyes were still rather foggy, like those of someone trying to swim up from a dark dream into the consciousness of a new day. "What's the problem?"

"The problem is, he lost the boat in a poker game. And boats are in short supply now."

Thad was about to begin beating his fists again when Julian pointed upstream to the bend in the river. "Why, here comes one right now."

The boat was named the *Morgan B.* It was traveling heavy. Even from the landing, they could see there would be no room in the hold or on deck for a seven-hundred-pound dinosaur head.

"Yeah, I see it." Thad sighed. "But what can we do?"

Rap Stevens studied the steamer as it pulled in to closer range. "Looks like it's got a load of timber and wood shingles," he said. "I know the captain of the *Morgan B.* I've played poker with him a number of times."

"Play for it now, Mr. Stevens," Julian said.

"What's that, son?" Rap asked.

"Play for the boat," Julian replied calmly. "Play for it and win."

An amused look crossed Rap Stevens's face.

"Don't say it, Rap!" Thad barked. "It's your fault. It

didn't have to be a gamblin' business, moving this head. Now play for it like Julian said."

"All right, gentlemen. I'll do my best."

No sooner had the captain's feet hit the dock than Thad had Rap Stevens's Colt .45 jabbed into his ribs.

"Welcome to Cow Island Landing, sir."

"Yes, yes. What's the meaning of this?" the captain stammered. Julian had regained his composure and was playing the role of the genial host.

"I believe you know Mr. Stevens? We really regret being so insistent about this poker game."

"Poker game?"

"Yes, my dear sir. For the *Morgan B.*"

The captain squinted at him in the sun. "Where you from, boy?" he demanded.

"England," said Julian. "You know, Queen Victoria, the British Empire, the sun never sets . . ."

"I demand to know what this ridiculous—"

"Oh, forget it," Julian said, "just play cards."

Thad poked the man with his gun toward a rope spool turned on end that was to be the card table and where Rap now sat on a keg. A member of the crew had started down the gangplank, saw Thad's gun in the captain's ribs, thought better of it, and turned around. The captain looked wistfully in the direction of the crewman. Julian noticed this.

"Look," said Julian. "You don't want to say you've been robbed by two scrawny kids and this dandy." He nodded toward Rap. "You want to know that you lost fair and square in a gentlemanly manner. You are a gentleman, I can tell. I could tell the moment you set foot off that boat. I said to Thad, 'This is a gentleman!' Now play!"

Within minutes, a small crowd had materialized like ants around a puddle of honey. It wasn't sugar that drew them, of course: just two men, a deck of cards, and a steamboat in the pot. Nobody moved to stop the game. For years, people would remember it as the best thing that had ever happened at the Cow Island Landing. As gambling stories went, it ranked right up there along with the legends.

Thad and Julian had forced the captain to raise, or bet, the *Morgan B.* Rap Stevens won it for them with a flush in hearts. He might have palmed a heart, but Thad and Julian did not care how Rap had won the *Morgan B* for them as long as he'd won it. After all, they planned to give it back to the captain in Omaha, where the head would be loaded onto a railroad car for the rest of the trip east.

They could see Fort Buford in the distance as they swung out of the deep bend in the river. Thad and Julian had fixed up a deck camp of sorts, just in the shadow of Lunge and Plunge's horns. Most of the days they had spent on deck, guarding their precious cargo. As they approached the fort, three scows came poling toward them.

The next thing Thad knew was that the deck was flashing with gold braid, epaulets, and scabbards. The army had boarded. They were at the moment reading some sort of declaration to the captain while Julian and Thad listened.

There were fragments of phrases like "state of war . . . security of the nation . . . martial law . . ."

"We're being commandeered," Julian whispered.

"No. It can't be!"

"Wait, we must stay calm. Let's look at this calmly."

"Calmly!"

"As long as we can stick with Lunge and Plunge, it will be all right."

"Stick with him—where? They're going to take this boat down the Yellowstone! We're going to be heading south toward the Powder River country and there are no railheads around those parts. We want to go east across the Dakota territory, down into Nebraska—on the Missouri, not the Yellowstone." Thad was almost shouting.

"Be quiet. Here comes an officer," Julian warned.

"You the owners of this boat?"

Thad could hardly concentrate on the man's words. He couldn't take his eyes off the man's blue coat. Suddenly there were Bluecoats swarming all over the foredeck.

"Yes, sir, we are the owners," answered Julian. "Welcome aboard."

"We're taking over the *Morgan B.* As you know, there's trouble down in the Indian country, round the Powder and the Bighorn rivers. Custer marched from Fort Abraham Lincoln nearly three weeks ago. General

Crook's coming up from the south and Colonel John
Gibbon from the west. We need this steamer to bring
in supplies."

"Fine," said Julian.

"Fine!" muttered Thad. What was Julian talking
about?

"Our only concern, sir, is that we are carrying classified U.S. government fossils bound for Omaha."

"What?" The officer looked confused.

"Fossils. You know, the bones of ancient creatures.
This is part of a joint British-American effort. I am with
the British paleontological team. My esteemed colleague, Mr. Longsworth here, is with your government.
We don't mind going out of our way. We know emergencies are emergencies and we . . . uh . . . feel that the
sooner these savages are whipped, the better. We just
ask that our fossils here be left undisturbed."

"Well, you're welcome to unload it at the fort. But
I can't guarantee that any civilian boats will be coming
through here for some time. Take it you want to get it
to a railhead?"

"Yes . . . well, uh . . . I think it's best if we stick with
you. Moving it could be a problem. This particular
species of dinosaur, by the way, is named after your
President—*Triceratops grantus.*"

"You don't say!" The officer was clearly impressed.
"Well, you can count on me as soon as this little fuss
with the Indians is over—and it's going to be quick—
we'll get your fossil right back a-heading east."

But for now, the *Morgan B* turned south and slightly west as it reached the point where the Missouri and the Yellowstone met.

"I can't believe this is happening. I just can't!" Thad whispered as he leaned over the rail and watched the water of the Yellowstone curl in frothy swags off the bow. They were loaded mostly with ammunition, several howitzers, and medical supplies, and with enough men to transport these supplies to the Powder River country and to Colonel Gibbon, who would be coming in from the west in need of some provisioning.

CHAPTER
➤ 39

Hundreds of deep creeks and tributary rivers flowed into the Yellowstone. Thad and Julian listened anxiously as they heard the commanding officer order their captain to turn off the Yellowstone and follow one of these rivers in an attempt to deposit the men and the provisions closer to Colonel Gibbon. Then they had taken yet another smaller tributary. This didn't seem risky, because the heavy spring rains had swelled these tributaries into mad rushing rivers, but the water suddenly became too shallow for the boat's draft. And they were forced to stop.

The soldiers had disembarked to try to meet up with Colonel Gibbon. According to the commander, they were far enough north to be unconcerned about Indians. The intelligence reports had them several miles to the south. But Thad was uncertain as to where exactly they were, because all the maps of the region had become classified documents and not available to "civilians."

Julian and Thad had tried to talk the captain into turning around and taking them back down to the Yellowstone. The current would be in their favor. The captain, however, stoutly refused and this time pulled a gun on them. "You want to get court-martialed?" he yelled. "This is treason!" However, the *Morgan B* had a flat-bottom tender, a scow that could sustain the weight of Lunge and Plunge. They struck a deal on that. The captain seemed only too happy to see the two boys and their crazy head float off downstream. He had even helped them put Lunge and Plunge into the rope basket and lower it with the deck crane onto the scow.

They had only gone a short distance when Thad thought he recognized the river that would take them to the Yellowstone. But it was a "false river," as Julian called it later, and simply dead-ended. For the next day, they started down numerous false rivers, creeks, and channels that Thad thought he recognized, but then they would dead-end. In short, they were lost somewhere in the vicinity of the Yellowstone River, not on the river and not yet meeting up with a stream that could carry them to it.

"I can't believe this is so impenetrable!" Julian exclaimed. "All water flows downhill—why aren't we just flowing with it into the Yellowstone? It's like a water maze."

It was then decided that Thad would scout the surrounding region to try to establish their location and, more importantly, that of the Yellowstone River. Julian would remain moored, awaiting Thad's return.

Thad had been gone a full day when he experienced the same curious sensation he always got when Black Elk was nearby. Suddenly a holy man from Black Elk's tribe stepped out of the woods.

"Man-Who-Runs-Through-Fire!" he exclaimed softly as he recognized Thad. Thad followed him to the encampment that was near the Rosebud Creek in the heart of the Cheyenne and Sioux country of the Powder River region.

Black Elk came out to greet him.

"You are here, brother," he said to Thad. "You are no longer lost."

"You knew I was lost?"

Black Elk's English seemed to fail him at this point and he looked around for Standing Eagle. He motioned him over from a gathering.

"Black Elk has felt you here for two, three days now."

Thad then explained to Standing Eagle how he and his other brother and the fossil head had become lost in the network of creeks and rivers.

"We shall help, but have patience." Standing Eagle translated Black Elk's words. Then together, in a mixture of Sioux and English, the two young men explained that the great chief Sitting Bull was in this very camp and that this was the third day of the dance of the spirit of the sun, in which the great chief sought a vision. Thad must join them in the circle to witness the dance, which was about to begin.

Thad watched for an hour as Sitting Bull bled himself and then, throwing his head back and staring at the sun, danced, seeking the vision for his people. He seemed to enter a trance. Thad felt himself jump as the chief suddenly fell over, stunned. It was only a few minutes before he rose again and began to tell his dream to the people. The parched voice cried out in Lakota, the Sioux language. Black Elk and Standing Eagle translated.

"When I look into the sky, I see soldiers falling like grasshoppers with their heads down and their hats falling—falling, falling, falling—falling right into the Indian camps." A murmur passed through the people.

"Wakan-Tanka, the Great Spirit, was giving the soldiers to the Indians to be killed." Then Sitting Bull stopped.

Black Elk turned to Thad and spoke with intense pride. "Sitting Bull's vision make our people strong in heart."

Thad was anxious to get back to Julian, but on that very day the Cheyenne spotted the first columns of Bluecoats, led by Three Stars Crook. When the word came, Thad knew that there would be no way he could get back to his friend quickly. Criers were sent out to warn the Indians camped in the Rosebud valley. A war party of one thousand Sioux and Cheyenne set out to meet the Bluecoats. This time it would not be like the slaughter on the Little Powder River. Thad, Black Elk, and several women went to help with the spare horses. The leaders were Crazy Horse, Sitting Bull, and Two Moon.

From the crest of a high hill on the western ridge of the Rosebud valley, the two boys watched.

"Watch Crazy Horse," Black Elk said. "Watch him dance his horse. When the horse begins to dance, Crazy Horse leaves the shadow world and enters the real world of the spirit. In this way, he leads his men. He feels nothing but the spirit."

But it was Crook's men that they saw first. Then there was a cry from the soldiers: "Sioux! Sioux!"

In that instant, Crazy Horse swooped down the flanks of the hill toward Rosebud Creek. The troops, used to moving in skirmish lines, had become scattered on both sides of the big creek. Crook gathered one group together for a charge. They began to race forward on their horses, sending a screen of fire from their carbines ahead of them.

"Watch!" Black Elk urged.

Crazy Horse had begun to dance. He darted here and there. The other warriors did the same. Refusing to lock into a defensive stance against the charge, the Sioux and Cheyenne warriors kept moving in a myriad of directions, coming back in for isolated assaults against the weak spots in the Bluecoats' lines. Crook's troops were thrown into total disarray by the repeated darting attacks from all directions.

"Look, the fire's grown too hot for Crazy Horse," Thad said. "But that fellow over there, he's luring away a few soldiers."

"That is Good Weasel," Black Elk said. "Crazy Horse's lieutenant. Now watch."

Suddenly Good Weasel wheeled his pony and with six other warriors turned on the Bluecoats with a fury and pursued them.

From directly below them, they heard a cry and, when they looked, they saw a young woman who had helped with the horses. She was riding her pony into the thick of the battle. She rode straight for the warrior known as Chief-Comes-in-Sight. Dazed, he stood by the body of his horse, which had just been shot out from under him. In an instant, however, he was on the woman's pony, behind her. The woman was his sister, Buffalo-Calf-Road-Woman.

It was called by the white people the Battle of the Rosebud, but the Indians would always know it as the Battle Where the Girl Saved Her Brother. The Bluecoats had fallen. Three Stars Crook was badly beaten and returned to his camp to wait and hope for reinforcements.

But Sitting Bull's vision had not been fulfilled entirely. And the Indians knew that there were more soldiers coming. So it did not surprise Thad to learn the next day that the chiefs had decided to break camp and move west to the valley of the Greasy Grass, the one the white men called the Little Bighorn.

There must have been nearly ten thousand Indians in the villages scattered in almost three miles along the twisting banks of the Greasy Grass. There were the Hunkpapas, farthest downstream, then the Minneconjous, the Blackfoot, the Sans Arc, the Brulé, and finally the Cheyenne and Black Elk's Oglala. They were all on the south side of the river. And looming up just beyond the banks of the river, Thad saw something unbelievable—three horns, thrusting through the tall buffalo grass. It was old Lunge and Plunge! And in the throng of curious Indians surrounding the skull, Thad spotted the bright flaming head of Julian DeMott. He was trying his best to explain to the Indians what the creature was.

It was a most joyful reunion.

"It's unbelievable, Thad!" Julian kept saying while he patted his friend's shoulders as if to convince himself that indeed Thad was really standing before him. "You're here! I was sure you had perished."

"Me, perish? How did you get here?"

"That is probably even more unbelievable. This band of Sioux found me. I think they thought I was rather special, you know, with old Lunge and Plunge here, and even my hair seems to intrigue them. They haven't seen that many redheads, I guess. The children simply can't keep away from me." Indeed there did seem to be eddies of children swirling around Julian, pointing at his hair and jabbering furiously. "In any case, I think you can say I've been captured, more or less—in a strictly friendly sort of way. Apparently things are really heating up around here. You know they've been so hospitable, I don't want to press them about when we can get away. I'm sure we can make a graceful exit when things are resolved with the soldiers—presuming, of course, we aren't killed."

"But how did you get here with old Lunge and Plunge?" Thad was baffled.

"By this river—the Greasy Grass, they call it, or one fellow says the white men call it the Little Bighorn."

"But is that where I left you?"

"Yes, indeed! Most convenient, eh? Except for the fact that the darned thing flows the wrong way. The Indians actually poled me up it. Getting back will be much easier."

The next morning, Thad and Julian had been helping Black Elk and several of the boys water the horses. The day grew hotter, and as the sun climbed in the cloudless sky and the wind died, a milky whiteness of heat and still air settled over the valley.

"Let's swim!" a cousin of Black Elk's had said. So they stripped off their clothes and plunged into the cold water of the river. Thad had been swimming near Black Elk when suddenly a queer look came across the Sioux's face. Black Elk stopped swimming and stood perfectly still in the waist-deep water. Just then they heard the cry.

"Nutkaveho! The white soldiers are coming! *Nutkaveho!"*

Thad and Julian were out of the water, throwing on their clothes. The Indian boys hardly bothered, however, and would ride half-naked. They could hear the cry pass from camp to camp like ripples on the water. Hundreds of people began to run for their horses. The boys' horses were right there. Thad picked a sorrel, Julian a gray, and they followed Black Elk on his buckskin.

Ahead, they could see the dust rising in the Hunkpapa camp. Already the word had spread that the soldiers' first victims had been the two wives and the three children of the Hunkpapa chief, Gall. Gall, in a fury, had turned on the company of soldiers and was forcing them back. When the boys arrived downstream at the Hunkpapa village, the water in the river was raging with men and horses and gunfire. Gall quickly forced the Bluecoats to the other side of the river and chased the company, Major Reno's command, up into the deep ravines between the bluffs on the north side of the river. Gall and his warriors were far ahead of the other

Indians who were coming from the Oglala and Cheyenne camps upstream. When they realized how far ahead Gall was, many of the boys that Thad and Julian had been swimming with turned back toward their own camps. But they did not turn back until they had stripped and scalped the soldiers who were dead or dying on the banks.

Thad and Julian returned with Black Elk to the Oglala village, and as Black Elk's mother walked out of the tipi and saw her son alive, she made the tremolo—the shrill warbling cheer to welcome her son from battle. Shortly after, Black Elk, armed, came up to Thad and Julian. "It is time for you to leave. The battle is coming this way. You must go now with your earth spirit." He nodded in the direction of the scow. "Go under this screen of battle fire and dust." His eyes were focused on something in the distance. "We see already Long Hair Custer's column on the ridge." Black Elk paused. "And know, my friends, the power of peace." It was the last Thad would see of Black Elk for a long time.

From the ridge near the coulee called Medicine Tail, George Armstrong Custer got his first view of the valley of the Little Bighorn. There were more villages and more Indians than he had anticipated. Grim-faced, he turned to his trumpeter. "Orderly, I want you to take a message to Major Benteen. Ride as fast as you can and tell him to hurry. Tell him there is a big village directly below and I want him to be quick in bringing ammunition packs."

"Yes, sir," the trumpeter replied.

Custer lifted his field glasses again. "And, trumpeter, what the devil is that floating down the river on some sort of raft?"

He handed the field glasses to the young man.

"I'll be darned if I know," he replied.

"You don't suppose they got some sort of howitzer on that thing—a floating offensive strategy?"

"I don't know, sir."

"Wait. I'll give you a message for Benteen." He got out some paper and scrawled a note on it, then handed it to the trumpeter. Trumpeter Martin was the last soldier to see Custer and his command alive.

Thad and Julian had already started downstream heading north, back toward the Yellowstone River. They had proceeded barely a half-mile when they saw an old man carrying a muzzle loader and striding toward his hobbled pony. The old man stopped for a moment and looked over the tipis and across the river to the high, broken ridges.

"Pahuska!" he cried.

Just at that moment, Thad looked in the same direction. A column of Bluecoats rode at a dead run down the Medicine Tail coulee and at the head of the column, his blaze of golden hair flying behind, was the Son of the Morning Star.

"It's Custer!" Thad cried hoarsely.

"No," Julian uttered. A simple, flat no. And there would be no talking themselves out of this one. There would not be time for talk about British-American relations and *Triceratops grantus.*

"They're hard on us. They'll be down here in no time!" Julian cried.

"Keep poling!"

"He's slowing up," Thad said. "He must be worried that those big cavalry horses with their iron shoes will skid on the bank or at the fording place on the rocks."

Custer and the foremost ranks of calvary entered the water with caution. Thad recognized a young warrior from Black Elk's band, the one called Blue Moccasin, ahead on the bank of the river. He was pointing downstream and seemed thrilled by what he saw. Then Thad saw them, too.

"Julian! It's the Hunkpapas. That must be Gall in the lead." More warriors appeared on the bank and they began to cheer. Gall and the Hunkpapas, fresh from beating back Reno, were racing down through the cottonwoods along the banks of the river.

"Fast! They come fast!" cried Blue Moccasin. *"Hoka hey!"* The Indian war cry crushed down upon them as Gall and his warriors surged toward the troops trying to cross the river to the villages.

Thad watched as Custer advanced, firing his favorite weapon, the Remington sporting rifle with the octagonal barrel. In his unsnapped holsters, at the ready, were the two English self-cocking bulldog pistols. Covering him from behind were his troops. The fighting was so heavy, the white gunsmoke so thick, that it was difficult to see. Thad strained to keep his eye on Custer. They were within thirty feet of him, and Thad blinked as he saw Custer stop and wheel his horse around midstream. He faced Thad directly. Then Thad saw the blossom of red unfurl like a rose on his breast. And then he fell. An Indian bullet had caught him in the heart. It might have been Gall's or even Standing Eagle's, whom Julian spotted a short distance away, jubilantly holding his Springfield rifle high in the air as his pony thrashed through the water. Most of the Indians didn't even know Pahuska was down until they saw his men carrying him out of the river and up toward the ridge. Then, in a great charge, they closed in around the Bluecoats.

The Little Bighorn flowed directly into the Yellowstone. They found the steamer *Morgan B* exactly where they had left it. The officers who had gone to join Gibbon had presumably been killed in the greatest defeat ever of U.S. troops by Indians. There was no trace of the captain or his crew. Perhaps they had abandoned the steamer and run scared back down the river, or perhaps they had perished, falling prey in the woods to some remnant band of Indians who had not made it to the big battle on the Little Bighorn.

Thad and Julian loaded Lunge and Plunge onto the foredeck. They threw wood under the boiler and started a fire. Within twenty minutes, steam was up. As the engine turned over, the piston began to hammer at the crankshaft. They swung into the stream. Thad took the wheel.

"Going the right way now, Thad." Julian smiled.

"Downstream. Downstream!" Thad answered.

And it was. All the way from the Yellowstone to the Missouri to Omaha, where Mr. Woodfin's train was waiting—all downstream.

CHAPTER
40

There was a cordon of roses, bright yellow roses, roping off the area in which they stood. It must have been nearly fifty feet long, and Thad and Julian were standing on either side of Louis Woodfin in front of the skull of the New World Museum's first major acquisition. *Triceratops grandis montaniensis,* or as Mr. Woodfin had just informed the press, "old Lunge and Plunge," the young discoverers' nickname for the creature. The press had loved it. The news of the disastrous battle of the Little Bighorn, in which the entire Seventh Cavalry had been wiped out, had made it back to the east just in time for the huge centennial celebration of America's independence. But now, finally, some good news had come out of the west. Woodfin had cautioned the boys to avoid all mention of their presence at the battle. For all intents and purposes, the world thought these boys had simply had a leisurely float down the Missouri.

The reporters were now asking them questions. Thad was uncomfortable, to say the least. He wasn't used to so many people. He didn't know whether it was the tight collar on his new shirt, but every time he tried to answer a question, his voice either cracked or sounded strangled.

"So, Mr. Longsworth, you're just an ordinary cowpoke who stumbled onto a good thing."

Now how in the heck was a person to answer a question like that, Thad thought. "I'm a tracker, sir. I learned about fossils through working with Professor George Babcock of Harvard. And yes, there's a lot of luck hunting fossils."

"And you, Mr. DeMott, do you hope to follow in your late father's footsteps?"

Oh Lordy, thought Thad, how's Julian going to answer that one.

"Not exactly, sir. Mr. Longsworth and I shall continue our research and collections in the west, funded by the New World Museum." Julian paused. Thad could tell he was thinking about how to word what he would say next. "My father was a theorist, and devoted to remaining first and foremost a university scholar. I'm interested in how museums can bring this knowledge to people, all people. In exactly two hours, five hundred schoolchildren who have never seen a fossil will come streaming through those doors. When they go home, they will have a new word in their vocabulary—*dinosaur.*" Julian stopped and then smiled broadly at Thad. "And we propose to make *dinosaur* a household word!"

EPILOGUE

The Masonic Hall in Greeley was packed. The tiny lady wore her years well. Her hair had turned gray now, but she still kept the same style she had had as a young wife at Fort Abraham Lincoln. Her dress, too, with its high collar, was reminiscent of a previous era. Pinned to the collar was a cameo with the likeness of her husband, the late George Armstrong Custer. The crowd quieted as Elizabeth Bacon Custer walked across the stage to the lectern.

In the audience, fifth row back, Thaddeus Longsworth leaned forward slightly and, locking his hands over the head of his cane, rested his chin on his knuckles while he listened. It had been fifty-six years since he had last seen her, since they had stood in the ballroom of the Custer headquarters at Fort Abraham Lincoln and she had described in detail Indian methods of torture. Thaddeus sat next to his wife, Abigail Cabot Longsworth, and listened as the same delicate voice spoke.

"My life changed forever one day in June, fifty-four years ago." She spoke about the custom of the officers' wives to follow the men on the first day of the march and to camp out on that first night with them and then to rise at dawn to bid them farewell. She described the mist that morning as the band struck up the general's favorite, "The Girl I Left Behind." And then she told about her vision as the bright sun began to shine through the morning mist when the soldiers were leaving. "I had a vision that morning. A scene of great beauty and wonder appeared, but my vision was one of terror, for as the columns of scouts and cavalry and infantry moved out, the sun broke through the mist and a mirage loomed, so that the line of horsemen appeared to float unto the heavens, and for a little distance the column seemed to march both in the sky and on the land." She paused. "I knew then that I would never again see my husband, the Son of the Morning Star."

Thad settled back in his seat, remembering another vision: that of Sitting Bull's in the Dance of the Sun on the Rosebud Creek.

After the lecture, there was a reception for Mrs. Custer. The Longsworths were invited, along with other prominent citizens of Greeley, Colorado. Thad had no desire to go but did so for Abigail's sake.

"I'm fascinated, Thad. Can't help it. She's very bizarre, don't you agree?"

"Agree. I'd be the first to say so. She scares the bejeezus out of me. She did fifty-odd years ago when I met her."

"But it's as if her husband has never really died," Abigail said. "It's as if she still sees him and speaks of him as that gallant, golden-haired boy general. I wonder if she sees herself still as a young bride. Jonathan would have fits if he knew I'd passed up this chance to meet her. I remember him describing her in a letter when you were both at Fort Lincoln.".

"Well, I always thought both she and her husband were caught up in follies, follies of time, too, I guess." Thad laughed. "Come on. Let's go in and meet her."

There was a receiving line and the mayor of Greeley was doing the introductions.

"Madame, I would like you to meet Mr. and Mrs. Thaddeus Longsworth, owners of the Dundee Ranch. Mr. Longsworth is well known for his work in paleontology." Mrs. Custer, who was a bit deaf, had lost part of the introduction but she paused a minute. "Your face is familiar—you didn't by any chance have the honor of ever serving in the Seventh for the general? You know, I never forget a face."

"No, no, never served. I had the honor of never serving," he said, and quickly moved on.

"Rascal!" Abigail Longsworth gasped as soon as they were out of the room. "I hope the mayor didn't hear it. You'll be kicked off the town council." She laughed.

"I hope he did hear it!" Thad grinned.

That evening, Thad sat alone in his study. He picked up his pipe from its rest on a chunk of fossil metatarsal from a trachodon. Abigail Longsworth had long ago given up on Thad's study in terms of housekeeping. There were bones everywhere. He preferred to shelve fossils, photographs, and Indian mementos rather than books. So there were stacks of books, articles, and papers written by Thad and others piling up in all corners of the room, plus all the paperwork required to run a ten-thousand-acre cattle ranch.

In a large casserole dish filched from Abigail's pantry, there were scores of teeth. The grandchildren liked to play with them. They played a guessing game with their grandfather. "Which one's the carnivore?" he would ask. "And the plant eater? And who's the big killer—the neighborhood thug, the one who could eat it on the hoof?" "Tyrannosaurus rex!" they'd squeal, and one of their grubby little hands would come up with the seven-inch tooth. Thad swiveled around in his chair and looked at the photograph on the wall. It was a picture of a young man, T. Barnum Brown, with his great discovery of the gigantic killer. Pictured with him, of course, were two older men—Thad and Julian— "The Deans of American Dinosaurs," as the paper called them, a title Thad loathed.

Visitors to his study never really seemed to mind the

disarray; never even noticed it. There was always a new
bone to ask about, or the fascinating old photos and
newspaper clippings; Thad and Julian DeMott as teen-
agers on the front page of the *New York Herald,* arriving
in Grand Central Station with the great triceratops head,
Teddy Roosevelt visiting the famous fossil hunter and
excavator at the Dundee Ranch. There was, of course,
the framed letter informing him that he had been named
the sole heir to the estate of the late J. W. Dundee, which
included the market value of the cattle sold in the summer of '74, as well as the land in Greeley. There was the
clipping of Julian DeMott's appointment as the director
of the New World Museum. And, of course, one of
Thad's favorites, from the museum's twenty-fifth-
anniversary celebration, with the picture of Julian and
the headline HE MADE DINOSAUR A HOUSEHOLD WORD.

There were no pictures of Indians. Thad hated pictures of white men with Indians. Every politician in the
west seemed to have one of himself taken with Red
Cloud, or there was a lineup of the great chiefs at some
meeting where the government was cheating them out
of more land. He kept his eagle's feather on a letter tray
on his desk and he was a mite fussy about letting the
grandchildren touch it too much.

Thad lit his pipe now and reread the letter that had
come that day from Julian DeMott.

> *Dear E. C.,*
> *I think you're dead wrong about dimetrodon's spiny back*
> *sail. This must be Abigail's side, the Cabot's coming*

through—all those sailing yachts they run around in up in Maine in the summertime. What else could account for this harebrained idea of yours that dimetrodon's back helped the poor critter tack across Permian ponds? Next thing we know you'll be proposing him for membership to the New York Yacht Club.

So it looks like Dakota Sweet River and I shall be going out west for our granddaughter's graduation from Stanford. We'll stop in on the way. Please arrange for a suitably newsworthy fossil to be excavated. The Depression has not affected museum attendance but a spiffy, first-rate find, something to set up in the Great Hall, might loosen some purse strings.

Have you noticed in the last ten years that all paleontologists run around in the field in these silly little shorts with their kneecaps sticking out and these nutty trooper hats? Are they trying to edge us old codgers out? I don't know about you, but I've got terrible-looking legs. Are we just getting too old?

Best to Abigail.

Always,

Julian

Dear Household Word Maker,

About dimetrodon. You know I hate sailing and as far as proposing the creature for the New York Yacht Club, the last thing they need is another fossil over there. I have another notion about its back sail. Maybe it served some thermal function—distribution of body heat. In regard to your other concerns: Of course, we're too old. I have to take four kinds of pills to keep my circulation and my plumbing in working

order. Doctors tell me I have no cartilage left in my right
elbow and ask me if I play tennis! Me, tennis! I have a few
vertebrae that have frozen up in my neck, so it's bad news
when I try to back up the automobile because I can't turn
my head. Abby says I'm a road hazard. But every day, I
manage to heave myself onto my old sorrel, who's in nearly
as bad shape as I am, and we ride out toward the mesas.
There's a serenity out there that's as good as liniment for
the spirit, and once the kinks are out of the spirit, the body
seems to follow suit . . ."

He stopped writing and twirled the pen between his fingers. Maybe what really healed him,
he thought, was riding through that ancient terrain and knowing that he wasn't looking for a
killer anymore. He was not thinking of the newspaper picture of Brown with the Tyrannosaurus
rex. He was, instead, thinking of the small child in
No Creek, Texas, who nearly sixty-five years ago
had tried to press himself harder into a patchwork
quilt under the bed of his murdered mother at the
Hole in the Hat saloon.

He turned around and picked up his trifocals to
look at the piece of paper he had rolled into his
typewriter. He'd only written two paragraphs so
far. A long distance to go yet. He read the first
sentence of the second paragraph.

His ma must not have known that the buffalo hunter
was coming. . . .

AUTHOR'S NOTE

The Bone Wars is a story that is fiction but rooted in history. As a novelist of historical fiction, I have worked within a tradition where facts are used and, at the same time, on occasion transcended. I would like to be as clear as possible as to what facts I have based my story upon and what facts I have altered. It must be pointed out that when I have altered facts, I have tried to remain faithful to the historical period in which they occurred. They were not altered to subvert history but, rather, to serve the purposes of storytelling. It would not be good storytelling if the essential fabric of the historical period was sacrificed in the process.

Through the 1870s and 1880s, there was a fierce competition in American paleontology for dinosaur fossils in the west. The basis for the characters George Babcock and Nathaniel Cunningham were the American paleontologists Edward Drinker Cope and Othniel C. Marsh. Cope was an eminent paleontologist from Philadelphia. Considered the more brilliant of the two, he had worked independent of an academic institution. He was one of the last scholars to work in this manner. Marsh worked at Yale University, and it was through his family's money that the Peabody Museum of Science at Yale was started. The two men entered into a bitter competition for fossils. Their battle for the main part was centered in the region of Como Bluff, Wyoming, although Cope had traveled extensively in the Judith River Badlands and made many significant discoveries in that terrain, which became known for its species of horn-faced dinosaurs. The two scholars' behavior was poor to say the least, especially when one considers their stature in the scientific community. They were petty and self-centered in their quests and often sank to distinctly ungentlemanly tactics, which involved suborning each other's teamworkers, bribery, and on occasion even the wrecking of some fossils they did not have time to excavate, in order to prevent the other team from benefiting. In the beginning, it was the sleazy behavior of such honored men that appealed to me enormously as a novelist and inspired me to write this book.

The excavations of both Cope and Marsh were taking place at the same time as the Indian wars for the Black Hills and the efforts to institute the reservation system. Buffalo Bill Cody had at one time served as a guide for Marsh, and Marsh had been a friend of Red Cloud's and an advocate of the Indian cause, many say to his own self-aggrandizement.

Algernon DeMott is modeled loosely after the great English paleontologist and anatomist Richard Owen, who invented the word *dinosaur*. He was known to be cold, arrogant, and rigid in his views of religion and evolution. He would not have been a contemporary of Marsh and Cope, but about twenty-five years older. I know nothing of Owen's family life, and Julian DeMott is my own invention.

Thaddeus Longsworth, on the other hand, is a composite of several wonderful characters I have encountered in western history. For the most part, he is based on the cowboy J. H. Cook, who served as a guide for Marsh, and Charles Sternberg, the most famous of the free-lance fossil collectors who worked with Cope extensively in the Judith River Badlands.

The real characters in this book, such as Buffalo Bill, Red Cloud, Black Elk, and Crazy Horse, were all involved in the historical events that I have mentioned in my story. For example, Black Elk was really at the Battle of Little Bighorn as a thirteen-year-old boy and was bathing in the river when he first spotted the members of the Seventh Cavalry. It is recollections from his book, *Black Elk Speaks*, on which I have largely based the accounts of the Battle of the Little Bighorn, as well as that of the Rosebud. His encounters with Thad, as well as Crazy Horse's and Buffalo Bill's, were, of course, invented. But every detail of those inventions is based on something that really did happen. Black Elk was really considered a seer or spirit traveler. Sitting Bull really did have his vision during the Dance of the Sun before the Battle of the Rosebud Creek, and Mrs. Custer, as well, had her own vision of her husband's death and the defeat of the Seventh Cavalry. There really was a comet that streaked across the Dakota sky during the Black Hills expedition of 1874, which the Sioux interpreted as a sign of Wakan-Tanka's anger.

In regard to the scientific information in the story, I have tried to be as accurate as possible about what was known then of fossils and the geology of the earth. It is important to remember that radiometric dating was not used until well into this century. Therefore, scientists could never specify absolute dates in terms of years but could only speak of the relative age of a fossil.

Geologists of this era tried to establish rates of deposition of the modern sedimentary strata and then estimate the time represented by similar ancient rock units. They thought that if they could guess the thickness of sedimentary rock, and where a fossil was in that strata, they could come up with a relative date for the fossil. Fossils found higher up in the sequence of strata were, of course, younger. Those lower in the strata were older. When scientists did speak in terms of numbers of years, for the most part, they meant less than 100 million. On two or three occasions, Jonathan

Cabot and Babcock mention billions of years in casual conversation. That would have been considered by most as stretching it. But as a novelist, I had the privilege of making them just a tiny bit smarter. Perhaps they had their fingers crossed when they said it. They could now, as we know from the radiometric dating, uncross their fingers in reference to the age of the earth.

The first triceratops was discovered by John Bell Hatcher in the early 1880s, a few years after Thad and Julian discovered old Lunge and Plunge. And the great thug of the Mesozoic neighborhood, *Tyrannosaurus rex,* although leaving many clues in his wake, was not excavated until the early 1900s by T. Barnum Brown.

After a year of working on this book, I had become so drawn into the story of the Bone Wars, Montana, and the background of the Indian wars that I knew my research would remain incomplete until I had done two things—dug a dinosaur bone and walked across the fields of the Battle of the Little Bighorn. Through the enthusiastic help of my old grade-school friend, Jeannie Kitchen Hanson, my son Max and I were able to join her and her children, Jennifer and Eric, on a University of Minnesota paleontological expedition conducted by Dr. Robert Sloan in the Badlands of Montana. Dr. Sloan was the soul of patience, answering our hundreds of questions as we scrambled over the buttes. We found a triceratops tooth, a fragment from a terrapin's shell, as well as a piece from an ancient crocodile and numerous garfish scales. There were no big bones on that trip, but we certainly became hooked on that time before time in a land so vast and so silent that, as my friend Jeannie has said, "only your imagination can fill it."

K.L.
March 1988
CAMBRIDGE, MASSACHUSETTS